Fallin' for a Hustler Like Me

Fallin' for a Hustler Like Me

Natisha Raynor

and

Blake Karrington

www.urbanbooks.net

Urban Books, LLC
300 Farmingdale Road, N.Y.-Route 109
Farmingdale, NY 11735

ISBN 13: 978-1-64556-543-7

First Trade Paperback Printing October 2023
Printed in the United States of America

10 9 8 7 6 5 4 3 2 1

Distributed by Kensington Publishing Corp.
Submit Orders to:
Customer Service
400 Hahn Road
Westminster, MD 21157-4627
Phone: 1-800-733-3000
Fax: 1-800-659-2436

Chapter 1

"What the fuck are you doing?" Khelani asked through clenched teeth as she trained her Glock on Malachi. She stared at the sight before her with a shattered heart, but she would be damned if she let a single tear fall from her eyes.

Malachi looked over his shoulder, and when he saw her standing there with a gun trained on him, his left eyebrow hiked up. Temporarily abandoning the treasure before him, Malachi stood up and turned around to face Khelani. There really was no way for him to explain what he was doing with her safe open. Thirty pounds of weed and a few stacks of cash stared him in the face. From the moment the door swung open, he had to decide between leaving the weed and money there or crossing Khelani and robbing her. He was in a jam—a jam that could cost him his life. He owed someone a lot of money, and rather than just being a man and coming to Khelani to maybe get fronted some work, he was going to take the grimy route and rob her. Right after fucking her, he planned to get what he needed while she was in the shower, dip, and explain himself later, but his plans had been ruined. He didn't miss the pained expression that was etched on Khelani's face or the hurt that lay in her gray eyes.

He was trying to survive. It wasn't anything personal. Maybe he'd be able to convince her of that, but he could tell from the way she was glaring at him that wouldn't be an easy task.

"Khelani, I know how this looks, but just let me explain." Funny thing was, after that, he was quiet. He wasn't saying anything. Because he didn't have anything to say. How was he going to explain what he was doing in her safe and make it sound believable? Khelani was far from dumb.

His lack of words did it for her. He was going to die anyway, but as soon as he hesitated with his explanation, Khelani pumped his body full of bullets. The bullets made his body jerk slightly before he fell backward into the wall. Khelani watched as his body slid down the wall and traces of his blood stained the paint. His eyes were locked on hers the entire time. As soon as his bottom tapped the floor, blood spilled from his mouth, and his head fell to the left. He was dead.

Khelani backed out of the room and headed for the bathroom, where her phone was located. With trembling hands, she picked it up from the sink and called Kasim. He would know what to do. She wasn't about to say too much over the phone, but as soon as he heard her voice crack, he knew she was indeed in trouble.

Khelani wasn't one to show emotion, and Kasim dropped everything he was doing to rush to her. It was a good thing he only lived one block over. He was there in no time, and when she took him to Malachi's body, he knew what he had to do.

"What happened? Are you okay?" He looked her over and saw that she was only dressed in a black silk robe.

"He tried to fuckin' rob me. That's what happened," Khelani replied with a hint of anger in her tone. "'You're too powerful, Khelani. You'll never find a man unless you submit. No man can take you outshining him.'" She mocked the words that Kasim had spoken to her months before. "Now you see why I don't let men get close to me?" she snapped.

Khelani walked away and left Kasim to clean up the mess she'd made. Her father told her not to come to the States and fall in love. Love and money didn't mix, and she was to always, no matter what, choose the money over love.

Khelani placed her hands on the back of her neck and blew out air as she looked up at the ceiling. For the first time in a long time, she had started to like someone, and it had ended with her painting the wall with his blood. It only confirmed what she already knew. She couldn't trust any-fuckin'-body, and love wasn't for her.

Kyrie Richmond pulled up at the location his partner Ghalen had provided him with. He pulled around to the very back of the warehouse. It was pitch-black out, but Kyrie spotted Ghalen's Audi right away. He also noticed Montana's motorcycle. Montana was the head of Kyrie's security team. Kyrie shut the engine off and looked over at Taina.

"I'll be right back," he told his date of the evening. She nodded, and Kyrie emerged from the car.

She had no clue where they were, but she wasn't afraid. She wasn't afraid because she had never seen the dark side of Kyrie. She only knew him as the head of a successful record label. Taina didn't know about Kyrie's street dealings. She had no clue what he was doing at a warehouse that looked desolate, but she didn't care. Taina just wanted him to hurry back to her so they could go back to her place. It was only their first date, but she wanted to fuck. No questions asked. To be on the arm of a man like Kyrie was a privilege in itself. She didn't take any pictures with him and post them herself because she didn't want to seem like a groupie. But Taina prayed that someone would snap a picture of them and post her on a blog. Not only did she hope to get in good with Kyrie, but being on the arm of a man of his caliber would make other rich niggas want her. The shit was weird, but that was how it worked. There was a reason IG models got passed around the industry. If a man saw his peer fucking with a bad bitch about her bread, it would stroke that man's ego if the same female gave him the time of day. Being spotted out with Kyrie would make her stock go up for sure.

Oblivious to the mental plotting that his date was doing, Kyrie walked swiftly to the back door, and as if Montana could sense his presence, he swung the door open for Kyrie.

"What up, boss?" Montana gave Kyrie dap before leading him farther into the room.

Kyrie smiled when he saw a man tied to a chair. The chair sat in the middle of the empty space, and Ghalen stood in front of the chair with a shiny object in his hand. Kyrie walked over to Ghalen and gave him dap before taking the $65,000 chain from him.

Once the necklace was in his hand, he glared over at the man in the chair. His eyes were almost swollen shut. His nose was crooked, letting Kyrie know that it was broken, and there was a huge lump on his forehead. He'd been beaten senseless for sure.

"What made you think it was a good idea to rob one of my artists for his chain? Then you took it a step further and tried to make him pay you to get it back. Big, bad-ass gangsta nigga." Kyrie turned to look at Ghalen. "This can't be the same nigga who was on his Snapchat boasting and bragging about taking Kilo's chain. He's real quiet right now."

Ghalen smirked. "That's because he's missing a few teeth."

Kyrie turned his attention back to the man in the chair. "Damn, they fucked you up. You know, on the way over here, I had all kinds of devious thoughts. I almost stopped by my crib to get my ax because the idea of cutting your thieving-ass hand off excited me. I mean, damn near made my dick hard. But I'm a businessman. I'm not savage-ass Kyrie anymore, and I won't risk a murder charge for me or anyone in my camp. So you better thank God that I'm choosing to let you live. But don't be shy now. Don't stay off Snap 'cause you all fucked up. Show your face and let your viewers know how robbing Kilo turned out for you. Sucka-ass nigga," Kyrie growled before walking off. "Let this bitch go," he instructed Montana.

Montana eyed the man, who was barely clinging to life. He understood very well why Kyrie didn't want to risk having the man killed. It was no secret that he robbed Kyrie's artist, and if he turned up dead, that would bring heat to Kyrie and his team. It was something that they didn't need. But Montana had been in the streets for years, and he just didn't think letting this kid live was smart. Kyrie was the boss though, and he had to do what he was told. He just hoped that not following his gut wouldn't come back to bite him or Kyrie in the ass.

Chapter 2

Two Months Later

"I really wish you would call Dad," Khelani stated as she walked into the living room and saw her sister, Anya, stretched out on the couch eating yogurt.

Anya peered at her sister as she placed diamond studs into her ears. "You look nice." She took in the black high-waist slacks that hugged Khelani's hips, and her red silk blouse. Khelani was barefoot, and the red polish on her toes matched the shirt she wore perfectly. Her thick, dark, curly hair was pulled up into a high bun.

"Thank you, but you not acknowledging what I said doesn't mean that I won't say it again. He always calls my phone when you don't answer for him. I'm a little sick of being the messenger for two people who are capable of talking for themselves."

Anya groaned and rolled her eyes dramatically. "Call him for whattttt? All he's going to do is threaten to make me come back to Trinidad as if I'm not a grown woman. He's the fuckin' fun police," she grumbled, and Khelani shook her head.

"Anya, we were sent to the States for a reason. We knew from day one that we were supposed to be here working. But no matter where we go, I'm always the one working, and you just bullshit."

"Because I'm not a slave. I never even said I wanted to be a drug dealer. He can't just make us sell his shit," Anya stated with a face full of disdain.

At 23, Anya was still young, but Khelani felt that it was time for her to grow up. They'd been in the States for two years. After they set up shop in North Carolina and got a steady line of income for their father, who was the plug back in Trinidad, they hit the road to take over Atlanta next. Their father, Kemp, was a very powerful man, and he didn't send them to the States alone. That would be too much like feeding them to the wolves. They had a driver, Kasim, who also doubled as their muscle. Once they got settled, it became very clear to Khelani that she was a one-woman show. All Anya cared about was having fun, partying, and fucking.

"Daddy sent us to North Carolina with three hundred thousand dollars and four hundred pounds of weed. Us getting set up in North Carolina was his money, but this condo"—Khelani swept her hand around—"this twenty-five-hundred-dollar-a-month condo came from all the drugs I sold. The allowance he sent you last month was just that, an allowance, because you damn sure don't earn the shit."

"And you never mess up, right? The last time I checked, you were the one who almost fucked shit up for us the last time, not me."

"I may have fucked shit up, but I still got the job done. All you did was sleep all day and party all night. It's not going that way this time. So get off your ass and start helping me, and start answering Dad's phone calls, today. You have until the end of the month or I'm making a phone call of my own." Khelani pointed at her sister.

Khelani stood five foot seven with dark brown skin and the most beautiful gray eyes. She was thicker than a bowl of oatmeal and a no-nonsense kind of woman.

As she eyed her sister, who had skin the color of heavily creamed coffee and gray eyes that mirrored hers, all she could do was shake her head. Anya stood an inch taller and had more than a handful of hips. She was a beauty indeed. But she was also a big brat. Not only was their father's drug empire Khelani's business, but she had to spend her free time babysitting Anya, and she was over it.

"Why should I have to earn it when my father is a multimillionaire? Make it make sense," Anya snapped like the spoiled brat she was. "You just defend him all the time because you're his favorite."

"Nah, I'm just tired of doing all the work while you reap the benefits. I made fifty-four thousand dollars yesterday off pounds, and I'm still up bright and early to go to my first day of a job that I don't fuckin' need, but making the right connections in this city will be worth my while. And if I'm Dad's favorite, then you're damn sure Mom's."

"It goes beyond having a favorite. He has always treated you like the perfect child. It's no secret that you're his heart and he hates me."

"He doesn't hate you, Anya. You're just irresponsible, and you make it hard for everyone around you. How do you think I feel knowing that you're our mother's favorite? All because you have light skin like hers. She acts like I'm so ugly just because of my dark skin. She is a colorist, and that's what I don't fuck with."

"You are reaching."

"Am I?"

Khelani's phone rang before either of them could say another word. She looked down and saw that it was her father calling again. He was the last person to call her the night before and the first person calling her this morning. Khelani let out a sigh of irritation before answering the call and placing it on speakerphone.

"Hey, Daddy. I only have ten minutes before I have to leave for work. You're on speakerphone. Anya is right here."

Anya's eyes widened at her sister's betrayal.

Kemp cleared his throat, and when he spoke, his voice boomed through the speaker on the phone. "I'm pretty sure that my money is what pays your cell phone bill, and since you can't answer my calls, I won't pay the bill. I sent you with your sister to be an asset, not a liability, and there's no need to get mad at your sister. She works for me. Kasim works for me, and when I ask them a question about your behavior, I expect an answer. They are not to cover for you. You're cut off. Until you can prove to me why I should be sending you three thousand dollars a month, you won't get another penny from me."

The call ended, and Anya was so angry that she was seeing red. In her ungrateful world, $3,000 wasn't shit. She didn't have to pay her rent, utilities, car payment, or even her own cell phone bill, so her entire monthly allowance went toward, clothes, shoes, hair, and nails. She didn't even consider that if she helped Khelani the way she was supposed to, she would have been making more money, and that would be enough to afford her the luxurious lifestyle she wanted to live, but Anya wanted everything handed to her.

Khelani knew that her sister would be angry for a minute, so she went to her bedroom, stuck her feet into her red Louboutin heels and grabbed her purse. She left the apartment and headed to the parking garage where her burnt orange 2021 BMW X5 was parked. For her first day as an administrative assistant at a record label, she didn't want Kasim to drive her.

Kemp was a rich and powerful man, and since he didn't have the son he wanted, he groomed Khelani to be as savage as any nigga. He saw to it that she was educated and well-spoken and could shoot a gun, cook a brick, and eyeball a gram of weed before she could drive. His businesses in Trinidad were so lucrative that when he decided to take over the States, he didn't send one of his henchmen—he sent his daughters.

Khelani was to play it safe. She couldn't just show up in town and start moving work. She would blend in with the right crowds, entertain the right people, and develop business relationships. She'd then become their supplier and open up the pipeline for them to deal with Kemp's people directly. Since marijuana had become legal in a few states, Kemp had way more competition now than he did years ago. He had to match the high quality of the weed that was now so easily accessible in the States, and he had to have plenty of it at competitive prices. Khelani felt that getting in good with rappers and high-profile businessmen in Atlanta would be her best move. Her résumé was impressive. She had never worked a "real job," but she used Kemp's legal businesses as references. With her stellar résumé and her good looks, she was hired on the spot. Khelani knew that it was important to show up and show out. She had to prove that she was a boss bitch and not just some groupie looking to fuck her way to the top.

Khelani pulled up to a tall building that was located uptown about twenty minutes later and parked her car. The streets were crowded, and everyone seemed to have somewhere to be. Grabbing her purse off the passenger seat, Khelani opened her door and stepped out of the car. She tossed her purse over her shoulder and then closed her door and hit the lock button on her key fob before following a few other people inside of the large building. As soon as she walked in, she saw the place was even busier than the streets had been. Khelani looked all around trying to remember what floor she needed to be on. From her understanding, the record label didn't own the entire building, but they occupied four floors. The building had ten floors total.

"Hey, Khelani, right?"

She immediately remembered that the man approaching her was the person who interviewed her, and she offered him a big smile.

Ghalen was five foot ten, and he had a stocky build. His skin reminded her of dark chocolate, and his long dreads were braided up and hanging down his back. He wore an expensive black suit and an even more expensive pair of black shoes. Ghalen looked like the definition of distinguished. His cologne infiltrated her nose, and she even peeped that his nails were neat, short, and manicured.

"Yes, that's correct."

"Nice to see you again. Kyrie is really excited to have you join the team. Ninety percent of the staff here is black. People might hear the words 'record label' and automatically think about diamond chains and a bunch of niggas walking around in sagging jeans, but that's not the case here. This label makes Kyrie a lot of money, and he takes it very, very seriously. Professionalism is a must. Knowing your job is a must. He doesn't mind helping his own, but coming to work and doing things half-assed is like not coming at all. I'm the accountant, but I'm on the third floor where you will be. I will introduce you to the office manager, Kim. She will train you and get you all set up."

"Okay, and thank you so much. Sounds good to me." Khelani followed Ghalen onto the elevator.

The elevator stopped on the second floor, and a pretty black woman wearing a form-fitting black dress and a black headwrap got on. She gave a small head nod to Khelani and Ghalen. Atlanta was nothing short of amazing to Khelani. Every city had boss bitches, but Atlanta took it to another level. It truly was the black mecca. Khelani was a boss bitch in her own right, and no other woman intimidated her. She liked seeing women on their shit, but she also knew women could be catty, envious beings who liked to keep some shit going. She was giving this job six weeks. Since she'd only been in Atlanta for a month, she didn't have a lot of clientele, so she wasn't really missing out on money by being at the job, but she didn't need the job. She was there for a reason, and she couldn't bullshit with that reason. She'd do a good job while she was employed there, but when she made the connections she came for, she was gone.

The elevator stopped on the third floor, and all three occupants stepped off. Ghalen introduced Khelani to Kim, and then he went on about his business. Kim was a brown-skinned woman who stood five foot seven without heels, and her hair was in long locs that hung down her back, and the tips were dyed blond. Khelani hadn't worn heels in a minute, and by the time Kim was done giving her a tour of the third floor, her feet were throbbing. The job didn't sound too complicated, and she was sure that she'd get the hang of it in no time. Khelani was smart as hell and a fast learner.

After the tour was a walk-through of all of the software on the computer, how to use it, and what was expected of her each day. Every time someone walked by, Kim would stop them and make introductions. Two hours later, Kim was done, and Khelani was mentally exhausted.

"I pushed back a meeting to be able to get this done with you. I have to go. Do you think you'll be okay out here alone? I have to meet with some record execs, and that will probably take me about two hours."

"Oh, I'll be fine," Khelani assured her as she glanced at her computer screen and saw that she had nine new emails for the email address that had been set up for her.

"Good. Email me if you need me, and you can go ahead and take a fifteen-minute break. At one, you can take your hour lunch."

Khelani nodded. She was going to run to the restroom, then get right to work. Time was money, and time was something that Khelani never wasted.

"What can I get for you?" The bartender at the restaurant that Anya was occupying walked over to her. It was only one in the afternoon, but she needed a drink, badly.

"Let me get a double shot of Don Julio and a splash of pineapple juice. Also, I want to go ahead and order my food. I want the wings fried hard, a side of fries, and ranch."

"Coming right up."

Anya let out a small breath and looked around the bar. To say she was pissed would be an understatement. Her father was rich as fuck. To cut her off would just be flat-out cruel. *How dare he want his pretty-ass daughters to pump drugs like niggas?* All Anya wanted to have to worry about was being the best dressed, prettiest bitch walking the streets and living off her father's dime until she snatched a baller of her own.

With her face and her body, Anya was a hot commodity among most dope boys, scammers, and legit niggas who came across her path. In North Carolina, she had quite a few heavy hitters on her team, and she was almost sad when she had to leave. Almost. Anya knew Atlanta would be a come-up for real. She could see herself right now being wifed up by a rich-ass rapper or athlete. When Khelani got the job at the record label, Anya damn near creamed her panties. She wanted to get into all the parties and dope events off her sister's name, and she could do the rest.

Kemp and Khelani wouldn't even let her have that though. Anya had been chilling, but it looked like she was going to have to get serious about landing a baller. She was too fine, and her pussy was too good for her to be walking around broke. The bartender came back with her drink, and Anya wasted no time picking the glass up. After placing the tiny brown straw between her heavily glossed lips, Anya took three long sips.

"I see I'm not the only person who likes to day drink during the week." A pretty light-skinned chick just as tall as Anya with just as much body sat down beside her. She may have been a bit thicker than Anya. The woman gave her Megan Thee Stallion vibes as far as her body type. Anya did a quick evaluation of the woman, and shorty looked like a boss bitch indeed. Or she could have just looked the part and been as broke as Anya.

"It's five o'clock somewhere," Anya replied and took another sip. She wasn't exactly the friendly type, but when ol' girl removed a pair of $1,200 shades from her face and placed them on the bar, Anya decided this was the type of bitch she needed to be running with.

"My type of bitch. I'm Camila." She removed the strap of her Chanel bag from her shoulder and placed the purse in her lap. When she looked over at Anya, her light brown eyes flickered a bit, and a smile graced her face.

This bitch is bad, and she looks paid, Anya thought. *She for sure has to know where the ballers are.* "Hi, I'm Anya."

"Anya, that's a pretty name. Fits your pretty ass perfect. You from the A?"

Before Anya could answer, the bartender came back over and took Camila's drink order, and Anya ordered another drink. She was feeling all warm and tingly inside, and just that fast, her previous agitation had melted away.

"I'm not. I'm actually from Trinidad. I've been here for a month now. Just trying to get a feel for the city and shit. I don't know anyone here but my older sister, and she has a stick up her ass."

Camila giggled.

"I'm dead ass. All she wants to do is work. Real independent-type bitch, but me? Shit, if God wanted me to work hard, He wouldn't have made me so pretty. I need a nigga to spoil me. Period."

"Yoooooo," Camila laughed. "On God, you my type of bitch. I have a feeling we can be great friends. So you not working?"

"Nope. I didn't need to, but I have to make something shake soon."

"What about that ass?" Camila eyed her as Anya's eyebrows dipped.

"Huh?"

"I own a strip club. It opens at four p.m. to cater to businessmen who might not want to have business meetings in traditional places. It also caters to dope boys and scammers who might want to see some tits at four in the afternoon rather than four in the morning. Business has been booming lately, and your pretty ass, baby, can make some bread in that muhfucka. Might even meet the nigga who takes ya ass up out of there. Feel me?"

Anya's eyes lit up. "I feel you." She'd never considered stripping because she didn't have to. Kemp or her niggas always spoiled her, but a lot of bad bitches were old strippers who were now the girlfriends of rich niggas. The days of niggas not wanting to wife strippers were over. Men didn't care about that shit anymore.

Camila didn't look to be too much older than her, and she was a boss bitch with her own club. Anya was willing to bet her last dollar that it was a nigga who put Camila on.

"Where is the club at?" she inquired as she finished off her drink.

"About ten minutes from here. Rappers love that muh-fucka. They come in at least five nights out of the week blowing bags. So do the scammers and dope boys. I'm telling you. Yesterday, four white corporate niggas were in there running up a check with black cards."

Anya felt all tingly inside, and she knew it wasn't just from the liquor. "Say less. When can I start?"

Camila smiled wide. "You can start tonight, baby." She pulled out her phone. "What's your number? I'll text you all the details."

The drinks came along with Anya's food, and she and Camila laughed, drank, and conversed for an hour. By the time they were ready to part ways, Camila paid Anya's tab, and when they did separate, Anya peeped Camila getting into a cocaine white Maserati.

"Oh, I can fuck with that bitch fa sho'," she said as she headed to her black Jeep. "I'm 'bout to run this muhfuckin' money up and show my dad I don't need his help." Anya smiled to herself.

Growing up in Trinidad, Anya hated it. Because her father was such a powerful man, she never had any pri-vacy. She couldn't ride the bus to school with her friends. Her father's driver took her. Even when her parents weren't home, there was always someone there, be it a maid or a chef. Sneaking boys in was impossible, and Anya couldn't be the wild, carefree teenager she wanted to be. Even though she was spoiled, she often felt like she was in prison, and she hated it. When her father asked her and her sister to come to the States, Anya jumped at the chance, and she didn't care what the requirements were. She'd been able to bullshit her way through North Carolina, but Kemp was finally tired of her shit.

However, now things were looking up for Anya. She didn't view stripping as a real job. She'd be able to turn up on a nightly basis and get paid for it. That was right up her alley. It was a given that Kemp would be furious, but Anya didn't care. If she was taking care of herself, there wasn't shit he could say, and he couldn't make her go back to Trinidad.

Chapter 3

"Yeah, I'm just now walking in my hotel room," Mozzy said, using his foot to close the door behind him.

He had his iPhone on speakerphone in one hand, and his suitcase was in the opposite hand. He walked farther into the penthouse suite and placed his bag down on the floor beside him. Mozzy looked around and smiled to himself. He was feeling the layout, and it was a whole lot more lavish than what he was used to back in Houston. Mozzy knew right then and there that Atlanta was going to be good to him. The air smelled different, and the money was looking a lot longer.

"I can't believe Big Man got you all the way out there," Judah, his cousin, said on the other end of the phone.

"I can't either. I was skeptical about coming to unknown territory, but I can fuck with this shit. Working for a nigga who has a record label and moves that work could be the kind of come-up I need in my life."

"Damn right it is, my nigga. You coming home off a bid. To have this kind of setup waiting for you is a blessing. You lucky as hell. Nigga, you were about to go down for a long-ass time for a murder you didn't even do."

"That's how that shit goes, man. Them motherfuckers don't give a fuck as long as they can close the damn case. I've been out for a few months though, and I still haven't seen any real money like before I got locked up. Hopefully, this shit will change all of that. If I like the way shit is going, I may set up shop here."

"I don't see how shit can go wrong."

"I hope that's the case, but no matter how sweet shit looks, it can always go wrong. I have to get going. I'm supposed to be meeting Kyrie in about fifteen minutes, but I'm only ten minutes away."

"I heard that Atlanta traffic is a whole different ball game, so you might want to double the time."

"I'm 'bout to head that way. I'll hit you later."

"A'ight."

Mozzy took a moment to look around the suite and take in his surroundings before he slid his phone in his pocket and headed back out of the room and down to the garage where his rental was. His current accommodations were very different from the cell he'd called home for more than a year. Kyrie had gotten him a suite and a rental. Mozzy couldn't wait to see what else came along with the job.

Back in Houston before he got knocked, he had worked for a hustler by the name of Big Man. Mozzy had gotten locked up when he was 22 for murder—a murder he didn't commit. Money had been good when he was on the streets, but it wasn't good enough for him to be able to afford the kind of lawyer who could get his case thrown out. Being innocent didn't mean shit. All the DA had to do was convince the jury that Mozzy had done it, and he was as good as sent up the river. Big Man believed in him though, and for that, Mozzy was eternally grateful. He sat in jail for over two years, but when he finally went to trial, the lawyer Big Man hired showed why he was worth the $500 an hour he charged.

Everyone had encouraged him to sue the police station that locked him up, but after everything that happened, Mozzy wasn't fucking with the police at all. Plus, he may not have committed that murder, but he'd done plenty dirt. As he sat in his cell day in and day out, he felt that karma had come to pay his ass a visit for all the wrongs he did in the past. When he was finally freed, he tried the straight path for two weeks and was right back in the streets. He knew that didn't make any sense, but he had to live, and he didn't know anyone who would be eager to give him a job.

Even though Mozzy was glad to be free from the belly of the beast, he came home not knowing how he was going to get back on his feet. He'd already never be able to pay Big Man back for the lawyer, so he didn't want to ask the man to front him any work, but once again Big Man came through like his personal savior. Apparently Big Man's cousin had his hands full, and he needed an unknown face to come in and help him out with some things. Mozzy didn't know exactly what he was going to have to do, but he was down for putting some money in his pockets.

He finally made it to the garage and then hopped in his whip before pulling off to go find Kyrie's office building. Exactly twenty minutes later, he was pulling up to his destination and parking after getting lucky by spotting a car pulling out of a space that was fairly close to the entrance of the building. Mozzy got out of his car and rushed inside knowing that he was already a few minutes late.

"Excuse me," he said, walking up to the front desk, and a red-haired woman held up a finger as she talked on the phone. Mozzy tapped his foot and looked down at his watch. It was five on the dot, and he was trying to catch Kyrie before he left. He knew Kyrie was expecting him, but Big Man had also told him that Kyrie waited for no one. "I need to speak with Kyrie," Mozzy said rudely.

"Sir, just a minute." The woman pursed her lips.

"Hell nah, you hold on. I got a meeting with Kyrie."

"Are you on the schedule to speak with Mr. Richmond?" she asked, pulling the phone away from her ear.

"I don't know shit about no schedule, but the nigga expecting me," Mozzy said, making the woman's eyes widen from his audacity. At the same time, a guy with long dreads braided to the back spotted him and rushed over.

"I got this, Carey," he said and then directed Mozzy away from the front desk. "Mozzy?"

"Yeah, how you know, and who the hell are you?"

"I'm Ghalen, Kyrie's accountant and right-hand man. Little rough around the edges, I see. You're about to be making a shitload of money, so when you come into the office, I'd tone down the street shit. Though you won't be here much, this label is Kyrie's business. He keeps this and street shit separate, so all that hoodlum shit gotta go."

"Shit, I didn't know y'all niggas was doing it like this around this bitch. Niggas wearing suits and all," Mozzy stated, amazed. He wasn't even offended at how Ghalen had checked him. All he knew was hood shit, but that legit paper was looking good as fuck.

"People serious about their business act accordingly. Kyrie doesn't require us to wear suits, but I'm a fly muhfucka, and I dress as such," Ghalen chuckled. "I'll show you to Kyrie's office."

As they headed toward the elevator, he saw the secretary scowling, and he almost threw up his middle finger, but he had to remember where he was. This record label shit wasn't just a front. Kyrie was legit as fuck. When they reached the third floor, Mozzy followed Ghalen. Mozzy took in the hustle and bustle of the office before they stopped in front of Kyrie's door.

"Image," Ghalen spoke and winked before heading back to the elevator, and Mozzy just shook his head and knocked on the door.

Mozzy was six foot one with skin the color of a new penny, and he rocked a low fade. He was tall and muscular from all the weights he had lifted while he was locked up. Once he came home, he kept the workout regime up. He had grills in his mouth, and everything about him screamed thug. That was mainly because of the two teardrops that were tatted right under his left eye and the fact that he kept an expression on his face like he was two seconds away from killing a nigga. He already knew he didn't fit in, and he hoped Ghalen was right. While all that Kyrie had going on was quite impressive, he would rather be in the streets putting his work in. Mozzy didn't want to have to be constantly worried about doing or saying the wrong things and feeling out of place.

"Come in."

Mozzy opened the door and stepped inside. He didn't even try to hide that he was further impressed. Kyrie's office was spacious with floor-to-ceiling windows and decorated like something out of a magazine.

"This shit is nice," Mozzy said, sitting in the white leather chair in front of Kyrie's desk. There was a matching couch tucked away in the corner with black pillows on it. Most of the office decor was black.

"Thank you. I had to make it comfortable because I spend a lot of time here. I'm glad you could make it though. Did my cousin run shit down to you or did he just send you out here blind?"

"Nah, he told me you needed help with some shit. I didn't know you was doing it like this though."

"Don't let any of this faze you. The business side of shit is just as crucial as the streets, especially with the shit that goes on behind the scenes. Don't worry about all of that though. What do you say we hit the strip club tonight and we'll talk more then? I just wanted to see your face and see what was up with you. Ya feel me?"

"Hell yeah, that's understandable. I'm down though. Ain't shit like watching some naked hoes and discussing business."

"Exactly. I'll send you the time and address."

"Okay, cool," Mozzy said, standing up. He slapped hands with Kyrie once again and then made his way out of his office. He may not have known how big Kyrie was doing it at first, but after seeing everything Kyrie had going on, he was trying to be doing it big just like him one day, no matter how he had to get there.

Kyrie slouched down and got comfortable in his seat as he cruised down the streets of a suburban community, pushing his brand-new Rolls-Royce, which he had paid a pretty penny to be customized. The outside was snow white, and the inside was charcoal black. It had all of the latest features, and he was blasting Jay-Z's classic album *Reasonable Doubt* through his Bluetooth system. Kyrie bobbed his head to the music as he made a right turn and then pulled in front of the house at the end of the street. He parked his car behind a matte black BMW coupe and exited his vehicle.

He walked up on the porch and then knocked on the door. Work had passed by quickly, and his day had already been pretty eventful. Kyrie wished he could have gone home and just called it a day, but he hadn't seen his folks in almost two weeks, so he knew he needed to show his face. Things had been busy for him lately, but his aunt and uncle would kill him if he didn't make time to check in with them. They had basically been raising him since he was 14, and they looked at him like he was their own.

Kyrie's mother had died from Lupus-related complications when he was 14, and her brother made sure to become his father figure since he had never had one. He was a football coach at Kyrie's school, and his wife was a nurse. He made sure to get Kyrie involved in football because he didn't want him hanging in the streets and continuing the lifestyle he had been living while his mother was alive. He lived in a nice neighborhood, and he wanted Kyrie to turn over a new leaf. Losing a mother couldn't be easy, but losing a sister wasn't either, and he was determined to make the best out of her child.

Therefore, Mario spent a lot of time with Kyrie on and off the field. When they weren't attending practice or a game, they were in the gym. Mario tried to train Kyrie as much as he could while making sure he left time for Kyrie to worry about school. Since Kyrie was tied up between the two, Mario didn't think he would possibly have time to entertain the streets, but he didn't know his nephew as well as he thought he did at the time. Kyrie finished up high school and went off to college on academic and athletic scholarships thanks to his uncle.

The truth didn't come out about Kyrie being involved in the streets until a year later when he got hurt on the field and lost his athletic scholarship. Since the pros were no longer in his future, he got involved in the streets a little deeper than he had been before, and word got back to his uncle. Before, it was just hustling to have extra money and the latest fashions. After he got hurt, hustling became a way of life. Kyrie was ready to quit college and just come back home since that was where he had been spending the majority of his time after losing his scholarship anyway. Mario refused to let him drop out though and told him just because he lost his athletic scholarship, it didn't mean he lost his academic one. He told Kyrie to make his mother proud and finish school.

Kyrie wanted to do that, but he was also stubborn. He had already become addicted to the fast money, and he wasn't thrilled with the idea of graduating from college and going to slave for someone else's dream. He couldn't even be bothered to sit in a classroom all day and listen to professors lecture. Nah, he would keep hustling, stack his paper, and start his own business. Kyrie loved his uncle, but every last one of his speeches about the streets fell on deaf ears.

Mario was just as stubborn as his nephew, and a part of him wanted to lay down the law—disown Kyrie, threaten to cut him off, all that—but he couldn't. Life was short, and he already lost a sister. He couldn't stand the thought of not being in his nephew's life and then, one day, Kyrie being gone. He made it clear that he didn't condone Kyrie's lifestyle, but the boy was now grown, and there wasn't a thing he could do about it except love him, give him advice, and pray for him.

It was a tough decision to make but the last thing he wanted was for Kyrie to keep going behind his back, and so he went with the first option. What Kyrie didn't know was that his uncle was also involved in the streets. He didn't make a living from just being a coach, but that was the side he never wanted his nephew to find out about. Since Kyrie had already made his own way in the streets, Mario figured it would be better to bring him in under him instead of allowing Kyrie to work for someone who would only care about the money he was spending and not his well-being. Mario taught his nephew the in's and out's of the game.

So by the time Kyrie graduated college, his uncle had taught him things about the game that he didn't know, giving him the ultimate advantage. He left college book smart and street-smart. Now Kyrie was running things, and Mario would only step in when he needed to. He had retired as a football coach, but he would always be a street legend. There were also things that Kyrie hipped his uncle to. Mario always felt it was best to keep your focus in one area, specialize in one kind of drug, but Kyrie didn't see it like that. There was a lot of money in weed, and there would always be money in coke. He didn't see why he should have to choose, so he sold both.

"What's up, Auntie?" Kyrie asked as soon as the front door was pulled open.

"Hey, baby, what you out here knocking for?" Candace asked, giving her nephew a big hug as he walked in the door.

"You know I have to knock before I come in."

"That's nonsense. You might not live here anymore, but this is still your house," Candace said, closing the door behind him. She had on a white pair of scrubs, and her hair was pulled back into a neat ponytail. Mario and Candace were both in their fifties, but they looked much younger.

"What's up, old man?" Kyrie asked, walking over to his uncle, who was sitting on the couch watching the news.

"Nothing much. What's up, stranger?" They slapped hands, and then Kyrie took a seat in the recliner next to the couch.

"I just left the office. It's been busy this last week."

"I see that."

"Would you like something to drink, Ky?" Candace asked, getting ready to head out of the living room.

"Nah, I'm good, but thank you."

"Okay. I'm finishing up dinner, so make sure you get a plate before you go."

"A'ight," Kyrie said as she walked out. "Camila been by lately?"

"She stopped by here a few hours ago. I'm sure she's down at that damn strip club now."

"Y'all still being hard on her?"

"We're not being hard enough, and that's the damn problem. Candace didn't want me getting her that strip club in the first place, but we both know how your cousin is."

"Yeah, you're right about that. Once she has her mind set on something, there's no changing the shit."

"Exactly. College wasn't what she wanted to do, and she wasn't about to be leeching off us for the rest of her life. So I gave her what she wanted, which was to own her own business. I'm glad she finally started taking the shit seriously and realized that running a business isn't so easy. She's not like us. You know we're both natural hustlers."

"True enough, but Camila is smart, so I'm pretty sure she has everything under control."

"Oh, she has it under control, but it's how she got it under control that concerns me. The last time I checked, the place was about to be shut down because of the lack of business and her spending money on herself before paying the bills, but now all of a sudden the shit is doing better than ever before."

"What, you wanted it to close or something?"

"I do now, but only because Candace is driving me crazy about opening the shit for her. She swears clubs are dangerous and Camila shouldn't be running one. You know she sits in here all day and watches the depressing-ass news."

"You know Auntie is kind of dramatic, but niggas get shot at the mall and in school. It isn't really safe anywhere."

"I told her that plenty of times, but she still worries. I got Camila the club to help her. Not to be a headache to me. You're a man, so I can get you wanting to do everything on your own without a handout, but Camila . . ." Mario paused and shook his head. "One day, she wants to be a grown, independent boss, and the next, she's back to being spoiled with her hand out. Trust me when

I tell you I'm glad business turned around, because it keeps her out of my pockets. It's just the way it may have turned around that has me concerned. Camila may think she's cool and shit because she dates dusty-ass niggas who tote guns, but she's not 'bout that life with her spoiled, sheltered ass."

"What you talking about?" Kyrie's eyebrows snapped together in confusion.

"I've been informed that Camila is pushing drugs out of the club. I swear, you kids are my karma. I don't know how true it is, but I want you to find out and shut that shit down. You hear me?" Mario looked over at his nephew, and Kyrie could see the anger in his eyes. Mario would go to war with the whole city behind his daughter, but at his age he would rather not. He just wanted her to lie low and chill out.

"Yeah, I got you." Kyrie was amazed at how much his uncle knew. Even as adults, it was hard for him and Camila to get anything over on Mario. His ear was to the streets hard.

"Good. Now go get your uncle a beer." Mario laid his head back on the chair and placed his hands over his protruding belly.

Kyrie just shook his head and got up to go to the kitchen. His uncle's house was nice and in the suburbs, but it was nowhere near as nice as what he really could have afforded. The thing about Mario was he had never been the flashy type. He did a short stint in the streets, and he felt that if he kept a low-enough profile, he wouldn't entice his nephew to follow in his footsteps nor would he bring attention to himself. The money he made from coaching football was barely enough to pay the monthly bills and take care of his wife's car payment, car insurance, et cetera. Yes, she was a nurse, and she had her own bread, but Mario was old school. He prided himself on being a provider, so what his job didn't pay for, he used the money he made in the streets. His wife used her money to do what she pleased, and she loved nice things, so it was nothing for her to have new furniture delivered or to take a nice li'l girls' trip with her sisters. Still, their life wasn't so flashy that Mario made himself look suspicious to anyone. In the eyes of those who didn't know him, he was just a simple man who liked working with kids, and he was middle-class. The money that he now lived off was from his days of stacking drug money, and since he was so modest with his spending, it would last him for a minute. When it ran out, his wife assured him that she would hold him down when she retired from the hospital in a few years. Her 401(k) was already at almost $300,000 and still growing.

"Here you go," Kyrie said, walking back into the living room after he had gotten a beer for himself and his uncle.

He chilled for a couple more hours, and he ate before heading home. An hour later, he had showered and gotten fresh before heading right back out the door. Kyrie's days were often busy, and he didn't get much sleep, but that came along with running a company and the streets. Kyrie was hoping that with the extra help he brought in, he would start having time for himself. He had been working nonstop, and a break was something that he could use. With everything going on uptown, he wasn't so sure if he would ever get one. He finally pulled up to his destination, and his phone started ringing from the cup holder.

"Yooo?" he answered after he had picked his phone up.

"What's up? Where you at?" Ghalen asked.

"I just pulled up at the strip club. I needed to come a little early and check shit out. I take it you're not coming?"

"Nah, Taylin tripping on a nigga." Ghalen sucked his teeth.

He was the same age as Kyrie, but he had been with his baby mama Taylin for a while. They had their only son, Tamir, when they were 16, and they had only been talking for a few months then, but their son had tied them together for life. They often bumped heads over shit like this, but Kyrie knew the two of them would be together forever. They were just crazy in love, and they both stayed showing out. At work, Ghalen was well put together, but off the clock it was a whole different story.

"Damn, if wifey said you can't come, then yo' ass can't come." Kyrie laughed.

"Shut up. You were the one who invited me out, so she's mad at you, too."

"Man, tell Tay to stop that shit. She knows everything is business with us."

"That's the same shit I be telling her, but every time I say it, I'm a lying-ass nigga."

"I ain't got shit to do with that." Kyrie chuckled.

"I was calling to let you know I wasn't gon' make it though."

"A'ight, pussy-whipped-ass nigga," he joked before ending the call.

Kyrie opened his car door and then got out. He walked past the bouncer and gave him a nod before proceeding inside of the club. The music was jumping, and Kyrie could feel the bass from the music. There were a few people sitting around the bar, and a couple of guys were watching a stripper dance while barely throwing any money. It was still early, and Kyrie knew the majority of the people wouldn't start pouring in until after one in the morning.

He walked straight through the club and then went upstairs to where the office was located. He tapped on the door and then opened it and walked inside before anyone responded. When he walked in, he saw Camila sitting at her desk by the door, going off on somebody on her phone. She was wearing a pair of black leather leggings, which looked like they had been painted on, with a black bra top that Kyrie assumed was meant to be a shirt. She had on a pair of six-inch heels, and Kyrie could only shake his head. Camila was going to always stand out and be well put together. One time he went to visit her when she had the flu, and even with a pale face, weak body, and a fever, she had lashes on, lip gloss coated her lips, and her bonnet matched her pajamas.

He walked over to the window and peeped through the blinds. The view overlooked the parking lot, and he could see a few people coming inside. Kyrie continued to watch for a few more seconds before closing them and turning around to face Camila. She ended her phone call and then stood up. She walked over to Kyrie and gave him a big hug before stepping back.

"Hey, what's going on?"

"Just came to check you out. Can you breathe in those damn leggings? I can already see somebody mistaking your ass for one of these strippers, and then I'ma have to body me a muhfucka."

"The perks of having a big brother," Camila said sarcastically. "Since when have you seen strippers walking around in leggings? I swear, you and Daddy stay reaching. Y'all about as dramatic as my mother." She rolled her eyes upward.

Kyrie frowned. "I'm a whole-ass man. There ain't shit dramatic about me. I leave that to females. You got that bread for me?"

"Yeah, the money is in the safe. Just make sure you get it before you leave tonight."

"Bet. But your dad is up on game. I swear we be underestimating his reach in the streets. We got a good li'l thing going on here, but I can't let him find out I'm the one supplying you. We might have to wrap this shit up sooner than expected."

"See, I hate when you start talking like that. Don't even think about cutting me out of the loop, Kyrie! My parents won't find out a thing. I just wish they'd let me grow the fuck up. Dang!" Camila stomped her foot like an over-sized child. "They were bitching when I wasn't making money, and now that I am making money, they're still not happy."

"Your parents just want you safe, Camila. You know that. They don't want to see you in jail or worse."

"But they don't say shit to you."

"Shawty, I got plenty of lectures that you weren't around to hear. Uncle Mario didn't want me in the streets either, but it's a bit different with me. For one, I'm a man, and right or not, there is a double standard."

Camila rolled her eyes. "Yeah, whatever. All I'm saying is let me stack some bread first before you try to call shit quits. I'm hoping that I can get money coming in the right way, too. I just hired a pretty-ass new stripper, and she has a body to die for. You should meet her."

"I'm not interested, but I was sticking around anyway. I'm meeting with someone, so just come find me in the VIP section if you need me."

"Okay, bruh," Camila said and then gave him another hug before he walked out.

By the time Kyrie made it back down to the club area, Mozzy was walking through the door. Kyrie walked over and slapped hands with him before leading him up to the VIP section. Kyrie stopped one of the bottle girls and ordered them a bottle before he took a seat on the comfortable couch. The place was already starting to get packed, and it hadn't even hit twelve yet. That was a good sign, and that was why he knew his cousin would be okay without all of the extra shit.

She seemed to get a thrill out of danger though, and she always had for as long as he could remember. So he knew it wasn't going to be easy getting her to go back legit. If he could, he'd kick his own ass for even asking her to help him wash his dirty money to begin with. He had started making more money out in the streets than he could wash through his own business, and he turned to Camila, who was eager to help.

Since she was willing to help him, he didn't have a choice but to return the favor last year when she came crying to him about her place possibly being shut down because of the lack of business. She may have washed his money, but that didn't make it hers, even though Kyrie had given her permission to use what she needed to keep her business afloat. When he started supplying her with drugs to sell in the club, she started getting a lot more customers, and now that she was seeing all the business she was getting because of the drugs, stopping wasn't her goal anytime soon.

"Damn, this shit nice. You know the owner? I saw you coming from the back when I was walking in," Mozzy said, sitting a few spaces down on the couch.

"Yeah, my cousin owns the shit. What's good with you though?" Kyrie pulled a pack of cigars out of his pocket and then pulled out a blunt that was already rolled.

"I'm just ready to get to this money."

"I know that shit right," Kyrie said, sparking the blunt. "I just basically need you to be ready. At all times. Stay ready and you won't have to get ready. Anything I need handled, when I call you, I need you to be on it. We'll start out small and move up as I see fit."

Mozzy nodded. He was no stranger to the game, and he knew that Kyrie would need to feel him out first. Test him. He didn't have a problem with that. "Ay, that's what I'm here for. Just say the word, and I got you."

The bottle girl finally came back up to their section and placed two bottles of Hennessy down in front of them. Kyrie tipped her, and then she smiled at him before walking away. Kyrie poured himself a drink and passed his blunt over to Mozzy. The DJ was playing nothing but hits from mad Atlanta artists, and the place was now packed to capacity. The vibe was lit, and Kyrie was just chilling and enjoying his night while trying to feel Mozzy out a little bit.

The new stripper his cousin had been talking about was finally about to perform. All of the spotlights were on her as the song came on that she would be performing to. "Throat Baby" by BRS Kash came on, and Kyrie's eyes were trained on the dancer. He thought she was a pretty girl, but he could tell she probably wasn't his type. Kyrie had nothing against strippers, but he just liked a certain kind of woman. He wasn't judging, but he liked a woman who was on her shit and who didn't have to use sex or her body to get there. As Kyrie narrowed his eyes, he thought about how much ol' girl on the stage looked like Khelani. In fact, if it weren't for the difference in their complexions, they could have passed for twins. He had only seen her in passing. He hadn't even had a chance to introduce himself, but he did peep that she was gorgeous indeed.

Kyrie thought Khelani was beautiful, and he wanted to get to know her more since they would be working closely together. He didn't get to where he was by not being a smart businessman, and he knew it might not be smart to start anything personal with her. It was tempting though as he thought back to how her ass looked in those black slacks. She was quiet and professional, and he could dig that. Plenty a hood rat had come to the office dressed nice trying to get a job because their mission was to land a baller. Kyrie had learned to be real careful when it came to who he hired. His last administrative assistant had a degree in business, but she was as ratchet as they came, and she had a nothing-ass baby daddy she let drag her down into the gutter with him. When she wasn't spending her time on the clock on the phone cursing him out, she was always needing to leave work early for some crazy reason. The only reason Kyrie had allowed her to stay around so long was because he had gotten used to her. When she did focus on the job, she did a damn good job of keeping shit running smoothly. However, the final straw had been when her baby daddy came to the office and pulled a gun out on her because he thought she was fucking someone in the office. Kyrie hated to let her go, but that shit was bad for business, and he was no longer able to deal with her shit.

"Hey, bruh, you all right up here?" Camila asked a few minutes later, and Kyrie looked over. He hadn't even noticed her walking up to the VIP section. She wasn't alone, however. She had the new girl in tow, and Kyrie noticed her gray eyes immediately.

"Yeah, I'm chilling." He had a slight buzz going on and was about ready to take it in for the night.

"Cool, I just wanted to bring Anya up here to meet y'all. This is my new moneymaker. She wasn't even dancing like this was her first time, was she?" Camila smiled, gassing Anya up.

"First performance? Damn, I couldn't even tell. Baby, you were working the fuck out of that pole." Mozzy looked over at Anya and licked his lips.

"See? I told you your ass killed that shit," Camila said excitedly. She knew Anya had a lot of potential, and she had already made a shitload of money her first night on the stage.

"I didn't know if you were just boosting my head. Thank you, sweetheart," Anya said, looking at Mozzy.

"I know we just met today, but if you haven't noticed yet, I don't sugarcoat shit. Bitch, you is bad on that stage!" Camila snapped, making Anya giggle. She then turned her attention to Mozzy, who was damn near eye fucking Anya. "Oh, I'm sorry I didn't even introduce myself. I'm Camila, Kyrie's people."

"Nice to meet you. I'm Mozzy." Mozzy was tipsy, but not enough to be disrespectful. He wasn't about to eye fuck his boss's people. He would just focus on fine-ass Anya. Mozzy licked his lips and bit his bottom lip as he zeroed in on Anya's pussy print.

Camila peeped the thirst in Mozzy's eyes. "I just wanted to say hello. You guys have fun and be safe." Camila looked at Anya and winked. "Go get them table dances, girl."

"Come here, let me get a good look at you." Mozzy licked his lips again, and Anya sauntered over to him. He was all up in a section and had his own bottle of Henny, so he must have had some paper, Anya assumed. She didn't know Kyrie paid for the bottles and the section was on the house.

Dressed in a black thong and matching bra, with clear six-inch stilettos on, she stood in front of Mozzy, and he grabbed her hand and made her do a little twirl so he could take all of her in. Her thighs jiggled like Jell-O, and he just knew her ass was talking to him. Her titties were sticking out of her top, and he was ready to French kiss them and wear Anya's ass out in the bedroom. He didn't even take into consideration that he really didn't have money to spare for a dance. Mozzy pulled her down on his lap, and she turned around and smiled at him.

"You sexy as fuck, but you already know that, huh?" he whispered to Anya, his breath tickling her ear. She had a regular ear piercing and an industrial piercing at the top.

"It wouldn't be my first time hearing it." Anya smiled. Flirting was her thing, so this job was right up her alley.

"And it damn sure won't be your last." All of his reservations about spending went out the window when she started gyrating on his lap to the Lil Baby song that was playing.

Kyrie got up in preparation to make his exit. Anya was exactly the type of female he had suspected her to be. She was just another bitch fucking and sucking for her next pair of Louboutin heels. He loved a woman on her shit, but there were more ways to get things than spreading legs for them. There were the strippers who just danced. They didn't fuck men from the club or sell pussy. Kyrie knew right away that Anya was the "anything goes" type.

He picked up his bottle of Henny and took a few more swallows. He knew he couldn't finish a pint to the head, but purchasing the bottle was business for the club. He didn't care about what got left in the bottle. Damn near every person he passed attempted to stop him and speak, but Kyrie simply gave a nod and kept it moving. Once he was in the back, he made his way back up the stairs and went into his cousin's office. He walked over to the closet and then opened the door with a kiss of his teeth before kneeling down to put the code in the safe that was inside of the closet. He had told Camila about not having the door locked. That was that careless shit that he hated dealing with. At times, running some shit with her felt more like babysitting than a partnership.

"You about to head out?" Camila asked, walking in the office.

"Yes, and keep this fucking closet door locked. What do I keep telling you about this shit?"

"Okay, Ky. I hear you." Camila rolled her eyes. "Who was that guy you were sitting with in VIP?" Camila asked as Kyrie got ready to walk out.

"Just a nigga Big Man sent to town to help me out with some shit."

"And you trust him?"

"I don't know him. That's why I have to feel him out. Why? You know something I don't?"

Camila shrugged. "I'm just saying he has that money-hungry look in his eyes. I know it when I see it, and he definitely has it."

"That could be a good thing for me as long as he doesn't get the bright idea to try to cross me, but these days, that's a chance you take with anybody. I got this," Kyrie assured her.

"I hear you. So you weren't interested in Anya at all? She's beautiful, and the bitch has body for days."

"Nah, I told you I wasn't interested off top."

"That was before you even saw her. For as long as I've known you, I've never seen you with anyone. I know you have trust issues, but I was just trying to help."

Kyrie chuckled, "Baby girl, when I'm ready to fuck with somebody, she for damn sure has to have more than a pretty face and a nice body. Atlanta is full of superficial, cappin'-ass wannabe YouTube stars and IG models and 'build a body' females good for pussy and head. That's it."

Camila shook her head. "Don't act like the A isn't full of some boss bitches, too."

"You're right, and I want a boss bitch who didn't become a boss from selling pussy."

"Whatever, Kyrie. Good night." Camila tried not to be too offended by his words, but she was damn near what he described. She wasn't a stripper, but she would give her pussy up to the highest bidder. And she didn't see a damn thing wrong with it.

Chapter 4

"And where have you been?" Khelani asked Anya as she peered over the red coffee mug that was resting against her plump lips. It was almost six in the morning, and Khelani had to be at work in three hours. She needed enough time to go get some weed and give it to Kasim so he could make a move for her. Khelani was exhausted and glad the next day was Saturday so she could sleep in. She kept telling herself that there was no money in sleeping, but her body was tired. She didn't have a life outside of hustling. Grabbing work was shit that Anya could have been doing to help her, and Khelani was starting to resent her sister more and more.

Anya's eyes were barely open, but she managed to roll them. She was drunk as hell and high as fuck and not in the mood to be questioned by her sister. Khelani stood in the kitchen dressed in a red pencil skirt, a black-and-white polka-dot blouse, and gray house slippers. Her curls were popping, and she looked like a damn librarian—a cute librarian, but she still looked like one, and that made Anya frown.

"Work," she snapped and opened the fridge for some juice.

Khelani jerked her head back. "Work? Where in the hell do you work?"

Anya smirked. "A strip club."

Khelani peered at her sister with her mouth agape and waited for her to give an indication that she was joking.

When she saw that Anya appeared to be serious, she placed her cup on the counter.

"Are you trying to make Dad come snatch your ass up?"

"I am grown!" Anya shouted. "He already cut me off. What more can he do? I don't want to sell drugs. I just don't. I'll move out and get my own place. Tell him to send someone else over here to help you and Kasim. You and he both can stop threatening me. I don't care anymore. I'll be out of here in a few days."

Khelani just stared after her sister as she walked away. Life was going to have to kick Anya in the ass a few times before she grew the fuck up. Their mother spoiled her, and Khelani often made excuses for her. Khelani loved Anya to death, but Anya couldn't be her problem anymore. If she wanted to be grown, then she could go be grown. Anya wouldn't always have the luxury of having someone to clean up her messes, and at that moment, Khelani was done. Anya could move out, she could strip, she could defy their father, she could do whatever it was that she felt she needed to do. Khelani finished her coffee and went to put her shoes on. She had to go handle her business. Time spent thinking about Anya's bullshit was time she didn't have.

Once she reached her destination, Khelani scanned the sixty pounds of weed that sat before her. Once she was sure that every pound was accounted for, she grabbed ten and placed them in a black duffel bag. The pounds were in bubble wrap and Saran Wrap, so their potent smell didn't overpower the air. Once the duffel bag was zipped up, she closed the safe back and exited the room. She handed the bag to Kasim.

"I don't wish to sit on the phone half the morning with my father and answer questions about Anya. Call him and tell him he needs to send more help. I'm giving this job at least another five weeks, and I'm tired already. I won't ask you to help me alone. Since Anya isn't pulling her weight, one more person should help."

Kasim nodded. "Got it."

He had known Kemp for more than twenty years. Ten years before, Kasim's wife died from breast cancer. They never had children, and when she died, he was left all alone. His mother had also lost her fight with cancer when he was 19, and Kasim was bitter with life. He was angry, and he had no desire to get close to anyone else. With no one at home, he threw himself into work. He proved himself time and time again and became one of Kemp's most loyal and trusted workers. For Kasim, going with the girls to the States and keeping them safe was an honor, and he was paid handsomely. Kemp sent him $10,000 a month for his bills and personal money. He also sent Kasim money to purchase the black Escalade that he drove the girls around in. Kasim was nothing more than a glorified babysitter, but he didn't mind. Not for what he was getting paid. His bills and living expenses barely came to $2,000 a month. That left him with around $8,000 a month to do with what he pleased.

He knew just like Kemp that Khelani was the smart one. Anya was a rebel and had more than likely given Kemp a few gray hairs. Kasim got paid to do a job, but he didn't necessarily agree with Kemp. He should have sent a nephew or a male cousin to take over the States. Not his daughters. Khelani was headstrong, and she was damn near the male version of Kemp, but she was still a woman. In Kasim's eyes, she didn't need to be risking her life or her freedom to be a queen pin. She should be somewhere getting married and making babies, but she had no interest in that. She was taking over various cities in various states and ensuring that Kemp's empire continued to grow. And as long as she was doing that and he was breathing, Kasim would be by her side as her protector.

Once that was taken care of, Khelani hopped in her car and headed to work. Khelani looked the part of an office worker. It was her second day at work, and she was wondering if she'd at least meet Kyrie. Many would kill for the $2,400 salary she was getting every two weeks, but that barely covered the rent on her condo. Khelani could make that in one day. She needed to figure out how to meet the people she needed to meet—the ones who would buy weed by the pound. Several pounds at a time.

"You're too powerful. You know that right? No man will ever want to be with you because you'd steal his shine. You need to be softer. More submissive."

The words that Kasim spoke to Khelani played over and over in her mind. Most days, she loved being who she was. Khelani loved being strong, determined, smart. She'd seen other females laugh and giggle and play the role of a dumb bimbo just to stroke a man's ego, and she would never. She saw the women who broke their necks to chase niggas with a bag. She also would never. Khelani had her own bag, but she was a woman by nature. Sometimes, just once in a blue moon, she wanted to be soft. She wanted to be dainty and not have to worry about running a drug empire. Anya was right about one thing. They'd never been given a choice. Khelani just always did what was expected of her, whatever it took to make her parents happy, and she soon found it was easier to make her father happy than it was her mother. Her mother criticized everything, and nothing was ever good enough for her. Khelani could bust her ass only to be ridiculed, but Anya could throw together the bare minimum and their mother would be elated.

She could relate to Anya when she complained about Khelani being her father's favorite. If Khelani ever had kids, she couldn't see herself having a favorite. But then again, she didn't have kids, so she didn't know what she'd do or wouldn't do. It just didn't seem fair.

Once Khelani arrived at work, she parked her car, grabbed her things, and headed inside. She ran into the elevator just before the doors could close, and she came face-to-face with a very handsome man. He was six foot four with skin the color of melted caramel and a thick, full beard. His head held a mass of curls, and he had an athletic build, like that of a football player. His cologne filled the air inside of the elevator, and he was dressed in black jeans that weren't too loose or too tight, a black button-up shirt, and a pair of wheat-colored Timberlands. He didn't look too street, and he wasn't really dressed up, but he didn't look out of place at all. If Khelani was looking for a man, her job would be the perfect place to find one because there wasn't a shortage of them at the record label.

"What floor?" The man in the elevator had a voice so deep that it made Khelani's pussy quiver. That was something powerful indeed. She had to squeeze her legs together to stop the sensation.

"Third. Thank you."

The stranger cocked his head slightly to the left. "Khelani, right?"

Khelani turned her face toward his. "Yes. Khelani Touissant."

The man extended his hand for her to shake. "I'm Kyrie. The owner of the label."

Khelani wasn't sure what to expect with Kyrie, but she damn sure didn't expect for him to be that fine. She shook his hand and gave him a small smile. "It's a pleasure to meet you."

"Likewise. I've heard good things about you so far. Keep up the good work."

The elevator stopped on the designated floor, and Kyrie tipped his head in her direction and stepped off.

Khelani was right behind him, and her eyebrows shot up as she headed toward her desk. The perks at the record label were looking better and better. She ruled out the thought of love long ago, but the fiasco in North Carolina had for sure reminded her that she was naive as hell. She was naive to think that happily-ever-after fairy-tale love bullshit was true. There were people who were happy and in love, but in most instances, it was a facade. Khelani learned with her parents that what people often showed the world was a different story than what went on behind closed doors. She didn't have the desire nor the energy to fake any damn thing, and she had no desire to change who she was to get a man to claim he liked her, maybe even loved her, only to take her for granted.

Khelani gave a smile and a hello to those around her before sitting down to log into her computer. From what she knew, Kyrie wasn't only a successful businessman, but he flooded most of Georgia and South Carolina with coke. He also dabbled in weed. From what she understood, he got the majority of the money from his coke. Khelani's plans were to eventually become the most sought-after marijuana connect in Georgia, and Kyrie could do one of two things. He could either fall in line and start buying from her, or she would take his clientele and there wouldn't be shit he could do about it.

After logging into her computer, Khelani got right to work. Being about her business came natural to her, so she worked diligently. Kasim knew not to bother her unless it was an absolute emergency, and she didn't have friends or a social media page. Her phone was on vibrate, and it wasn't a distraction. Khelani worked hard, and before she knew it, three hours had passed. Little did Khelani know, she was being watched by a lot of the people in the office, and they admired her hard work. To them, she didn't appear to have a motive. She didn't constantly ask questions about the rappers signed to the label, and she hadn't asked when any of the parties or events were. She was a breath of fresh air, but no one was watching her harder than Kyrie.

Since being close to her in the elevator, all of his common sense went out the window. Sleeping with the employees would more than likely end up bad every time, but he wouldn't be him if he didn't at least attempt to get to know Khelani.

"Knock knock." Kim stuck her head in the door and said the words instead of actually knocking.

Kyrie tore his eyes away from the monitor on his desk. There were cameras in every room at his label, and he watched his employees regularly. Kim had been working for him the longest, and she knew him almost as well as he knew himself.

"Looking at the new girl?" She entered his office without being invited.

Kyrie smirked. "You think you know me."

"I do know you, nigga. Remember what happened last time?" She sat down in front of him and crossed her legs.

Kyrie smiled and shook his head. "Nothing bad happened last time."

"Nothing except one of the damn cleaners became obsessed with you after you fucked her. You would go days without coming in just to avoid her."

Kyrie laughed at the memory. "But then she got pregnant by Sway, and I haven't seen the bitch since."

"Anyway, I won't be here tomorrow. My daughter has a doctor's appointment, but I think Khelani can keep things running. She's a fast learner and about her business."

"So I've been hearing. Ghalen said the same thing. I think I'm going to invite her to Kobie's party tomorrow."

Kim's eyebrows hiked up. "Are you inviting her so she can get to know some of the artists on the label or for personal reasons?"

"I'm your boss, shawty. You're not mine. Chill on the interrogation."

Kim put her hands up in surrender. "You got it, boss. She's a hard worker, so don't mess this one up, because you might be in charge, but when the admin assistant slacks, it makes my job harder."

Kyrie kissed his teeth. "I got you, damn. You don't have no faith in your boy."

"None at all." Kim was half joking and half serious as she stood up and walked away.

Kyrie picked up his phone and dialed Khelani's extension. He licked his lips when the melodic tone of her voice came through the speaker of the phone. "It's Kyrie. Can you pause whatever you're doing and step inside my office for a minute?"

"Sure. I'll be right there."

Kyrie sat back in his chair and waited for Khelani. "Come in," he called out after she knocked lightly on the door.

When Khelani entered the office, Kyrie's dick got harder than steel. He wasn't sure if it was the hair, her eyes, her curves, or what. He was so used to women with weaves hanging down to their asses that her natural hair was sexy as hell to him. Her nails were short and a nude color. Everything about her was classy and simple. Khelani was his definition of a bad bitch. She didn't have to do too much at all and she could still gain a man's undivided attention. "Have a seat." He motioned his head toward the chair.

Khelani sat down, and Kyrie tried to read her. She looked confident and sure of herself. There wasn't the slightest hint of nervousness displayed. Kyrie found it odd that he was damn near lost on how to come at her.

"Tell me a little bit about yourself. What made you want to work for a record label?"

"I'm twenty-four, and I am from Trinidad. I've been in the States for two years, and I've only been in Atlanta for one month. I didn't necessarily set out to work at a record label, but when I read the job description, I felt that my experience and skills would be an asset to the label."

Her answer made Kyrie's dick even harder. There was nothing like a smart, sexy chick.

"Word. Your résumé is definitely impressive. What brought you to Atlanta?" His eyes scanned her finger to see if she was wearing a wedding ring.

"I love the fact that there are so many professional black people here."

"Indeed, there are. You have kids? A man? I ask because one of my artists, Kobie, is having a party tomorrow night. All the artists on the label will be there. It will be a good way for you to meet everyone. We're like family around here."

"I don't have kids, and I am single. My sister is the only person I know here, so a networking event will be nice. Just give me the information and I'm there."

"I'll get your number off your résumé and text you. Enjoy the rest of your day."

"Thank you."

Kyrie lustfully watched her as she walked out of his office. She was new in town and had only been in the States for two years. He wondered what her story was, but he didn't want her to feel like he was interrogating her, so he cut the Q&A session short. If she was single, there would be time to get to know her later. He already knew that the men at the party would be on her like dogs on meat.

It was time for lunch, so Kyrie left the office to head down to one of his favorite restaurants. As he was heading toward his car in the parking garage, he saw Khelani getting into a burnt orange Beemer.

Goddamn, and she got bread, too? I need to find out what's up with her for real.

Kyrie's phone rang, breaking him from the trance that Khelani had him in. He saw that his homie Tae was calling. "What up?"

"Yo, we have a slight issue. Kenyatta didn't re-up this month, and neither did Jimmy or Vato. There seems to be a new connect in town with some fire-ass weed."

Kyrie pinched the bridge of his nose. There were a total of six dope-ass rappers and singers signed to his label, and they were all making him money out of the ass. He wasn't broke. The money he made from the label was what he paid his bills with, and there was often money left over even after he looked out for different people and spent money on dumb shit. The money he made from coke went into his retirement fund, and the money he made from weed was his bullshit money. Like when he wanted to go to Dubai for five days or spend $120,000 on a watch. It for damn sure wouldn't cause him to run up on hard times because a few people didn't re-up, but that wasn't what he was trying to hear.

"And who is this person?"

"I don't know yet. I'm trying to find out."

"Do that."

Kyrie ended the call and started his car with a scowl on his face. He was the man to see in Atlanta for weed, and he needed to know who was trying to step in on his territory so they could be handled accordingly.

Chapter 5

"What's this?" Anya asked Camila as she pulled into the parking lot of a white building. There was a sign on it that said CUTZ AND GRILLZ. As soon as Anya woke up for the day, Camila was texting her and asking her if she wanted to hang.

"My girl Caresha does hair in the front, and her nigga Snow does grills in the back. I have to come pick my shit up from him, but Caresha is one of the dopest stylists in the city, and she doesn't charge celebrity prices. You should check her out."

When Anya straightened her hair, it touched the middle of her back, so she didn't really see the need to spend a crazy amount of money on bundles. She had her own thick mane, but she did like to rock braids every few months. She got out of the car and followed Camila into the establishment. If she kept having nights at the club like her first night, she'd be able to move out of Khelani's condo and into her own place in no time. It was time to finally show her dad and sister that she was grown and could take care of herself. A nice-ass one-bedroom was attainable as long as she kept seeing good money from dancing.

When Anya and Camila entered the building, the first thing Anya noticed was that it was hood as hell. A pretty brown-skinned chick with a purple lace front on was standing behind a swivel chair doing a sew-in. There was one person under the dryer and another waiting.

"Hey, boo," the girl with the purple hair spoke to Camila.

"Hey, love. This is my girl Anya. She's new in town, and I told her you do the best hair around."

"That I do." Caresha smiled.

Anya smiled back, but she could feel the other patrons of the shop eyeballing her. With her face and her body, she was used to glares from jealous bitches. She didn't care as long as nobody said anything to her.

"Snow back there? I have to pick my grill up."

Caresha rolled her eyes upward. "Yeah, his trifling ass is back there. Bitch-ass nigga," she mumbled, and Camila chuckled.

"Y'all on that again? You hate him at least once a month, but neither one of y'all not going nowhere."

"Keep thinking that," Caresha stated with a suck of her teeth.

"Don't worry. I am." Camila started walking to the back, and Anya followed her.

When they reached the back, Anya peeped a brown-skinned dude with shoulder-length dreads. They were dyed blond, and ordinarily, she wouldn't care for a guy with dyed hair of any color, but Snow wasn't bad looking at all. He was a little short for her taste. He looked to be about five foot nine, but he couldn't have everything. If his pockets were deep, that would make up for his height. For a second, Anya thought she was getting beside herself, but she didn't miss the way Snow looked at her before greeting Camila.

"What up? I was just about to text you. I got that all wrapped up for you."

"I can't wait to see them," Camila squealed while Anya looked around.

"How long would it take for me to get a bottom grill?" she inquired while looking at various pictures on the wall of grills that Snow had made.

"If you have time, I can do the mold now, and you can come back and get them tomorrow."

"Bet." Anya looked over at Camila. "We got time for that?"

"Sure."

Camila watched as Snow grabbed some gloves while Anya got comfortable in his chair. Snow was the average man. He would eye fuck any decent-looking female and try to actually fuck most of them. Caresha had caught him in so much shit over the years it wasn't even funny. They had an intense history. Snow and Caresha met in middle school. He took her virginity at the age of 15, and they had been together off and on for the past eleven years. In that eleven years, they had three kids, and he'd given her four different STDs. The longest they ever stayed apart was four months, and Caresha had the time of her life being really single for the first time. She was having too much fun, because when Snow caught wind of that shit, he damn near committed suicide. Camila didn't understand why Caresha put up with his shit, but she didn't need to. At the end of the day, Camila was her girl, and she had her back. That was why, as soon as they were done and in her car, she put Anya up on game.

"That nigga Snow is gon' flirt with you. I bet my bottom dollar on that shit, but he's off-limits. No matter what Camila says, she and Snow are locked in. Don't even mess with his ass."

Anya simply nodded. She wasn't going to throw herself at Snow, but if he came on to her, she just might see what he was talking about. She respected Camila's loyalty, but Caresha was her friend. Anya didn't know the bitch, and she said out of her own mouth that she and Snow were broken up. It had been over a month since Anya had some dick, and she was ready. Mozzy had been on her hard as hell when she gave him a lap dance, but she was on the fence about him. He was a'ight, but Snow looked way better.

Camila cut into Anya's thoughts. "My cousin, the one in VIP last night, he has a record label. One of his artists is having a party tomorrow. You trying to come?"

Anya looked over at her newfound friend with wide eyes. "Fuck yes, I want to go! Shit, I need a new outfit. Wait, my sister works for a record label. I wonder if his is the one. What's his name again?"

"Kyrie Richmond."

Yep, that's him. Small world. Camila's cousin was the plug and the person Khelani was trying to get connections through. "Sounds familiar. I have to ask her, but I'm in."

"Awesome. I'm telling you, stick with me, kid, and Atlanta will be good to you."

All Anya could do was smile because, for some reason, she felt that this was true, and she was all for it.

The next day, Anya went to the mall and picked out an outfit that was sure to turn heads at the party. Since her father had cut her off and she knew Khelani wouldn't give her money, she had to use the money she made the night before, which was damn near a stack. Anya had a pair of black Gucci tights that would set the outfit off just right. They were see-through with the Gs on them. She was going to rock a pair of denim booty shorts, a black bra, and some strappy black heels. Anya could pull a man in sweats and a hoodie, but to go to the club, she was putting all the goods she'd been blessed with on display. She needed to hit a lick. And in her mind, any sexy-ass nigga with money was the lick she needed to come across. Honestly, he didn't even have to be sexy. An ugly nigga with deep pockets would do the trick, too. A middle-aged white man was the person who purchased her first Fendi bag for her. Even though Anya came from money, a man still had to be on his shit to have sex with her. In her eyes, she was a princess and needed to be treated as such. And what better way to treat a princess than to spoil her relentlessly? She wasn't Khelani, and she wasn't working for a damn thing. Unless one counted her working that pole at Camila's club.

Anya was glad that when she went to get her grills from Snow, the hair salon portion of the shop was closed and empty. She knew that, whether Snow was single at the moment or not, if she pulled up without Camila while Caresha was there, all eyes and ears would have been on her.

"Hey," she greeted Snow as she entered the room and saw him perched on a stool, head down, scrolling through his phone.

He looked up and smiled at her. "What's good, baby girl? I got your shit right here." He stood up, and Anya's eyes fell on his dick print in his gray sweatpants. It looked like he was working with a monster for sure.

"Good. I'm going to a party tonight, and I want to rock them."

"Oh, yeah? That all you doing tonight?" Snow tossed Anya a curious glance.

She eyed him intently to look for a clue that he was flirting. She didn't want to take his kindness and casual conversation to mean something more if he wasn't actually trying to get at her, but she could read the look in his eyes. Snow was flirting with her. "Is there something else that I need to be doing?"

Snow smirked and licked his lips. "I'll leave that up to you to decide. I'll probably be out tonight too. Take my number."

Anya bit her bottom lip and looked Snow up and down. He was dressed very casual and plain in gray Polo sweats and a plain white tee that fit snug on his muscular frame. He was lean, but Anya could tell he worked out. Her eyes took in the veins that bulged down his arms, and she wondered if he had protruding veins in his dick. The only jewelry he wore was a watch. A lot of people rocked grills, but Anya couldn't look at Snow and surmise how much he was holding. Maybe he had money. Maybe he didn't. There was something about him though, and even if he didn't have bread like that, maybe he could scratch her sexual itch until she found the baller to come along and scoop her.

"Nah, it ain't gon' be that easy. You gon' have to call me, and if I'm free, we might be able to link."

"I heard that." Snow unlocked his phone, and Anya rattled off her number to him.

She smiled even wider when he rang her up and gave her 50 percent off her grills. She definitely didn't want to spend all of her money, especially since she was missing a night of work to go to the party with Camila, but she wasn't even mad. If she played her cards right, missing work would be worth it. After putting her grills in, Anya smiled at her reflection in the mirror. Yeah, she was that bitch for sure. After flirting with Snow for a few more minutes, Anya got in her car and headed home. Tonight was going to be a movie, and she was excited as hell. When she pulled into the parking garage, she saw that Khelani was home, and she decided to ask her about the party. They hadn't been seeing much of each other lately, and Anya wondered if she was still mad at her. More than likely she was, because Khelani could hold a damn grudge.

When Anya entered the condo, she saw Khelani standing at the island in the kitchen pulling a plastic bag containing a seafood boil out of a plastic bag. She was dressed in a gray robe, and her hair had been straightened and was pulled up into a high ponytail.

"Damn, that smells good." Anya's stomach growled as the aroma from the food wafted into her nostrils. When Khelani didn't speak, Anya kissed her teeth. "Damn, K, you still mad? Get off that shit already. You know I love you, and me not helping was nothing personal against you."

Khelani untied the plastic bag and removed a shrimp. "Oh, you actually love someone other than yourself? Interesting."

"Really?" Anya's feelings were low-key hurt. "Say I didn't help you in North Carolina. Say I didn't tell you that I didn't want to do it anymore time and time again. Say I didn't encourage you to let this shit go and give Malachi a chance when you started feeling him."

"Well, that would have been the wrong thing to do. He would have robbed me blind, and I would have defied Dad for nothing."

"Okay, so besides that. I get that some niggas aren't shit, but are you truly happy living like this? If you choose not to fall in love, do it because that's what you want and not what Dad is telling you. He can't dictate your life. 'Don't fall in love. Choose the money.' What? You don't want kids one day?"

"Anya, none of that changes that you've seen me running myself ragged working a job and hustling and you never offered to help since we've been here. You just sleep and party and leave me to figure shit out on my own, but it's all good. Delante is coming over to help me and Kasim out."

"K, please stop being mad at me. I'm sorry. I miss my sister. We are all we have here."

"Okay, whatever." Khelani pulled her corn on the cob from the bag and began eating it.

"So the owner of the club that I dance at, Camila, is Kyrie's cousin. We're going to some party tonight that he's throwing. How is it working for him?"

Khelani shrugged one shoulder. "It's a job, and it's serving its purpose. I'll be at the party too. I haven't met any of the artists at work, so tonight will be my chance. It won't be tonight, but once I'm in good with a few of them, I'll ask them who they cop their weed from and ask them if they want to try my shit. No true smoker ever turns down the chance to taste different kinds of exotic weed."

"See! You have a good plan. It might not even take you six weeks at that job to gain the clientele you need. Once a handful of people get their hands on that shit you're pumping, word of mouth will do the rest."

"Hope so."

Anya could tell Khelani still had a slight attitude, but she was softening up a bit. She was a natural hard ass, but if she loved you, you'd know it.

Anya walked over to the fridge to look for something to eat. Khelani's food smelled so good, she wished she had stopped and gotten something, but she wasn't going back out. Anya knew she had to put something on her stomach before she started drinking. She and Khelani stayed on the go too much to ever spend a lot of time cooking, so there wasn't a lot to choose from. Anya quickly decided on a bacon, egg, and cheese sandwich, and she gathered the necessary ingredients. She playfully looked over at Khelani, who was eating in silence.

"Dang, I know you're mad. You didn't even offer a nigga a shrimp."

A small smile graced Khelani's beautiful face. "You know I don't play 'bout my shrimp, but you can have a cluster of crab legs."

"Ohhh, thank you." Anya's eyes lit up as she reached for the crab legs.

When she was done cooking and eating, Anya saw that it was almost ten, so she took a shot of Don Julio and went to take a shower. She blasted her music, and an hour and a half later, she was dressed, her makeup done. She entered the kitchen and saw Khelani standing in the living room scrolling through her phone.

"Sis, you look amazing!" Anya gushed, and she wasn't exaggerating either. It had been a long time since she'd seen Khelani dress up in something other than work clothes. She hated how her sister was so all about business and never let her hair down. She loved money too, but damn, what good was having the money if you never took time off to enjoy it?

Khelani was dressed in a nude bodycon dress that looked painted on. The dress clung to every curve of her body like it had been tailored just to fit her. On her feet were peep-toe black platform heels, and her hair hung down past her shoulders.

"Thank you," she replied to her sister. "My Uber is almost here."

"Wait! You have to take a shot with me." Anya ran over to the island and poured Khelani some tequila in a shot glass. She was going to drink hers straight from the bottle.

Khelani did want to let her hair down a bit and have some fun, so she grabbed the glass without protesting and tossed it back. She scrunched up her face as the harsh liquid made its way down her throat.

"Okay, I have to go. He's a minute away, and you know sometimes the elevator is slow."

"Byeeeee, sissy." Anya was feeling good off her two shots, and she took another one. Her phone chimed, and she ran to her room to get it. Seeing a text from Camila that she was on the way made Anya smile.

By the time she put gloss on her lips, heels on her feet, and sprayed some perfume, Camila had arrived. When Anya got in the car, the smell of weed smacked her in the face.

"Okay, you smoking that premium gas," Anya declared.

"And that's all I smoke." Camila passed her the blunt, and the women danced in their seats and turned up all the way to the club.

Anya was on a mission. She had Snow in her back pocket when she wanted dick, and now she needed a money man. She didn't come to the A to play, and it was time for her to leave her mark.

Chapter 6

"Nigga said he got it from a bitch," Tae informed Kyrie as they sat in the back of his Bentley. Kyrie had a whole fleet of cars, six to be exact, and he kept a driver on standby for occasions like these. Tonight was a celebration, and he had already kicked it off. He sat in the back of the luxury car with a bottle of Belaire in one hand and a fat-ass blunt in the other.

"A bitch?" He frowned up his face before placing the blunt between his lips and taking a deep pull. "What's her name?" His voice came out choppy as the smoke left his lungs.

"Kenyatta claimed that she just told him that he could deal directly with a nigga named Kasim, but he knew she was running shit."

The scowl on Kyrie's face deepened. "How you do business with a bitch and you don't even know her name?"

Tae shrugged. "He just said she was a pretty-ass bitch. Not from around here, and he could tell she was on some boss-type shit. Said her weed is like that. Shorty got some mochi, gelato, and some other kind of weed. Platinum skunk or some shit."

Kyrie kissed his teeth in agitation. "So this nigga was so mesmerized by the bitch's beauty that he didn't even ask her name? Ain't no fuckin' way. What if her ass is the law? Is her being pretty gonna save his dumb ass?"

Tae shrugged. "I'm just the messenger. If her weed is potent like that, we'll find out how to get in touch with her soon enough."

Kyrie hit the blunt feverishly to keep his agitation at bay. It was supposed to be a night of fun. He had accomplished a lot and had several multimillionaires signed to his label. If he was being honest with himself, Kyrie knew that it was his ego that had him tripping about this new weed supplier. He didn't need the money he was missing, but he certainly wanted it. Of course, he wasn't the only person in the A who sold weed, but he was still pissed that someone came in and took several of his customers away at once. What if more followed?

As his driver pulled up in front of the club, Kyrie placed the bottle of champagne to his lips and took a swig. Fuck all that. It was time to celebrate. He put the bottle down and exited the car. As he stood on the sidewalk and waited for Tae, he saw Khelani walking toward the entrance, and his dick reacted as it normally did when he saw her. The effect that she had on his manhood was crazy. He peeped that she was alone, and he eyed her through hooded lids.

"I'm glad you could make it," he stated, stepping closer to her. He saw some niggas turn around and stare at her ass, just as he'd predicted. Men would be on her all night unless he kept her close.

Kyrie wasn't even concerned with her presence potentially hindering females from trying him. He had one or two females he rocked with when he got horny, and they didn't play the club like that. In fact, one of them went to church every Wednesday and every Sunday. She played that good-girl role to a T, but she was one of the biggest freaks he'd ever met.

"Thank you for inviting me," Khelani replied, showing off stark white teeth.

"You can roll with me. I have the entire VIP section on lock."

"Damn, who is this?" Tae inquired as he looked Khelani up and down.

When Kyrie answered, he shot Tae a look that only he could read. He was silently telling him that Khelani was off-limits. "This is Khelani. She's my new administrative assistant. Khelani, this is my homie Tae."

"Nice to meet you."

The small group headed inside the club and was immediately ushered into the VIP section. The club was packed, and when they entered the section, Kobie and around thirty more people were already lit. Thick weed smoke lingered in the air, and the bottles of liquor seemed to be never-ending.

"What up, boss man?" Kobie greeted Kyrie with a homeboy hug.

Kyrie introduced Kobie to Khelani, and then he passed him the black box that he brought inside the club.

"Happy birthday, my nigga. May this year be even greater than the last."

Kobie opened the box and lost his cool when he saw the diamond-encrusted chain. "This shit is sick," he screamed and bounced around the club section, showing it off.

Kobie was a good kid. He was 20, and he signed his deal at the age of 18. With his advance money, he bought his mom a house, and he bought his dream car. After that, he worked hard, and the fame came fast. He had a whole slew of cousins and friends who felt entitled to his money, and finally after spending thousands upon thousands of dollars loaning people money that they never paid back, paying the bills of a good five people every month, bailing niggas out of jail, et cetera, he got fed up and cut a lot of people off. He had purchased jewelry for himself, but the $19,000 necklace that Kyrie gifted him was the most expensive gift he'd ever received in his life. Shit, aside from Kyrie and the other artists at the label, nobody else even got Kobie a birthday gift except his mom and his girl.

He damn near cried when his girlfriend gifted him ten pairs of sneakers. It was the thoughtfulness. Everyone else assumed that because he was rich, he didn't need other people to buy him gifts, but Kobie just wanted to know he was appreciated. The gift didn't even have to be expensive.

"You give good gifts," Khelani stated as a bottle girl came by and handed Kyrie a bottle of Hennessy.

"Thank you. He works hard. He deserves it." He eyed a stack of cups on the table. "Would you like a drink?"

"Umm, sure, but I already drank some Don Julio. I can't do that dark."

"No problem. I see some right over there. I'll be right back."

Khelani watched him walk over to retrieve the bottle. Kyrie was handsome indeed. She killed Malachi a month before she left North Carolina, so it had only been two months since she'd been with a man. She wasn't pressed, and she stayed too busy to be lonely, but she wondered for a brief moment what it would be like to wet his beard up. Shit, she was still human, and she still got urges. If she was going to let him get her rocks off, she knew she'd need to do it before he found out who she was. Sometimes all women wanted was the dick too. Kemp had been on her ass since she was a preteen, so Khelani had never been in love. Not even once. She came close to it at 17, but when Kemp found out, he deaded that shit. Khelani didn't lose her virginity until she was 20. In her entire life, she'd been with two men.

"Thank you." She took the drink Kyrie handed to her.

"Would it be awkward if I asked you out? I'm not even gon' stand here and pretend like I'm not intrigued by you. You working for me makes me a bit hesitant to cross the lines, but I see you as being mature enough to handle it. No pressure. Just two grown single people hanging out off the clock. What do you say?"

He was cute enough for her to fantasize about, but Khelani hadn't really expected him to ask her out. Even if there would be no love connection, in an effort to keep him close, she agreed. "What do you have in mind?"

"Maybe dinner tomorrow evening. I can get my homie to close up his restaurant and cook us a gang of good shit. His food is the truth, and I'm a silent partner."

"Impressive. Sure, we can do that."

"Bet. I'm going to go mingle a li'l bit instead of staying stuck up under you like a sucka. Watch out for these niggas 'cause they gon' be on you. Better yet, maybe I should stay."

Khelani laughed. "I'll be fine. I see Kim over there."

Kyrie did a double take as he saw Camila and Anya entering the section. "Yo, that chick right there, do you know her? The two of you could pass for sisters."

"We are sisters."

"Damn. At least I know I'm not tripping. Well, now I feel better about walking off. I'll text you a time for our date."

"Got it." Khelani smiled.

"Okay, I see you with the fine man all in ya face," Anya joked as she hugged her sister while Camila smirked.

Anya's sister was just as gorgeous as her, and she looked like Kyrie's type, especially if she was the stick in the mud Anya had described. Kyrie didn't like lit bitches. He liked boring women, and he still didn't even wife them, so Camila knew all he wanted to do was stick dick to this chick.

Anya made introductions and right away, Khelani got bad vibes. "This is my sissy, Khelani, and this is my boss and friend and Kyrie's cousin, Camila."

"Nice to meet you." Khelani gave her a fake smile. Camila was dressed in a black dress that was completely see-through. Her nipples were on full display. She didn't even try to put on pasties or anything. Khelani could see right away why Anya gravitated to her, because that was for sure some shit she'd wear.

The women chatted for a few, and when Kyrie came over, Khelani could damn near feel the heat radiating off of him.

"Girl, what the fuck you got on?" he spat in a tone full of disdain. "Ay, I'm 'bout to walk the fuck away from you 'cause you tripping like a muhfucka. Have some respect for yourself."

Camila rolled her eyes upward. "Here you go being all extra and shit. They're just breasts, damn. I can't help it if I'm not one of those boring-ass church hoes you like to fuck."

Kyrie didn't even respond. He simply walked off. Khelani peeped the slight shade. She wasn't dumb. She didn't like Camila's ass off rip, but unless she came right out and disrespected her, she'd spare the little thot. Khelani wanted to stay far away from her, and she hoped that Anya didn't find her way into trouble with this ho.

Just as Khelani finished off her drink, her phone rang. When she looked down and saw that Kasim was calling her, she walked off. There wasn't a place in the club that she could go where music wouldn't be loud, but she didn't want to talk to him in front of Anya or a stranger. Anya was no longer a part of the family business. Khelani walked toward the bathroom and stuck one finger in her ear to block some of the noise.

"Hello?"

"Just hitting you to let you know that I'm about to go meet James. I told him I don't do this late-night shit, but he just got back in town. I'm making an exception because he's spending double what he spent last time."

Khelani's eyebrows furrowed. Delante wasn't in town yet, and she didn't like the thought of Kasim going to make a play at damn near one in the morning alone. "Swing by the club and get me. I don't want you going alone."

"Khelani, no. Don't insult me. I'm a grown-ass man. I can conduct business without you being with me."

Khelani rolled her eyes upward and kissed her teeth. "It doesn't matter what my gender is. I'm an extra set of eyes, and we don't know this nigga to trust him. I'm going with you. I'll text you the address, and you just call me when you're outside." She ended the call before he could protest.

"Oh, my bad," Khelani stated when she turned around and ran into Kyrie.

"Nah, it's my bad for not paying attention. That damn Camila has me hot." He shook his head.

Khelani chuckled. "If she's anything like my sister, she keeps you hot then. I learned long ago to stop even caring. Let her figure life out on her own. She's grown."

"I feel you, but the shit she be doing isn't even called for. You good though?"

"Yeah. Something actually came up, and I have to leave in a few."

Kyrie eyed her intensely. What could come up this time of night but sex? Maybe a nigga hit her and told her he was about to come scoop her. She told him she was single, but that didn't mean she wasn't fucking someone. He peered into her eyes and envisioned what it would be like to slide up in her. Was another nigga about to do that? "We still on for tomorrow?"

"Yes. Of course."

"A'ight. Be safe, and I'll text you."

Khelani smiled and walked away while Kyrie shook his head to himself. He was putting too much thought into where she might be going. Technically, it wasn't his business. He wasn't even on that kind of time to be caring what a female did, but he was learning fast that Khelani wasn't too much like most women, and that shit had him curious as hell.

"Damn, you fucked up." Snow bit his bottom lip and narrowed his eyes at Anya, who was sitting on the couch in his friend's den. He damn sure couldn't take her to his mama's house, and he didn't want to get a room when he wasn't sure if they would link. He kept thinking she was bullshitting, but in actuality, she was trying to get away from Camila.

Snow stayed with his mom or different homeboys whenever he and Caresha were on the outs. If he fucked Anya and the pussy was good, he'd have no problem splurging on hotel rooms to fuck her thick ass in. Caresha had a pretty face, and he loved her to death, but not even birthing three kids gave her an ass. He always joked that he was going to buy her one, but they broke up so much, he was scared to. He would be damned if he paid for her to get her body done and she went and fucked the next man. He'd kill her ass for real.

"I feel good as shit. Why you all the way over there?" she purred. Her lids were so low from weed and liquor that it looked like her eyes were closed.

"You want me over there with you?" Snow licked his lips. He walked over to Anya with his hand on his semi-hard dick.

"Let me see that shit," she giggled, moving his hand out of the way and reaching inside to feel what he was working with. There was nothing shy about Anya.

She didn't have as much luck at the party as she had anticipated, but she was so drunk and high that, at the moment, she didn't care. A famous producer asked for her number, but there was no guarantee that he'd call. A rapper wanted to take her home, but he wanted her to have a threesome with another bitch from the club, and she wasn't with that. Maybe she would have if she already had him locked in and she did it with him on some wild, fun shit. But she wasn't about to compete with another bitch the very first time that she had sex with a nigga. Anya knew she was a freak, and her pussy was good for sure, but if he couldn't be satisfied with just her, fuck him.

"Ummmm," she moaned when she saw he was working with a nice size. It was thick and long. Not huge, but she could definitely work with the shit.

"You like that shit?" he asked in a low tone.

Anya didn't answer. She just pulled it out and studied it for a bit. She had no interest in playing the good-girl role. She didn't have to wait until the fifth or sixth time to give him head. Anya enjoyed giving head. She liked seeing the faces men made and the whimpers and moans that her fellatio caused. The ultimate foreplay for her was making a nigga putty in her hands. Anya took Snow's dick into her mouth, and he let out a low, guttural moan as the head of his wood touched the back of her throat. Anya slowly pulled back, then laced his shaft with spit. She rotated her wrist and slowly began to jack him off while she sucked him. Anya's eyelids fluttered as she went in on his dick, and seconds later, Snow was moaning and fucking her face. Anya's dick-sucking skills had his toes curling and his breathing shallow.

Anya pulled her head back, smirked, and wiped her mouth as she stood up to undress. Her pussy was wet from sucking Snow off, and now she wanted to be pounded. Snow followed her lead and undressed as well. After securing a condom on his dick, he grabbed Anya's C-cup breasts and ran his tongue back and forth across her large nipples. Ready to get the party started, Anya slipped a finger between her moist folds and rubbed her clit while he sucked. She had the engine humming, so by the time he twirled her around and bent her over the couch, slid his dick in her, and hit her with a few strokes, Anya was screaming bloody murder while she came all on his dick.

Remembering that he was a guest in someone else's home, Snow clasped a hand around Anya's mouth to silence her cries of pleasure while he continued to drill into her. His balls slapped against her pussy as he fucked her savagely with one hand around her mouth. When she quieted her cries, he moved his hand down to her neck and began to choke her, and that instantly made Anya have another orgasm.

"Goddamn," Snow panted as Anya creamed on his dick a second time. He was fascinated by the sight of her fat ass and loving how wet and juicy her honeypot was.

Anya reached behind her and spread her ass cheeks wide. "Goddamn, you got some fire-ass pussy." Snow gritted his teeth as he tried to hold back from cumming so fast.

Anya let go of the back of the couch and leaned down and grabbed her ankles. Snow hissed as he slowed his strokes and watched his dick slide in and out of Anya's tight pink flower. His body jerked slightly, and he knew she had him. He was hooked on Anya's pussy already. Once he quickened the pace of his strokes, it didn't take long for his seeds to shoot from his dick and into the condom. He wished he could have spent the entire night in her pussy, but it wasn't his crib. Snow slid out of Anya and smacked her ass.

"We def' got to get a hotel room next time. Or do you think your sister would trip if you had company?"

"Boy, I'm grown." Anya rolled her eyes. Khelani couldn't tell her not to have company, but Anya did want freedom.

She didn't want to have to pay bills, but she wanted to be able to do what she wanted without Khelani breathing down her neck. "Plus, I'm getting my own spot soon."

Snow's eyes lit up at the sound of that. He made good money customizing grills, but he also sold a little coke on the side, so he wasn't broke by far. The idea of Anya having her own crib that he could fuck her in for hours had him ready to trick. "Let me know when you find a place. I'll def' put something on that deposit for you."

Anya only smirked. Shit, he needed to have the whole thing. What the fuck was something? She told herself to just be patient and she'd find the baller she needed to come and be her savior.

Anya was low-key irritated that she had to take an Uber home rather than just curling up and going to sleep. She gave Snow a pass this time. The sex was good, and she'd keep him around. For now. But it was clear to her that Snow wouldn't be that nigga who came in and tricked on her heavy. At this rate, Anya needed about two more niggas to add to her team. One thing was for sure—she wouldn't be missing another night of work anytime soon.

Chapter 7

"This is a cliché-ass question, but why are you single? It's got to be by choice," Kyrie inquired the next day over dinner. He wanted to pick Khelani up, but she had insisted on meeting him at the Brazilian Steakhouse.

She showed up dressed in a tight black dress and red peep-toe booties, and her hair was back, curly. Three gold chains with different charms graced her neck, and on her wrist was an iced-out Cartier watch. She matched his fly for real, and Kyrie wanted to know her story.

"My father has always had high expectations of me. There was no room for boys when he wanted me to get straight A's, and every time I met one goal, there was another for me to cross off the list. I just never slowed down enough to get into anything serious. The few times I attempted, my trust was broken, and I quickly found out that there was a motive or lies involved. I don't have time for that. I'd rather get to the money than have a man playing me and stressing me out."

"I can relate for sure, but it seems weird to hear a woman say that. There are really niggas out here fucking over beautiful-ass, smart women who get their own money? That's crazy."

Khelani chuckled. "Yes, there are really men out here doing that, but I'm good. I'd rather be the way I am than stuck in some relationship I hate or bouncing from man to man because I don't know how to, or I don't want to, take care of myself. A man can provide me dick and companionship. That's about it, because I take care of myself. Oddly, that's what most men have problems with. They have no problem throwing money and fucking, but ask them to be honest or emotionally available, and it's crickets."

"Damn." That was really all Kyrie could say because she had described him. He was emotionally unavailable like a muhfucka. He damn near loved that women would fuck him with no conversation based on just who he was. It was rare that Kyrie had to work for the pussy. All this getting to know a person and going out on dates, he was doing it with Khelani because he wanted to. "So you're good not being in a relationship?" He knew some females who were too into running the streets and hoeing to settle down, but he knew most women really wanted white picket fences and babies.

Khelani thought about how stupid she felt when she let her guard down for Malachi and he attempted to rob her. She couldn't afford another slipup like that, and she wasn't trying to go to prison for murder. She needed to stay far away from niggas who made her want to pump their asses full of lead.

"For the moment, yes. Maybe in a few years, I'll have a change of heart."

Kyrie studied Khelani to see if she was just kicking game. Something was telling him that her cool ass wasn't playing a part. She didn't seem like the type to be too pressed about a nigga, and that low-key excited Kyrie. He wanted to be the exception to the rule, the one who made her fold.

"I hear that. What do you do for fun?"

"I like to read."

That got a laugh out of Kyrie. "I said fun, Khelani."

She raised her eyebrows and tried to figure out what was funny. "I know what you said, and I read for fun. When I have time."

"My bad." He continued to laugh. "You talk a lot about being busy. You just started at the record company, and you get off at five. You got other jobs I don't know about?"

Khelani smirked. "Maybe. Now let's talk about you. Why are you single?"

Kyrie cut into his steak. "It's just hard to find a woman about something." He thought for a second. "Okay, I'm lying. What I said is true, but I have trust issues as well. I like a different kind of female, one who is smart, classy, gets her own money without fucking for it, and not out here trying to be a hot girl. I have found some women over the years who fit that criteria, but I have trust issues. I don't trust easily at all, and it's hard to be in a relationship if you don't trust your partner."

"I feel you one hundred percent. I feel like if some shit is meant to be, then that's what it will be."

"Fa sho'. Listen, I'll be flying out to Cali next week for the BET Awards. You want to come?"

"What about work?"

"I'm flying out on a Thursday and coming back Sunday. You'll only miss two days in the office, but it's cool. It's a work trip. You can bring a laptop and work on my private jet. You can also work at the hotel."

Delante had come into town, so Kasim had help. Khelani wouldn't feel so bad about leaving him while she went to Cali. Unlike Anya, she didn't want to put everything on Kasim. It took a team to run an empire, but this trip could help her in the long run. Plus, she'd been working hard as hell for two years. She deserved a small break. "Sure. I can go."

A grin graced Kyrie's face. "Cool. I'll book your room when I get back home. I know you're against relationships and all, but maybe we can hang out a bit in Cali. Have some fun off the clock."

"You're not worried about rumors or what people may say?"

"Hell nah. I'm the boss. I run this shit, and I do what I want."

"I heard that," Khelani replied before finishing off her wine.

Their plates were both clean, and Kyrie damn near hated to go. "Dinner has truly been nice, Ms. Khelani. I enjoyed your company."

"Likewise."

After he paid the bill and left a tip, he walked Khelani out to her car. Kyrie was itching to taste her lips, palm her ass, suck her breasts, or something. He was going to play it cool, however. As if the universe knew he was done eating, his phone rang as he was walking back to his car.

"Yo?" he greeted Tae.

"We lost another one. Derrick not re-upping with us this time either."

Kyrie pinched the bridge of his nose and closed his eyes. When he spoke, his tone was low and even. "Find out who in the fuck is selling weed to all my goddamn customers." He ended the call without even waiting for Tae to respond. When Kyrie found out who this muhfucka was, he might just toss her ass in a river with bricks tied to her feet.

"You trying to come back to the room with me or what?" Mozzy spoke into Anya's ear as he hugged her from behind while she danced on his lap. His dick was harder than Chinese arithmetic, and he'd already tipped her ass $200. He was tired of flirting. He wanted to fuck.

Men had been buying Anya drinks all night, and she was feeling good. Being the new girl in the club got her a lot of attention, and it was all welcome. She had been at the club for four hours and had earned $945. There were two more hours before closing, so she knew she'd be leaving with over $1,000.

"I still have two more hours to dance. I need my money," she replied as she stood up because the song had ended.

Mozzy eyed her thick thighs, and he was ready to trick heavy on Anya's sexy ass. He had just started making money with Kyrie, but it was good-ass money. Kyrie told him that his suite was paid up for another two weeks. It was nothing to him because he used a business credit card, and he would write the room off on his taxes, but once the money started coming in, Mozzy would have to foot his own bill. Mozzy was still enjoying the free ride for the moment, and he was feeling good.

"How much will it take for you to leave with me right now?"

Anya smirked. She wasn't sure what Mozzy was working with, and she knew if she said too high a number, he may not be able to swing it. However, she wasn't going to completely lowball herself. He'd already given her $200, so she decided to cut him a little slack. "If I leave here now, I'll be missing out on no less than five hundred dollars."

That wasn't what Mozzy wanted to hear. He only had $1,000 in his pocket after splurging at the mall earlier, but fuck it. *You only live once.*

A group of niggas walking by openly admired Anya's ass, and that was the deciding factor for him. The cognac in his system had him feeling like a real boss nigga. The money he spent on Anya, he'd make it right back. That was the point of fast money, right? If you couldn't have fun with it, why risk your freedom and your life to make it?

"Bet. Let's roll."

"Slow down, daddy. I have to cash out and get dressed. Give me fifteen minutes."

Of what she'd earned, she owed Camila $141. Strippers had to give her 15 percent of their money at the end of the night. Anya was glad that Mozzy was giving her the $500 off the record and that she didn't have to give Camila a portion of that.

Anya knocked on the door and walked into the office before Camila even said to come in. When she stepped in the office, Camila pushed her desk drawer shut. "Damn, did you hear me say to come in?"

Anya could have sworn she saw a white powdery substance on the tip of Camila's nose, but she swiped her hand over her face fast as hell, so if it had been there, she swept it away before Anya could be sure. Maybe she was tripping. Anya frowned her face up slightly because it wasn't like Camila to be a sourpuss. She was normally bubbly and lit.

"My bad. Geesh, I was just coming to cash out. I'm about to head out."

Camila's eyes narrowed. "Why you leaving so early? There's money out there." She wasn't stupid. If a stripper was leaving the club while money was flowing, they were more than likely going to fuck, and that cut into Camila's money. Still, there was only so much she could say because the strippers were grown, and they didn't punch a clock. They could dance two hours or six hours.

"I'm about to go kick it with Mozzy for a bit."

Camila didn't even attempt to hide her disgust. "Mozzy? Ewww. He ain't got no money. That nigga is Kyrie's errand boy. You 'bout to miss out on scrilla for that lame nigga?"

Anya didn't give a damn about Mozzy. She didn't care what Camila said about him technically, but she didn't like the way Camila was looking at her. She acted like

Anya was about to go fuck a bum on the street. Shit, in all, she was getting $700 out of Mozzy in one night. He wasn't that damn broke.

"You act like you in that nigga's pockets. Him running Kyrie's errands don't concern me. Every night he comes in here, he tips me lovely. I'm just going to have some fun. Damn."

"I thought you were about your bread. Leaving the club two hours early to entertain a broke nigga isn't bad-bitch behavior, but do you, boo."

Anya was feisty by nature, but it intensified when she had alcohol in her system. "Who the fuck are you to be judging me? I don't have to sit in this bitch all night if I don't want. First, I couldn't fuck with Snow. Now you're telling me don't fuck with Mozzy. I wasn't aware you were the pussy police."

Camila eyed Anya with a sadistic smirk before she responded. "Slow ya muhfuckin' roll, shawty. I don't run you or your pussy, but I run this shit. Hell nah, you can't fuck with Snow. That's my homegirl's nigga, and I'd be a wack bitch to let you deal with him. As far as Mozzy, if you want to give your pussy up to broke niggas and bring down your stock, that's on you. Now you can get the fuck out of my office."

Anya was stunned. She and Camila had hit it off instantly from day one, and now they were getting disrespectful with one another. Anya could tell by Camila's dilated pupils that she probably had seen white powder on her nose. Anya was all about partying and having fun, but not even she fucked with coke.

Deciding to leave before shit got ugly, Anya got up out of Camila's office. At the end of the day, her father was rich, and her sister had big bank. She'd rather go crawling back to Khelani and work for their father before she kissed Camila's ass. Matter of fact, that was what she'd do.

With a smirk on her face, she headed for the dressing room. Her first order of business would be to try to secure Snow as a customer for her sister. Khelani only sold weight, but Snow smoked mad weed. Anya was sure that once he tried Khelani's shit, he'd at least cop an ounce. True weed smokers didn't cop a couple of grams a day. Not the ones with money. They'd go ahead and buy enough weed to last them a couple days. Maybe even a couple of weeks.

Yeah, fuck this raggedy-ass strip club. And even if she did want to keep dancing, there were plenty of strip clubs in the A, and Camila's wasn't the most popping by far. *Fucking bitch.*

Chapter 8

"You're going to the BET Awards? Man, what the fuck? I want to goooo," Anya whined like a damn kid.

Khelani shook her head at her sister's slight temper tantrum. "It's not my trip. Kyrie is the one with the private jet and the tickets to the show. Sorry."

"You could have given me a heads-up or something. Fuck." Anya was pissed. How was she in a city full of rich niggas and she hadn't snagged one yet? She damn near wished she hadn't gotten into it with Camila about Mozzy's ass. Whether he gave her money or not, he was the worst lay she ever had in her life. She was never sleeping with him again.

"I'm sure you'll be okay."

"Anyway." Anya let out a dramatic sigh. "I smoked a blunt with my homie this morning, and he wants to cop two ounces of weed from you. Since you're going out of town, you want me to get Kasim to serve him?"

Khelani couldn't believe that Anya rounded up some clientele for her. She almost told her to serve him, but she wasn't going to give Anya the code to the safe that her weed was stashed in. Nah. She hadn't proven herself to be worthy of all that. "Thank you. Yeah. Hit Kasim. I have to get ready to go."

"Uggghhhhhhh," Anya groaned loudly, and Khelani only laughed.

When she applied to work at the record company, there were a few vacant positions. When Khelani suggested she apply too, Anya looked at her like she had two heads. Anya didn't want to go out and work for shit. She wanted everything just given to her based on her looks, her body, or her name, and life didn't always work like that.

Khelani's Uber arrived, and she headed downstairs. It was in the back of her mind that Kyrie probably didn't invite her on the trip just for business purposes. Khelani knew that any fun she planned on having with him would have to be short-lived. When her six weeks at the label were up and she quit, she wouldn't be seeing him again. She wasn't even sure how she was going to explain leaving the label so soon after starting, but she'd think of something. Time was moving fast. She'd already been there for two weeks. Khelani only had four weeks left to do what she needed to do.

She had to leave the party early to go be with Kasim, so maybe the trip to the awards would make up for that. Quite a few of the artists and employees of the label would be on the jet. Khelani didn't want to just jump into business. She wanted to develop a nice, cordial relationship first, then ease into the fact that she sold weed. A lot of rappers popped various kinds of pills, drank lean, and some even snorted coke, but it seemed like all of them smoked weed. There was always money to be made in the marijuana business, and people with money loved paying top dollar for shit. It made them feel like they were purchasing something exclusive that the average person couldn't afford. Khelani knew how to take advantage of that.

Khelani had only been in the car for five minutes and she had ten new emails. Her job wasn't hard, but it wasn't exactly laid-back. She worked every hour that she was on the clock. There was never a moment to waste unless she wanted to get backed up. Khelani was so focused on replying to emails and trying to get caught up on her workload that she didn't even realize they had pulled up to the location the jet was leaving from until the driver opened the door for her.

"Oh, wow, I was in a zone for real. Thank you."

"You're welcome."

The driver collected her luggage, and she followed him over to the jet. Kyrie had pulled up in a black Hummer, and he exited the vehicle dressed in black sweats, a black hoodie, and black sneakers. The ice around his neck and encrusted in his watch seemed to shine brighter against his all-black attire. His beard glistened in the sun, and Khelani could tell he'd moisturized it. There was nothing like a man who took care of himself. The fact that he smiled when he saw her might have made Khelani blush if she were into that kind of thing. The last nigga who made her blush had tried to rob her, so she was good on that emotional shit.

"What up?" He shocked Khelani by giving her a one-arm hug. "How was the ride here?"

"It was cool. The driver was very polite."

"That's what's up. I need to run something by you."

Khelani looked at him curiously. "What's that?"

Kyrie looked a little hesitant to respond. He swiped his hand across the back of his neck. "So one of the chicks who be styling my artist, Swag, she's coming out tomorrow. She has her own room, and we're not together. But we've slept together more than a few times, and when she sees other women around, she tries to be on that territorial shit. She'll probably be doing little shit to make it seem like we're together, but we're not. I never lied to you. I'm single."

Khelani shrugged passively. "That's fine. You don't owe me any explanations. We're two people who had dinner together once. I am not tripping. Trust."

Kyrie nodded. "I just wanted to make sure."

Khelani followed him onto the jet, and she spoke to everyone who was already on board. Kyrie for sure seemed like the type of man to have sex with lots of different women. Khelani had never fucked him, and she was still on the fence as to if she would. She didn't care about one of his women being on the trip as long as the bitch didn't get disrespectful. She sat across from Kim, and the women alternated between conversing and working the entire trip.

"Yo, your eyes are pretty as hell. I know you be having niggas mesmerized and shit," one of the rappers assigned to the label, Draco, said to Khelani randomly. She was used to it. People had been admiring her eyes her entire life.

When she looked up from her laptop, she saw Kyrie looking in her direction. She turned toward Draco. "Thank you, but I don't know about all that," she chuckled.

Draco licked his lips. "You single, ma?"

Khelani had to stifle her laughter. Draco wasn't more than 19. Because he was famous and had money, he was probably used to pulling any woman he wanted regardless of his age, but Khelani wasn't with it. He was cute, but rich or not, she couldn't do a damn thing with a nigga who couldn't even buy her a drink legally in a bar. Rather than wounding his ego or hurting his pride, she just smiled at him politely.

"I am, but I don't mix business with pleasure. You cute though."

She was glad that Draco's phone rang, because he looked as if he was about to protest what she'd just said.

The jet finally landed in L.A., and Khelani was eager to get off and stretch her legs. There were eleven of them total, so they split up into three SUVs at the landing strip. Khelani ended up in the same vehicle as Kyrie.

"You trying to join me for dinner tonight?"

She looked over at him curiously. "Isn't your li'l boo coming tomorrow?" Khelani knew good and well he wasn't going to try to squeeze her in for a quick fuck and then be all up on the other chick when she came.

"I explained the reason to you why I even brought that shit up. Don't hold that against me. I haven't had sex with Rebecca in a minute, and I don't plan on it because she does too much. She's a good stylist though, and Swag doesn't want anybody styling him but her, so I tolerate her. I don't fuck with her like that anymore, but if she sees a beautiful woman around, she will try to make it seem like we're still rocking. I've checked her about the shit, and she still acts dumb."

Khelani didn't want him to keep explaining because it really didn't matter. She didn't care what Kyrie did or who he did it with. "We'll see. If I'm not tired."

Kyrie raised one eyebrow as if he felt like she was bull-shitting. He couldn't force her to fuck with him. He was trying to go with the flow and let things unfold naturally, but he wanted to rock with her for certain. He was pissed when Swag requested that Rebecca come on the trip, but he had to put business above all else. He knew Rebecca though, and as soon as she saw Khelani, she would start doing the most. He was dreading the shit. She wasn't the type to disrespect Khelani or try to fight her. She'd just be extra with the affection toward Kyrie.

"You do that," was all he said.

Khelani had spoken about not being interested in a relationship, and he wasn't really either. But he'd be lying if he said he wasn't attracted to Khelani or if he said he didn't want to see how things would play out with them.

Anya walked out of the bathroom with a towel wrapped around her thick body and steam from the bathroom wafting down the hallway behind her. When the song she was listening to stopped playing, she knew that someone was about to call her. She was shocked to see that Camila was calling her phone. For a brief moment, she started not to answer, but she went ahead and picked up. "Hello?"

"You coming to work tonight?" Camila asked in a pleasant tone as if they hadn't just gotten into it the night before.

Anya wasn't sure how to answer. Should she just say she was quitting because she didn't want to work for a bitch? She quickly decided that she wasn't about to let Camila or anyone else punk her into not being truthful. "I really hadn't planned on coming back since it seemed that we aren't on the same page."

Camila kissed her teeth. "Anya, my business consists of babysitting hella bitches who, half the time, don't do what they should be doing. I run an entire club alone, plus I have to keep my eye on everything and everyone, and sometimes I just get stressed the fuck out. It's not okay for me to get frustrated and take my anger out on anyone who works for me. It's not professional, and I'm working on my attitude. I value your presence in my club, and if you come in tonight, you won't even have to cash out. Don't tell those other bitches though."

Anya smiled to herself as she grabbed her bottle of lotion and sat on the bed. She liked how Camila was humbling herself. "Well, since you put it like that, I'll be there for sure."

"Great!"

Anya really wasn't feeling how Camila could switch up at the drop of a hat, but as long as she didn't have to cash out at the end of the night, she'd be there. She could already see how nasty Camila could be when she was angry, and she didn't like it. No matter how sincere her apology seemed, her coming at Anya wrong could happen again. Her father always told her that people show who they really are when they're angry. Camila was trying to appease Anya, but Anya was smart enough to know that Camila still had that boss-bitch mentality, and in the midst of an argument, she wouldn't hesitate to let it be known that she felt Anya was beneath her.

Anya chuckled to herself. "Bitch has no idea who my father or even my sister is. Couple of Chanel bags and a hole-in-the-wall club don't make you better than the next. Her net worth probably looks like lunch money compared to Khelani."

After standing up and letting the towel drop to the floor, Anya admired her naked frame in the mirror. She was too damn bad not to be on the arm of a rich nigga. She should have been on a jet on her way to the BET Awards. She honestly could have been even without a nigga if her father would just act right. Anya hated that he was so damn difficult. Why couldn't she just be a spoiled Trinidadian princess?

As Anya was stepping into a red thong, her phone rang again. She kissed her teeth when she saw that Mozzy was calling. This was his third time calling her since they had sex, and she hadn't answered any of his calls. She wished he would just get the hint already.

Her first issue with him was that his dick was too fucking small. The only way it wouldn't slip out of her every five minutes was if he put her legs all the way up until they were damn near behind her head. Her ass had to basically be lifted off the bed while she was damn near on her head in order for his tiny penis to stay inside of her. Anya was all for different positions, but having to stay that way for too long was uncomfortable. His sex game was just garbage. She even hated kissing him. The traces of saliva he left on her skin after kissing her disgusted

Anya. She loved money with a passion, but he couldn't pay her any amount of money for her to have sex with him again. If she got broke enough, she'd slang pounds with Khelani before she fucked him again.

Once her phone stopped ringing, Anya finished getting dressed and headed to the club. Since she hadn't planned on going, Anya arrived at the club later than she normally would, and it was already kind of packed. She rushed to the dressing room to undress. She wasn't trying to miss out on too much more money. When she came back out, she had fifteen minutes before she had to do her set on stage, so she sauntered through the crowd trying to find good prospects to flirt with.

Anya stopped dead in her tracks when she noticed Mozzy leaning against the bar, eye fucking her. As soon as they locked eyes, she turned in the opposite direction to go to the bar on the other side of the club. The sight of him turned her fucking stomach. Why wasn't his ass in California with Kyrie? Camila was right. He wasn't shit but an errand boy, and the thrill with kicking it with him was gone. Anya just hated that he could pop up on her at anytime when she was at work. It really didn't matter though, because like Camila, she could be a nasty bitch when she needed to be. If she had to hurt Mozzy's feelings in order for him to get the point, then she would.

Mozzy's eyes narrowed as he watched Khelani's plump ass walk away from him. The cognac he was sipping burned his throat, but that was no match for the boiling that his blood was doing. He didn't have an issue fucking a chick once and then cutting her ass off unless he'd spent a lot of money on her. Him giving Anya $700 in one night was more than he'd ever given any female at one time. Now this bitch was trying to play him? Fair exchange wasn't robbery, but in Mozzy's eyes, there was no fair exchange. For as much money as he'd given that bitch, he needed to be able to get some of that pussy a few more times. It was the best that Mozzy had since he'd been home from prison, and he didn't appreciate being curbed. Anya was the type of chick he could wife. It didn't matter that she was a stripper. Once he started making real money with Kyrie, he could spoil her, and she could quit the club.

His nostrils flared as he saw a nigga with blond dreads grab Anya by the wrist. She stopped to talk to him, and even from across the room, Mozzy could see the wide smile on her face. That was his bad for falling for a ho. It was a lesson that he was learning the hard way, but if it was up to him, he wouldn't be the only one learning a lesson. If Anya thought she was just going to ghost him, that bitch was about to find out just how Mozzy from Houston got down.

Chapter 9

Khelani was standing at the bathroom sink with a towel wrapped around her body, moisturizing her wet curls. She had taken a shower and was going to get dressed to go out with Kim and a few other employees of the label. There were parties going on everywhere. She was finally getting a mini vacation from running around selling weed and sitting behind a desk for eight hours a day, and she was going to enjoy it.

There was a knock on her room door, and Khelani's eyebrows snapped together. Who would be at her door? Maybe it was Kim. Khelani pulled the towel off her body and grabbed a white oversized shirt. After pulling it over her head, she stuck her feet in some slippers and walked to the door. Khelani didn't care how nice the hotel was. She wasn't walking barefoot on a carpet that strange people trekked on with their shoes on.

She raised one eyebrow after looking out of the peephole and seeing that Kyrie was standing at the door. After she slowly pulled the door open, both her eyebrows hiked up. "May I help you?"

"Yeah. I'm here to pick you up for our dinner date."

"Ummmm . . ." Khelani scratched her head. "I don't remember agreeing to go out on a date with you. Plus, you didn't give me a time, and as you can see, I'm not even dressed."

"I'll wait," he stated and walked into the room, leaving her looking confused.

After standing there for a few seconds stuck on stupid, she closed the door. "Why do you assume that I don't have plans? You do know that Kim asked me to go out with her, Bella, and Maria?"

"They can wait. It won't take us more than two hours to grab dinner. Damn, you act like I'm the worst person in the world to hang out with."

Khelani chuckled. "I never said that. Don't put words in my mouth."

"So I'll wait for you to get dressed, and we can roll." Kyrie sat down on the couch in the front of her suite, and Khelani let out a deep breath. He obviously wasn't taking no for an answer, so she headed back into the bathroom.

After moisturizing her face and skin, she grabbed an outfit from her suitcase, went back in the bathroom, and closed the door. Once she was dressed, Khelani emerged from the bathroom with light makeup on her face. Kyrie watched her in awe as she reached for her shoes. She had on a red see-through type of dress that was similar to the one that Camila wore with her breasts exposed, but Khelani wore hers in a classy way. She wore a black bra underneath, and even though it was a dress technically and came down to her ankles, she wore black skinny jeans underneath. On her feet, she put nude strappy heels. Nude lipstick coated her lips, and eyeliner accentuated her almond-shaped eyes. Hanging from her ears were large gold hoops, and a matching gold watch decorated her wrist. Khelani looked like pure fuckin' perfection. *Camila could take some tips from her on how to be sexy while having respect for herself.*

"You look fuckin' phenomenal," Kyrie admired as she grabbed her purse.

Khelani turned around with a smirk. "I don't look like a boring church lady, do I? I heard that's the kind of woman you like."

Kyrie frowned. "Camila thinks any woman who doesn't show everything God gave her is boring. I wouldn't listen to her hating ass. I like women who have respect for themselves and carry themselves like a grown-ass woman. That's what I like."

"Nothing wrong with that. I told you your cousin reminds me a lot of my sister. There is no reasoning with them or trying to get them to think normal most times."

"Tell me about it. You ready to go?"

"Yeah. Mind telling me where we're going?"

Kyrie held the door open for her. "I always have to hit the Melting Pot when I come to L.A. The food is amazing."

Khelani's eyes swept over Kyrie while they were in the elevator, and she had to admit that he was handsome as fuck. She could see why a woman with little self-restraint and low self-esteem may do the most in an effort to keep other women away from him. That would never be her thing, but Khelani knew not everyone was as strong as she. She couldn't imagine the heartbreak that weaker-willed women went through. For as tough as she tried to be, Malachi came along and made her feel things she'd never felt before. As soon as she went against the grain and let him in, he did the unthinkable. Killing him hurt her, but it also further numbed her. Khelani would be damned if she made the same mistake twice. It didn't matter how sexy, rich, or charming Kyrie was. Their time getting to know one another would be coming to an end soon. She was going to make sure of that. The only way she'd keep contact with him any longer would be if he decided to get his weed from her, and she doubted his pride would allow him to do so.

Kyrie led her out to a black Escalade, where a driver was waiting for him. He wanted to rent a Porsche or something fly as fuck for his short stay in L.A., but he figured there was no need. He planned to turn up and have fun, so with all the champagne and liquor that would be flowing, having his own personal driver was best. Kyrie also knew that if he was riding around L.A. with Khelani, paparazzi was sure to see them and take pictures. He didn't even know where shit with her was going to go, so he didn't want extra eyes and ears in his business.

Inside the car, Kyrie's phone was going off nonstop, but he gave Khelani his undivided attention. There was still a lot that he didn't know about her and there was a lot of mystery that left him intrigued, but he didn't need to be intrigued. He needed to know who she was. Kyrie got his people in HR to run a background check on her, and her record was squeaky clean. She'd never even had any kind of traffic ticket.

"When is your birthday?" Kyrie asked, causing Khelani to smirk.

The "getting to know one another" questions when a man and woman met was always sort of comical to her. Most men knew their intentions weren't good and they were going to waste your time, but they still put so much effort into the facade. It was sick. Rather than express these feelings to Kyrie, however, she simply answered. "My birthday is October tenth."

"That's coming up in a few months. You have anything planned?"

"Not at the moment. Holidays aren't really my thing." Kemp had money, and he always spoiled his girls with material possessions, but he wasn't affectionate by far, and her mother was affectionate with who she chose to be affectionate with. Being that she saved all of her praises and love for Anya, Khelani avoided her whenever possible. Her holidays weren't spent with her loving and doting family. Most times, they were spent with her in her room wishing for the day she could leave her parents' home and live on her own.

"Damn. I love holidays. Especially Christmas. Stick with me and we might be wearing matching Christmas pajamas," Kyrie joked.

Khelani shook her head. "I don't think that will ever happen. But it's a good thing that I don't do relationships and that you have trust issues. So we already know this isn't going very far."

Kyrie had seen women play that hard shit, and weeks later, their ass would be behind closed doors begging and crying for him to just love them and do right. He was confident that he had the skills necessary to break down the hardest woman, but her determination had him very interested. It was almost like his own personal challenge to make her ass deviate from all that talk about being against relationships.

"I do have trust issues, but I also know that we never know what life holds for us. I believe in just going with the flow. It's not that far-fetched to feel like when we meet the person we're supposed to be with, we'll know, and it will make us change our way of thinking. I don't know what I could be for you or to you unless we give it a try, and the same goes for you. I could end up being the nigga to change your life."

"I doubt it, but I can't knock how you feel."

"So you're saying I'm wasting my time? I should stop trying to get to know you? You're not interested in dates or seeing where this could go?"

"I'm saying that I don't do relationships, so this could only go so far. I'm also saying that I don't stay in one place for long, so after a year, no more than two, I'll be ready to move on to another state. My life is very unpredictable right now, but I do know what I won't allow to knock me off track, and that's a man. I have no problem with us being friends or hanging out, but I don't think we need to develop any kind of attachment toward one another, at all."

Kyrie was stunned. Khelani was something else. Most women would be elated that his rich ass was showing interest in them whether they had their own money or not. He was a good damn catch. What single woman was turning him down? He had to respect her wishes though. No matter how confused he was as to why she wasn't falling in his lap, vying for his attention, he'd never be pressed. For any woman. Maybe she was gay on the low. Kyrie nodded at her words.

"I have no choice but to respect that."

He wasn't about to be salty, and he was still going to enjoy their outing, so he kept the conversation flowing until they arrived at the restaurant. He continued to open doors for her and treat her the same way he did prior to being shot down. Khelani didn't sugarcoat shit for any-one, but she almost felt bad for the way she handled him.

"You know the way I feel has nothing to do with you, right? You haven't done one thing to rub me the wrong way. My mind was already made up about men way before I met you."

"Who hurt you, shorty? We're adults. Let's have a conversation. I'm just curious to know what has you so dead set against ever giving another man a chance. A nigga made a baby on you? Got married on you? What?"

Khelani smirked. If only it had been something so trivial. Once she made a name for herself in Atlanta, there was a huge chance that Kyrie would find out what she did for a living, but she wasn't ready to tell him that just yet. If she couldn't tell him what she did, then she couldn't tell him the real story. Khelani shifted her body in her seat.

"I let my guard down and let a man get close enough to me to attempt to steal from me."

Kyrie's eyes flew to the watch on her wrist. It looked to be worth a few thousand, but what kind of lame-ass nigga was going around stealing from women? Khelani appeared to be doing well for sure, but a man had to be super corny to steal from her. "What, he took some jewelry or something?"

"He got into my safe, and what was inside was far from petty."

That got Kyrie's attention. When he looked over her résumé, he saw she had a job history as an office manager. He didn't know too many females, or people who had legal money period, who kept their money in safes. He wanted to ask so many more questions, but he chose not to. Maybe later. There was something about Khelani, and no matter how hard she resisted him, he was going to get to the bottom of who she was as a person.

"So did you let the nigga explain? Or at least try to?"

"I don't know about you, but if I catch a person in my safe, a safe that I didn't give them the code to, there won't be a lot of talking."

Kyrie let out a light chuckle. "So you beat him up? I'm just saying. Once you were calm, did he try to come back and at least give an explanation?"

"Dead men don't talk."

The ice in her tone and the fire blazing in Khelani's eyes had him damn near at a loss for words. She said that shit like a real-ass gangsta. *She killed the nigga?* Kyrie's dick almost got hard. It had been confirmed that Khelani wasn't like most women at all. It also confirmed his suspicions that she had other shit going on. There had to be something she wasn't telling him. Maybe an ex got locked up or got killed and left her money. He didn't want to come across as being nosy, and he didn't want to overstep his boundaries, so he decided to chill on the questions for a bit.

"My bad, gangsta. All jokes aside, someone violated your trust in a major way, and you have every right to be guarded. I have never hit a woman in my life, but if I walked in the room and saw a woman in my safe, I might bust her ass that day. I can see why you wouldn't let the average person get close to you, but you're letting that fuck nigga win if you deprive yourself of happiness because of what he did. I don't steal, but I'd cut my dick off before I'd steal from a woman. Shit is lame."

Khelani appreciated his persistence, but she was over it. She wasn't about to keep explaining to Kyrie why she refused to take him seriously. More than likely, he didn't want anything deep with her either. He was just letting his ego lead the way. Khelani knew how to choose her battles, so she simply replied with, "You're right."

They finished dinner, and the food was amazingly good. They had just left the restaurant and gotten back to the car when Kasim called her phone.

"Hey," she answered right away.

"I hate to bother you, but I have bad news. Delante got robbed. He took a bullet to the arm, and the fuck nigga got away with twenty pounds."

Khelani's nostrils flared. It could have been much worse, but she was still livid. "Were you there? Are you okay?"

Kyrie's eyes shot over to Khelani, and he could see that she was pissed.

"I'm fine. I shouldn't have let him go alone, but we had mad people to serve and—"

Khelani cut him off. "Nah, I shouldn't have left. I'm on the next flight home."

Kyrie eyed her with concern. "Everything okay?" he asked when she ended the call.

"Yeah. I just need to go home. I'm sorry. I'll still get my work done."

"No worries, *mami*. I can get my jet to take you as soon as you're ready, but are you sure you're okay?"

All Khelani could do was nod, but she wasn't okay. She hadn't even been in town three months yet, and fuck niggas were trying her already. She needed to get back to Atlanta and make an example out of niggas.

Chapter 10

Tae counted the money a second time before zipping the bag back up and looking over at Camila. "You know I'm not gon' be able to keep covering for you, right?" He peered into Camila's glassy eyes.

"What you mean?" she said, attempting to play dumb.

Tae kissed his teeth. "Come on, man. The last two times I picked money up for Kyrie, the shit been short. Something tells me you're dipping in the product, ma."

Camila tried her best to be offended, but she was so damn zooted she couldn't have fooled Stevie Wonder. Her eyes were shifty and wild. Kyrie had some good-ass coke. It was pure, and Camila was becoming heavily addicted. She was no longer the casual user.

"Nigga, you accusing me of stealing from my blood? And low-key calling me a cokehead?"

Tae grabbed her face with his hand. "Chill with trying to insult my intelligence, ma. I don't give a fuck what you do, 'cause you're grown. You don't have to explain shit to me, but Kyrie isn't about to be looking at me like I keep shorting him. You gotta fix this shit."

The drug in her system and the intensity of the moment had her heart beating like a drum in her chest. "You know I like that rough shit." A lazy grin eased across her face. Tae's ass was fine. She'd always flirted with Kyrie's friends. Ghalen wasn't the best looking one, but his paper was long. He refused to touch her, however, out of loyalty to Kyrie.

Tae though, his fine chocolate ass had her kitty purring at the moment. He had money too, and he was sexy, cocky, and aggressive. All of the characteristics that she liked in a man. Anytime she subtly flirted with him, he might simply smirk or say some slick shit back. It never went past that, but with the way he was grabbing on her and checking her had Camila ready to bust it open for him right there.

Tae peered into her eyes for a bit as he contemplated his next move. It didn't take him long to decide that he wasn't about to let pussy knock him off his square. He needed to get at Kyrie ASAP about this problem. "I have business to handle," was his response as he let Camila's face go.

Tae grabbed the black bag that was on her desk and left the office. As soon as he was in his car and out of the noisy club, he called Kyrie. Tae was glad that Kyrie was a businessman and a smart man. Some people might be quick to take Camila's word over his because she was blood, but Kyrie knew that Camila was a wild card—a wild card who fucked up often.

"Yo, what up?"

"I have a few things to tell you. I found the first thing out right before I pulled up at the club. So you want the good news first or the bad news?"

"What's the bad news, nigga?"

"Money was short again, and Camila is tweaking. I think she's using that shit, man. On God, you know I would never steal from you."

There was a brief silence on the other end of the phone while Kyrie beat himself up. Camila was the reason he never wanted daughters. That damn girl was hell. Her snorting coke wasn't a reach at all. He could definitely believe it, and he hated that he even started supplying her ass. "What's the good news?"

"I found out who the person is who's taking your clientele. Bitch named Khelani."

"So the nigga Snow hit you up for twenty pounds of weed a day after he copped twelve ounces. Then you go to serve him, and he doesn't answer the door, but you get robbed on the way back to the car? You already know it was him, right?" Khelani's eyes darted from Kasim to Delante.

"Oh, we know that for sure," Kasim replied. "Problem is we ran up in the crib we met him at, and some bitch with a baby was in there. Claimed Snow doesn't live there and he'd only been there once to drop off a grill that he made for her nigga. If that baby hadn't been in there, I would have done her in."

Khelani clenched her jaw muscles. She didn't want unnecessary bloodshed. If she could help it, the only person who would be killed would be the nigga who robbed her. "Nah, no need for all that. We just gon' find out where that nigga be. And this the nigga Anya put you on to?"

Kasim nodded, and Khelani closed her eyes and blew out a small breath. She couldn't be too mad because Malachi almost robbed her ass. Getting close to niggas was just a bad idea period. Anya could be reckless, but she wasn't going to hold this one against her. Khelani pulled out her phone and called Anya's phone.

"Hey," she replied, sounding half asleep.

"Where the fuck that nigga Snow live at?"

Anya's eyes popped open. She was confused because she'd been jarred from her sleep, but hearing Snow's name was enough to catch her attention. "Huh? I don't know where he lives. Why? What's wrong?"

"You said he was yo' people, right? He robbed Delante, and that's his ass. Where you know him from?"

Anya groaned. Why were people so stupid? He really robbed the person she put him on to? The dick was superb. So superb in fact that it was he who had fucked her to sleep. She let him come over since Khelani went away. Something told her to make his ass leave before she went to sleep, and she now was glad she did. And he had the nerve to come smile in her face and have sex with her after he robbed her people? That was scandalous indeed.

"He has a li'l shop where he makes grills. I can look it up and text you the address. I really thought he was cool people. My bad, Khelani."

"It's all good, Anya. Shit happens. I just hope you don't have any kind of an attachment to this nigga because it's gon' end real bad for him. You know that, right?"

"I know." Khelani liked Malachi's ass, and she killed him with no hesitation. Anya hated to see how dirty she would do a nigga she didn't give a damn about.

Anya didn't allow herself to become too attached to men either because they were always doing dumb shit. They would either get locked up, get themselves killed, cheat, or something. All a man could do for Anya was give her dick and money. If the money and the dick stopped or the dick was trash, she was as good as gone. Mozzy had been calling her so much that she had to end up blocking his little-dick ass. She didn't care if she saw him in the club either. Anya had tried to spare him, but the next time he bothered her, she was going to let him know that his sex was trash and she never wanted to fuck him again. If he didn't like it, oh well. She wasn't stroking the ego of a nigga who couldn't even properly stroke her walls.

When Anya got off the phone with Khelani, her thoughts for some reason drifted to Caresha. She was going to be a single mother for real once Snow was dead. *Damn. Cold world.*

Since Anya's sleep had been disturbed, she decided to go ahead and get up for the day. She would get dressed, go get food, and go to the club a little earlier than usual. Anya was all about the money. She had quite a few prospects lined up. Anya decided to hold off a little on dealing with anybody else until they proved for sure that they were worth it. She knew off the rip that Snow wasn't a baller, but he was sexy, and she just wanted to have some fun. The sex made her glad that she'd given him a chance, but it was too bad that he decided to end his own life by being a cruddy nigga. Mozzy, that nigga was a hot mess for sure, but for a whole different reason.

Anya had been blinded by him always getting sections and bottles and tipping a little money. He worked for a boss-ass nigga, but he was far from rich. And even if he was, Anya wouldn't be able to stomach having sex with him again. She had to choose a little more carefully next time. The few guys she'd been flirting with lately all had ice, and they came into the club with stacks upon stacks of ones. They dressed fly as hell and appeared to be getting it, but Camila put her up on game. Half those niggas were scammers. They cracked credit cards and cashed fraudulent checks. A man could be in the club with mad jewelry on, dripping in designer clothes, ordering plenty of bottles, looking like that nigga, and go home to the slums. Some of them didn't even have cars, just designer clothes, jewelry, and electronics. When Anya thought hard about it, fucking with a scammer might not be too bad if he could use some of those cards to buy her nice things.

A few hours later, Anya was strolling into the club. It wasn't packed at all, but she expected that since she arrived early. She changed clothes and perched on a stool at the bar. She was going to get good and fucked up, and hopefully, it would be a good night. Most professional white men didn't frequent the bar after dark. They actually wouldn't be caught dead there, but there was one small group of lawyers who let time get away from them. All the beautiful women, the flavorful wings, and the strong drinks had them turned up. Anya was finishing up her first drink when a blond man walked over to her. She could tell by the lopsided grin on his face that he was drunk as shit.

"You are so fuckin' beautiful." His eyes roamed her body. "Can I get a table dance before I go?"

A big smile graced Anya's face. "You sure can, baby." She slid seductively off the stool and followed him back to his table, swinging her hips every step of the way.

The man's friends all looked on in amazement at the woman he picked, and Anya wasted no time getting down to business. She twerked, gyrated on laps while rubbing on herself, and gave all of the men a hell of a show. They were tossing money at her, and by the time they left, she had $395 in her possession. Anya smiled and mumbled to herself, "I knew it was going to be a good-ass night."

After heading over to the bar, she ordered another drink. Business was still kind of slow, but the night was young. She laughed and talked with a few other strippers and patrons of the club, but when she saw Mozzy, her mood was instantly ruined. His ass was like a fuckin' fly. Why wouldn't he just go away? Anya decided to head to the back to get out of his view. Just knowing he was near was killing her vibe, but she didn't move fast enough. She had just stood up when he grabbed her arm.

"Where you going, love? I'm trying to get a dance."

"I have to go to the bathroom." Anya gave him a fake smile while resisting the urge to roll her eyes. The cologne he wore smelled pricy. He was dressed nice, and she still wanted no part of him. Funny how bad sex from a nigga could make you look at him completely differently.

"Nah. I want my dance. It's not gon' take long, and we both know you like to ignore muhfuckas. Damn, my money not good enough for you no more?"

Anya was over it. The alcohol and the agitation she was feeling from his persistence didn't mix. "Look, take a hint, bruh. Goddamn. You don't have to be a pest. You were cool and all, but I'm not feeling it. Stop calling me. Stop texting me. You don't have to tip me when you come in here. There are plenty of females to entertain you. Leave me the hell alone. A'ight?" she snapped.

The smile that eased across Mozzy's face contradicted the anger blazing in his eyes. He was giving off weird-ass energy, and Anya wanted to be away from him. Just as she snatched her arm away from him, he eased his gun out of the pocket of the thin jacket that he wore. "Working for Kyrie has its perks. Security lets me in with this bad boy right here. Now follow me to my section or get dragged outside and eat a bullet. Your choice."

Anya's heart slammed into her chest. He was doing all this because she rejected him? Nigga was corny as fuck, and she hated the night she ever left the club with him. Camila's ass was right about him, and she was too damn dumb and stubborn to listen. Anya contemplated making a run for it, but she didn't know just how deep Kyrie's reach went. If the bouncers let him in with a gun on the strength of Kyrie, they might not stop him from dragging her out of the club. They might think he was her nigga or some shit. She would go do the dance for him, and then she'd let security and Camila know that either he couldn't come back in the club or she was going elsewhere to dance.

Reluctantly, Anya followed Mozzy to the section. His ass came in the club several times a week getting sections and tipping strippers. Meanwhile, his lame ass was living at a hotel. Mozzy sat down, and Anya began to dance in front of him. Since her back was to his, she didn't even notice him unzipping his jeans or pulling his penis through the slit. His perverted ass didn't even care that he was pulling his dick out in a strip club.

With lightning speed, he grabbed Anya and forced her into his lap. He put one hand around her neck from behind and choked her while pulling her thong to the side with the other hand. His grip on her neck was so tight that Anya couldn't scream or get up off his lap. His dick was so damn little that even him forcing his way into her middle while she wasn't aroused didn't even hurt her. Anya just felt disgusted and violated, and tears sprang to her eyes. She'd done a lot of shit. In her eyes, she was wild. You only live once, and she was nowhere near as reserved as Khelani, but being raped had her fucked up. Mozzy choked her while scooting to the edge of his seat and pumping in and out of her. She was tight and warm, and despite the act not being consensual, her body betrayed her. Anya began to get wet, and Mozzy was in heaven. At times, his grip would loosen a little on her neck, and then it would tighten back up. He didn't last long in the pussy, but by the time he came, she had begun to feel as if she was about to pass out. Her lips even had a blue tinge to them.

Mozzy pushed her off his lap, and Anya fell to the floor. She struggled to breathe, and she was dizzy, so it took her a minute to get up off the floor. Camila walked by and saw Anya on the floor. She also saw Mozzy breathing hard and zipping his jeans back up. Her eyes darted from him to Anya, and her eyes narrowed as she peeped that Anya's lips were blue, and tears ran down her cheeks.

"What the fuck is going on in here?"

Anya peeled herself up off the floor. *Fuck Kyrie's pull.* Even if she had to get Kasim to get at Mozzy, he was going to pay for what he just did. "He fuckin' raped me," Anya cried in a shaky voice.

Camila's eyes flew over to Mozzy, and he kissed his teeth. "That bitch is fuckin' lying. Why would I have to rape her when I've fucked her before? She's just a freak. She pulled my shit out and started riding it."

Anya's voice was raspy from being choked, and there were marks on her neck. It was easy to see who was telling the truth.

"Nigga, why are her lips blue? Why are there marks on her neck? Why was she on the floor?"

Mozzy shrugged passively. "She a freak. Bitch likes when I choke her."

"I told her the night she left with you that you were a broke-ass lame." That comment wiped the smirk off Mozzy's face. "You're pathetic as hell. You might be seeing a little bread from being Kyrie's do boy, but you're still corny in my eyes."

Camila's comment infuriated Mozzy so much so that he took a step toward her. "You better watch how you talk to me, bitch. Don't get fucked up trying to handle me."

Camila let out a snort. "Nigga, please. Kyrie made ya bum ass, and one phone call to him and he'll end ya bum ass. Get the fuck out of my club."

Her comment made Mozzy so mad that his upper lip twitched. He was two seconds away from knocking her out, but he had to remember who she was. He was in this city, and he had the money that he had thanks to Kyrie. He was still driving the rental that Kyrie paid for and still living in the hotel that he footed the bill for. If he wasn't trying to go back to Houston with his tail tucked between his legs, he had to put his pride to the side and leave. It took every ounce of self-restraint that he had, but he walked away.

Camila looked over at Anya. She knew nothing good would come of her dealing with Mozzy, but she had to learn the hard way. "You going to the hospital so they can do a rape kit?"

Anya was so shaken up that she was trembling. "No. They'll call the police, and I don't want that."

"Just go ahead and leave for the night. Get yourself together. You'll be okay. Don't let that fuck nigga break you. I'll get Arman to make sure he leaves." That was as deep as her pep talk went. Camila wasn't a very affectionate person. Anya was a tough girl, and Camila felt like she'd be okay.

Anya nodded and walked toward the dressing room. It literally felt as if bugs were crawling on her skin. She wanted to go home and scrub her skin off. If it was the last thing she did, Anya was going to make Mozzy pay for what he did to her.

Chapter 11

Kyrie sat on the edge of his desk, waiting for the knock to come. He had been waiting for this shit all day. When he found out that Khelani sold weed, he wasn't the least bit shocked. In fact, everything about it made sense. It would be hard for him to go all day at work without confronting her, so he didn't go into the office until later.

Kyrie played different events over and over in his mind, like her speaking on the nigga she caught in her safe and saying he was no longer alive. Anyone could look at her and tell she had her own money. Even her saying that she never stayed in one place for long, it was all adding up now. This entire time, he'd been smiling in the face of the person who came to town and started taking his clientele. Kyrie didn't like feeling played. If she had some fire-ass weed that she was moving like that, she didn't need to work for him unless she had a motive. Yet, her ass was always the one talking about how she didn't trust people. The more he thought about it, it made his blood boil.

He didn't go into the record label until four p.m. Most everyone left for the day at five, including Khelani. "Come to my office before you leave," he instructed her before going into his office and closing the door.

When she knocked, the anxiety he felt heightened. "Come in."

Khelani walked in dressed in a snakeskin-print dress that had thin straps and stopped at her knees. Underneath the dress, she wore a cream turtleneck sweater, and on her feet were black thigh-high boots. Khelani had a very unique sense of fashion, and she could be a stylist for sure. Even in his anger, Kyrie had to stop and respect her fashion sense. He quickly recovered though.

"I got niggas telling me that they've copped some pretty good weed from you. Seems like you just appeared out of thin air and started snatching up my clientele. So all that bullshit you spat about being an asset to my company was game, huh? You started working here to get close to me for what? To take my customers?" He didn't even know her that well, but he felt betrayed. He let that shy-girl, good-girl, classy-bitch act knock him off his square.

"I had no way of knowing who your clientele is or was. I deal with about nine people here in Atlanta. I did start working here to make the right connections in the city. Any of your clientele who came to me was a coincidence."

She didn't appear to be lying. She looked him in the eye as she spoke, and she appeared confident. Kyrie was still pissed though. "Who the fuck are you?"

"As I told you before, I'm from Trinidad. My father sent me to the States to start a pipeline for him back to Trinidad. He's the plug there. I set up shop in Charlotte, and Atlanta was my next stop."

Kyrie let out a brief chuckle. "So you like a goddamn queen pin or some shit, huh? You get up every day and come in this bitch and work hard like you need this li'l money. You're smart for sure. A woman who will do anything to get what she wants." His eyes bore into hers as he spoke.

"Kyrie, I came to Atlanta to sell weed. I didn't come with malicious intent or some kind of vendetta against you. I'm new in town, and it made sense to me to get on at the label and make connections. I'm sorry if you feel deceived. I did my job, and so far, I haven't even made any useful connections. I'm used to dealing with the big fish, and it's obvious that your clientele likes what I have. You could cop your weed from me and go back to serving them."

What she said made sense, but that didn't stop Kyrie from being livid. "I guess it's safe to say that you no longer work here." He refused to acknowledge what she said about him buying weed from her. His ego was wounded, and Khelani could see that clear as day.

"Okay." She removed her badge from the strap of her dress and placed it on her desk. "I can go log out of my computer and get my things."

Kyrie damn near felt panicked. Even in his anger, he didn't want her to walk out that door. He was surprised that, for as upset as he was, he didn't want to see her go. His emotions were all over the place, and that only added to his anger. What kind of hold did this woman have over him?

"Nah. As a matter of fact, you can work for the next two weeks. You leaving now will put Kim in a bind."

Khelani poked the inside of her jaw with her tongue in an effort to compose herself. She was done trying to stroke Kyrie's bruised ego. He had her fucked up. "So I'm not sure what you think this is, but you don't snap your fingers and I just do what you want me to do. Now I can work from home for a few days while Kim looks for a replacement. After that, you're on your own."

Kyrie stood up. "If you were anybody else, you might just get robbed of the work that you have and sent back to wherever you came from." His upper lip curled slightly.

Khelani cocked her head to the left and studied him a bit. "You run a multimillion-dollar company and you're crying because you lost a few niggas who don't even cop more than two or three pounds at a time? You're doing all this for what? You'd risk your career and your life by robbing me, 'cause don't think shit is sweet just because

I'm a female. My father runs Trinidad, and his reach is long. Remember that shit. You mad because you wined and dined me and you never got the pussy? I didn't fall at your feet and submit? Shit didn't go how you planned, and you're salty?"

"I get it. You must be a dyke. You wear the strap when you fuck bitches?"

Khelani smirked at Kyrie. "I take dick very well. Is that the issue, Kyrie? You want to fuck? Just say that then, and maybe we can work something out."

Kyrie wanted to say fuck her. He wanted to tell her to get out of his office and to stay away from his clientele, but the bulge in his jeans gave away his true feelings. In a matter of seconds, his dick was so hard that it hurt. He wanted to wipe the smirk off her face. Invading her personal space, Kyrie walked up on her, gently pushing her body with his.

"I think you're getting a kick out of playing with me. You might want to find you something safe to do, ma."

When Khelani didn't respond, Kyrie placed one hand around her neck as if he was choking her. Squeezing gently, he placed his lips on hers and snaked his tongue in her mouth. She smelled sweet, and her mouth tasted sweeter. It was what Kyrie had been craving, and he was determined to make her fold. His hand made its way up her skirt and ripped the red lace panties that she wore. Their kiss deepened as he fumbled with his belt buckle and freed his dick from his Marc Jacob boxer briefs.

Kyrie hoisted Khelani up, and she wrapped her legs around his waist. Staring into her face, he pressed the head of his dick at her opening, and she was already juicy for him. Crossing that line with Khelani might prove to be a mistake, but the sexual chemistry between them was so thick that it was damn near choking him. He pushed into her a little more, and she clenched her pussy muscles around the part of him that was in her. Yes, she was dangerous indeed, but Kyrie was determined to get some kind of reaction out of her. He pushed himself deeper into her, and it was his turn to smirk when her face crumpled slightly, and her mouth fell open. He had her ass.

With her back pressed against the wall and her legs locked around his body, Kyrie stirred Khelani's middle with passion and aggression. He was fucking her like a man just released from prison. Since he couldn't get to her breasts because of the outfit that she wore, his lips found hers again, and their tongues did a sensual dance. Khelani moaned in his mouth, and that shit turned him on. She wrapped her arms around his neck, and he carried her over to his desk. After sitting her down, he pulled back and bit his bottom lip as he watched his dick slide in and out of her pink treasure. She was so wet that her essence made his dick look glazed. He used his thumb to gently stroke her clit as he continued to massage the walls of her pussy, and Khelani let out a long moan.

Kyrie pulled all the way out of her and peered into her eyes as he used his dick to lightly beat her clit. He slid his dick up and down her slit, and Khelani lifted her hips slightly. She wanted him back inside of her. He watched her as she licked her lips.

"You want this dick?"

He was about to piss her off. Kyrie's ego trip was interrupting her impending orgasm. It was just like a man to want his ego stroked at the worst time. Khelani had always been a stubborn one, so rather than answering, she just narrowed her eyes into slits and peered at him. Kyrie chuckled. Her defiance was cute, but he wasn't willing to give up.

"Tell me you want this dick."

Khelani almost got up and told him to fuck himself, but Kasim's words echoed through her mind: *"You're too powerful, Khelani. You'll never find a man unless you submit. No man can take you outshining him."*

If he wanted to play, she could play too. "I want that dick. Please give it to me, baby," she moaned and had to stifle her laughter at the shock that registered on Kyrie's face. He hadn't even expected her to give in and say the shit.

"Kyrie, baby, please," she repeated, and that was all she wrote.

Kyrie slid back into her with a savage groan and went back to assaulting her pussy. The office was empty, and Khelani was glad because when waves of pleasure ripped through her body from an orgasm so intense that it made her toes curl, she cried out in pure ecstasy. She'd never had such an intense orgasm. It left her body trembling and jerking, and it didn't help that Kyrie hadn't eased his strokes up. His balls slapped against her pussy as he gritted his teeth and tried to fuck the taste out of her mouth. The orgasm made her already-soaked pussy wet beyond belief, and it was hard for Kyrie to hold off on his own nut. In fact, her pussy was so good and had him in such a zone that he didn't even pull out. Kyrie groaned as he came inside her with not one regret in the world.

A thin layer of sweat decorated her upper lip, and she looked so beautiful that Kyrie forgot about the slight power trip. With his dick still inside of her, he leaned down so that they were chest to chest and placed a juicy kiss on her lips. They locked eyes for a moment. Just for that moment, it was as if time stood still. Nothing else mattered, and the only people who existed were them.

It didn't take long for either of them to snap back to reality. Kyrie slid out of her, and Khelani stood up. Her panties were ruined, so she stepped out of them and put them in the trash. Without speaking a word, she headed out of Kyrie's office and headed to the bathroom to clean herself off. All he could do was stare after her.

"Muhfuckin' Khelani."

"What are you doing here?" Anya asked as she headed into the kitchen and saw Khelani sitting on the couch holding her laptop.

"I live here."

"Ha-ha. Why aren't you at work?" Anya tried to mask her agitation. She wanted to smoke, drink, and forget her sorrows. Who cared if it wasn't even noon? The rape she endured at the hands of Mozzy was still heavy on her mind, and she wanted to numb herself. Anya was a grown-ass woman, but she didn't feel like having Khelani looking down on her and judging her if she got shit-faced early in the day.

"I'm working from home. My cover is blown. Kyrie found out that I'm the person who's been taking some of his clientele, and he wasn't too happy about it. I told him he should get on the money train, but I don't think his pride will allow him to cop from a girl."

Anya looked over her shoulder. "Damn. He probably thought you were some low-level chick who would be impressed by what he has only to find out that you don't do too bad for yourself. Nigga would rather eat crow than cop his shit from you," she chortled.

Khelani sighed. "I know. I shouldn't even be helping his ass, but I'm doing it for Kim. Nigga fired me, then said, 'Nah, you're gonna help Kim.' I had to check him on that shit real fast. I know I threatened his manhood and all, but he had me fucked up."

"I'm sure. He was trying to wine and dine you and impress you, and then he finds out you're not who he thought you was. But I mean, now that the cover is blown, why not let loose? Why not give dating him a try? I know he'd still be open to it, because if he didn't like you, he wouldn't be tripping so hard. Kyrie is supposed to be about his paper. You come into town with some fire-ass weed and he's not trying to buy you out? That's his ego for sure."

"Because I don't want to date him. I don't want to date anybody. I just killed the man I was dating less than three months ago. I think I need to get over that first."

Anya kissed her teeth. "You liked Malachi, but you didn't love him. And the moment you saw him in your safe, any feelings you had for him disappeared. I know you. Been around you every day of my life for my entire life. The moment Kasim disposed of that nigga's body, he no longer existed to you. You're not hurt."

Khelani rolled her eyes upward. "Okay, I have work to do, and you're distracting me." Anya didn't take anything seriously, not even her own life, but here she was trying to read Khelani. It was almost comical.

Khelani didn't love Malachi. She never claimed to, but the sting of his betrayal didn't hurt any less. Khelani had no desire to ever again let her guard down and be disappointed by a man. Kyrie was rich, handsome, and very charming. To fall for him would be signing up to forever be in competition with the many females who wanted to be with him. Falling for him would mean trusting him to be committed to her and not sleep around, and Khelani would drink glass before she trusted a man to be faithful. Too much came with dealing with a man. It could never just be easy and fun. It might start out that way, but at some point, it would switch up. Someone would catch feelings, and the entire dynamic of the relationship would change. Plus, she moved around too much. Khelani didn't have time to be invested in one man.

But every time she thought back to their escapade in his office, her pussy throbbed. Khelani thought she'd had sex enough times in her life to be considered sexually experienced, but Kyrie showed her what she'd been missing. It was the absolute best sexual experience that she'd had in her life. The first orgasm she ever had was with Malachi, and he didn't even make her cum every time they had sex. She didn't cum with him until the fifth or sixth time they had fucked and she was very comfortable with him. He made her have an orgasm a total of two times before she found him attempting to rob her and killed him. Everything about Kyrie did it for her. The passion behind his kisses, the intensity of his gazes, the aggressive yet gentle way that he handled her. It sent chills down her spine in a good way.

She pushed thoughts of Kyrie from her mind and went back to work. Knowing that her job with his label would be over in a few days made her feel a sense of relief, but she was a little sad also. Although it was tiring, Khelani felt normal getting dressed every day in her cute little outfits and going to work. She enjoyed being in the presence of and having conversations with people other than Kasim and Anya. It was secretly nice to have Kyrie pining for her, even though she knew they'd never go anywhere. Khelani wondered what it would be like to pull an Anya move and tell her father that she no longer wanted to work for him. What if she just got a regular job and lived a regular life? She had enough money for a hefty down payment on a home. Her Beemer was paid for, and even if she put money down on a house, she'd be left with enough money to have a nice cushion for a few years. She could for sure make it working a regular job. Khelani once again took a mental break from her work and daydreamed. What would she do if she wasn't selling drugs? She loved fashion and could see herself being a stylist.

Khelani was jarred from her daydream when she got a text message alert. After picking up her phone, she saw that Kyrie had sent her a message that simply said, Let's talk numbers.

Khelani placed her laptop on the couch and got up to go get her burner phone. She didn't talk business on her iPhone. With bated breath, she called Kyrie and waited for him to answer.

"This is my business phone. What were you looking to cop?"

"I already know it's good because niggas are going crazy for it, so let me start with a hundred pounds, and we will see where it goes from there."

"I can arrange that. How soon would you like to get them? I can send my right hand, Kasim, to se—"

"Nah," Kyrie cut her off abruptly. "I'm only dealing with you."

Khelani breathed in deeply through her nose. Kyrie and his stubbornness were starting to irritate her. He was acting like a big-ass baby. If he wanted to see her, he could just say that instead of making demands. She was going to appease him, however. He was trying to cop a hundred pounds, and unlike him, she wasn't going to let emotions get in the way of money.

"When do you want to meet, Kyrie?"

"My place this evening. I'll text you the address. Does seven p.m. work for you?"

Now he was trying to be accommodating. "It does."

"Cool."

He ended the call without another word, and all Khelani could do was shake her head.

Chapter 12

Kyrie headed into the club knowing that shit wasn't going to go well. He'd been busy and had so much going on that he hadn't been able to confront Camila about what he was told, but today was the day. He nodded his head in the direction of anyone who spoke to him, but he was a man on a mission. He headed straight into the office and found Camila sitting at the desk scrolling through her phone. The first thing he noticed was that when she looked up at him, she looked a little flushed, but a sense of relief crossed her face almost immediately.

"'Bout time. You got that? One of the strippers hit me up twice already. She has regular customers who come in and cop."

"I'm not giving you any more coke, Camila."

You didn't sell drugs for as long as Kyrie had and not pick up on the traits and habits of users. Camila was antsy. She wanted more coke, and it wasn't to make money off of.

"Why not? Is it because of Dad? I told you he's not going to find out."

"It has nothing to do with him. When I picked the money up a few weeks ago, it was two hundred short, and I didn't say shit because you're family. The first time Tae picked it up, it was five hundred short. Last time, it was thirteen hundred short. You not about to keep stealing from me and thinking shit is sweet. On top of that, it's not like you're just stealing. You're using the shit, Camila."

Had she not been so livid, she would have seen the pain in her cousin's eyes. She'd done a lot of shit to disappoint him, but this took the cake.

"I'm not using shit. You keep listening to Tae. That nigga don't know me," Camila hissed. "Maybe ya man is stealing from you, but don't put that shit on me."

Kyrie shook his head. "You're dangerous, shawty. You know how I get down, and you know that if I really thought Tae was stealing from me, I'd hurt that man. You're my blood, and I love you, but I'm gon' distance myself from you for a bit. You need to get your mind right."

It felt to Camila like Kyrie was being mean to her, but his words to her caused an ache in his heart. Cutting her off would be like cutting off his sister, but she was going to stand in his face and blame Tae for some shit that she knew she did. It didn't get any worse than that. Camila did too much too often, and it had to come to an end. He couldn't keep entertaining her shit or enabling her. It was time for her to grow up.

"Distance yourself from me?" She snatched her head back. "You're acting real brand new right now, Kyrie. You want me to give you the li'l petty-ass two grand? Your rich ass is acting like you were missing some serious stacks."

"It's not about the amount. It's about the principle. That attitude right there is why I can't fuck with you. I don't need you to wash my money anymore. I'll handle the shit myself. You be easy." Kyrie left the office, leaving Camila fuming.

She knew plenty of niggas she could get coke from, but she wanted Kyrie's shit. She grabbed her purse and left her office to go and get some before the club started getting too packed. On her way out, she saw Anya and Snow conversing at the bar, and her eyes narrowed into slits. That was one ho-ass bitch. She'd just been raped by

Mozzy, and here she was all up in Snow's face. Camila had no idea that Anya was confronting Snow about robbing her people. He was playing dumb, but Anya knew better.

Camila's skin felt clammy as she headed for the door. She would deal with Anya and Snow another time. No one but Camila knew that the reason she was so against Anya and Snow had nothing to do with her loyalty to Caresha. She'd fucked Snow a few times herself. The last time, in fact, had been a month ago, and like Anya, she was hooked on the dick. Snow was a professional pipe layer. That was why Caresha's mouth was torn slam off her face. On one coke-induced night, Camila took it too far, and she had the best sex of her life with Snow. She felt guilty the next day, and she promised herself she wouldn't do it again . . . until she got horny, and he was the only man she wanted. The more they slept together, the more addicted she became. Seeing Snow make googly eyes at Anya burned her ass up because she knew that she and Snow could never be. Caresha would kill her if she ever found out about them.

Being that Caresha was on her mind, it really startled Camila when she walked out of the club and saw Caresha heading toward the entrance looking furious. Camila forgot all about her quest for coke.

"What's wrong with you?"

"I went through that bastard's phone. He's fucking that bitch! You bringing bitches around my nigga and they fuckin' him?"

"Hold up now, Caresha. You already know how Snow is. I told her he was off-limits. You act like I hooked them up. I went to go get my grills, and she was with me."

"Well, I'm about to beat her ass."

"I'll tell her to come outside. Don't cause a scene in the club, but if she wants to be bold enough to fuck your man, then whoop her ass," Camila said simply. She was agitated that she could no longer sell coke out of the club, she was agitated that Kyrie was pissed with her, and she was agitated that Snow was all up in Anya's face. All of those things were a recipe for disaster. Camila was like a ticking time bomb, and she wasn't anybody's friend. Not Anya's and not Caresha's.

Camila stepped inside the club and saw Snow walking away from Anya. She smirked before calling Anya's name.

"Yo, Anya. I need you to step outside for a minute."

Anya didn't second-guess Camila's request. She followed Snow, and he stopped dead in his tracks upon seeing Caresha, but she didn't say one word to him. She had beef with one person at the moment, and that was Anya. Camila folded her arms underneath her breasts and watched the scene that was about to unfold.

Anya looked confused as Caresha stepped in her face.

"You want to come in my shop smiling in my face and then fuck my nigga, bitch?"

Caresha didn't even give Anya time to answer. She stole off on her, causing Anya to stumble since she had on six-inch heels. Before Anya could recover, Caresha began raining blows down on her. Jealousy and rage overtook Camila's body, and she jumped in the fight. She was looking like the devoted friend, but she had her own motives. There was no way Anya could get to her feet with both women attacking her, so she curled into a fetal position until the fight was broken up. Snow pulled Caresha off Anya while one of the security guards grabbed Camila. They knew it was bad when blood began to stain the pavement. Anya got up slowly, and her nose and mouth were leaking blood along with a gash in her forehead. Her left eye was already beginning to swell. No matter how much pain she was in, Anya wouldn't let them see her shed one tear.

"You bitches had to jump me? Word? Camila, on God, next time I see you, I'm doing you dirty."

"Yeah, yeah, bitch. Just grab ya shit and kick rocks."

Camila was mad at the world. In that moment, it was fuck Anya and fuck everybody.

"This shit look like some fire." Kyrie inspected the weed that Khelani had brought into his home. He began to open one of the packages. When he glanced up at her, his dick jumped at the sight of her. "Have a seat. Smoke one with me. Or are you in a rush?"

Khelani remained standing. "Because you decided to purchase weed from me, that erases our entire conversation from yesterday? We just act like none of it ever happened?"

"Yeah. Just like we acted like it never happened when I was sliding my dick up in you," Kyrie spoke as he pulled buds from the package.

Khelani could only shake her head. This man was something else. When she still didn't sit down, Kyrie stood up and walked over to her. He grabbed each side of her waist as he invaded her personal space.

"All that hard shit is about to stop. You need that wall up when you out dealing with them niggas on your money shit. With me, you calm that shit down. You don't want a relationship, then so be it. You're not going to stay in the A forever, then that's what it is. But while you are here, we gon' do what we do, and you can stop fighting me on that shit."

Khelani didn't respond because the way he checked her made her pussy ache for him. And little did he know, she was tired of fighting him. Exhausted. When she didn't protest, Kyrie dipped his head and found her lips with his.

"You gon' act right?" he spoke into her mouth.

"Ummmhmmm," she moaned as he placed his face in the crook of her neck. All she could think about was having more bomb-ass sex with him, and that was enough to make her submit even if it was only temporary.

Pleased with her response, Kyrie pulled back with a smile. "Good. Now sit down so we can smoke. You hungry? I can get my chef to come through. He lives in this neighborhood."

"I mean, I could eat, but how are you going to call him on such short notice?"

"Because I'm that nigga. You let me worry about that." Kyrie picked up his phone from the cup holder of his leather recliner and shot his chef a text. He even told him that if he was available to come by on such short notice, he'd tip him an extra $300.

The duo sat in silence while Kyrie rolled the blunt. As soon as he lit it and took a long pull, his nostrils flared, and he damn near coughed. "Goddamn. This shit is like that for real." He took a few more puffs, then passed it to Khelani. He hated how into her he was. "Yo' ass had me hotter than fish grease yesterday." He shook his head at the memory.

"I apologize for that. That wasn't my intention. I'm just about my money."

The weed had Kyrie feeling real mellow. "I like that shit," he stated in a low voice. "You just being easy and not giving a nigga a hard time. I'd give ya ass the world if you knew how to act," he chuckled, but he was serious.

Khelani exhaled weed smoke from her lungs. "I can give myself the world."

Kyrie kissed his teeth. "That's the shit I'm talking about. You can, but why would you want to? You have a nigga who would do it for you. That shit is crazy as hell to me, but I have to respect who you are because plenty women damn near begged me to settle down with them. They weren't who I wanted though, so I gave them every excuse in the book. Guess that's the game you're playing with me, but it's all good. If you don't want me, that's what it is."

Khelani was high, and the last thing she wanted was deep conversations. She passed him the blunt back. "I'm gonna head out." She stood up, and he was right behind her.

"Fuck that, Khelani. Fuck all that running and all that tough shit. Goddamn, just tell me what's good. You don't want me?"

Good dick will make a woman emotional. That and all the shit she had going on was weighing heavily on her. Kyrie didn't know how bad she wanted to just chill out and be a woman. Not a damn drug dealer.

"In another life, Kyrie, I wouldn't want anybody but you," she confessed with tearful eyes. She couldn't believe this nigga had her about to cry.

Her vulnerability made Kyrie want her even more, and he cupped her chin in his hand. "We don't need another life when we have this one." He kissed the corner of her mouth, her nose, her forehead, and then her lips. Khelani's body relaxed as he began to suck softly on her neck.

He moved his mouth back up and spoke against her ear. "I wanna give you all this dick." Kyrie pressed his body into hers, and Khelani felt his erection. That turned her on, but his words made her giggle. "You gon' let me give it to you?"

He pulled back so he could look her in the face, and Khelani simply nodded. That was all he needed to see. Kyrie picked her up, and with her legs wrapped around his body and his hands on her ass, he carried her up the stairs to his bedroom. Kyrie took off Khelani's Louis

Vuitton combat boots, then peeled her black leggings and panties down her thick thighs. After placing his head in between her legs, the scent of cocoa butter on her skin filled his nostrils. Kyrie kissed her clit softly before French kissing it passionately. Khelani's back arched, and she bit her bottom lip as he probed her most sensitive parts with his mouth. When he moaned into her pussy, her body jerked slightly, and Khelani grabbed his curls as he devoured her. The things Kyrie was doing to her pussy with his mouth had her juices running down the crack of her ass.

Kyrie had a point to prove. He was that nigga, and he often made women fall before they got the D. Once they did get the D, however, it was usually a wrap. He'd be ducking and dodging them like crazy, but he welcomed the antics from Khelani. Making her act as if she gave a damn would be the ultimate pleasure for him. It was funny how the right woman could make a man change how he acted and how he moved in general. All he wanted to do was win Khelani over. He knew once he had her, she wasn't going anywhere. The feeling of an impending orgasm engulfed her, and Khelani was desperate to reach that peak. She began thrusting her hips and riding Kyrie's face until her clit swelled, and her pussy began to contract violently. Kyrie didn't let up off her, and he slurped her dry as she moaned and called his name.

He finally came up for air, and their tongues connected. Khelani tasted her juices on his lips. Kyrie's beard glistened with her essence, and she played in his hair while her body yearned for him. When Kyrie stood up to undress, Khelani sat up and took her shirt and bra off. They didn't use a condom the first time they had sex, and one wasn't on his mind the second time. Kyrie wasted no time guiding his dick to her opening and easing into her. Khelani let out a shaky breath as he filled her up. Kyrie was too rich to be going around having unprotected sex. He didn't need a bunch of babies to pay for or any STDs to get rid of. If he hit a woman raw, it needed to be understood that the pussy was for him and only him. He didn't feel the need to express his feelings because he doubted Khelani's difficult ass was fucking anybody else.

"That shit feel good?" he asked in a low voice before pecking her on the lips. He knew it did from the way her face was contorted, but he wanted to hear the words.

"It feels very good," she replied as he stirred her middle.

"I want this shit from the back. I want to see that fat ass jiggle while I fuck the shit out of you."

Kyrie pulled out of Khelani, and she got into the doggie-style position. Kyrie spread her round ass cheeks and began eating her out again. Khelani was losing her mind, and that shit stroked the hell out of his ego.

"Fuuccckkkk," Khelani squealed as he pulled out of her and smacked her on the ass hard as hell.

As soon as he slid back into her, she came again. She squirted just a bit, and the puddle that appeared on his bed along with the cum that shot onto his stomach and balls made him fuck her savagely. Her reaction to him was turning him on like a muhfucka. The wetter and tighter she became, the better it was for him. Kyrie felt it was safe to say that Khelani had the best pussy he'd ever had. He clenched his teeth together as he pounded in and out of her.

"This my goddamn pussy," he roared as he shot his load into her womb. He stayed inside of her for a moment before easing out of her. Kyrie admired her glistening pussy before she got off the bed.

"Where's the bathroom?"

He eyed her naked body and licked his lips. "You heard what I said? That's my pussy."

Khelani smirked. "I heard you loud and clear."

She and Kyrie engaged in a brief stare down. It would always be a battle of the egos with them, but if Khelani didn't learn anything else from her mother, she learned when to let a man shine. "As long as you act like this, it's yours. But how fair would it be for my pussy to be yours while your dick is roaming?"

"If it ain't you, fuck a bitch," he replied adamantly, making her blush.

"I hear you."

That satisfied him, and he kissed her before leading her to the bathroom. They had just cleaned up and put their clothes back on when Kyrie's chef rang his doorbell. He let Mike in just as Kasim was calling Khelani.

"Hello?"

"I know where that nigga Snow is. He finally went to his shop. Me and Delante are about to run in and fire his ass up."

"Damn, I wanted to be there," Khelani stated, but she knew they didn't have time to wait for her.

"There's no need for you to be here. We got this," Kasim assured her. He was overprotective of Khelani and never wanted her in harm's way.

"Okay. Be careful."

Kyrie's eyes shot in her direction. "Everything good?"

"Yeah. My right hand is just going to handle some shit, and I want to be there."

The way she bit her bottom lip was sexy, and Kyrie had learned her well enough to know that she was conflicted about something. He wasn't sure what the call was about, but he knew the kind of shit Khelani dealt in. If she was his girl, that shit would come to an end ASAP. He knew he couldn't tell her shit though. They were only fucking.

Khelani and Kyrie finished smoking the blunt he rolled while Mike prepared seafood pasta, garlic bread, and lamb chops. When they were done eating, she was stuffed and ready to be alone so she could talk to Kasim.

"I have to get going, but thank you for dinner. It was delicious."

Kyrie wished he could have gone to bed with her and woken her up the next morning by sliding his dick in her. "You're welcome. Let me know when you make it in the house."

"Will do." She turned to walk away, and he pulled her back. Kyrie didn't let her leave him until he'd placed a few pecks on her lips.

Khelani headed to her car feeling as if she were walking on a cloud. Kyrie made her feel things she didn't want to feel. If she could feel like this every day, he might be worth risking it all for, but this feeling was temporary. After the honeymoon phase came the bullshit. Khelani decided to stay in the moment and not think too much about the future, and in the moment, she needed to go get a Plan B pill. Khelani couldn't afford any slipups.

Chapter 13

"What in the fuck happened to your face?" Khelani asked Anya the next morning. Even though she and Kyrie were on good terms, she was still going to work from home. When Khelani walked into the kitchen for her morning coffee and saw the gruesome sight of her sister's face, her heart dropped into her stomach.

Anya's eye was swollen shut, and there was a gash on her forehead. Her lips were swollen, and she looked as if she'd been beaten mercilessly, and all Khelani saw was red. Anya dropped her head shamefully. The only way she'd been able to get to sleep the night before was to drink tequila until she was damn near sick. She needed something for the pain, but Anya didn't want to go to the hospital.

"Camila and her friend Caresha jumped me," she mumbled as she grabbed ice for her lips. "I was fucking around with Caresha's ex, Snow. They jumped me at the club."

It literally felt like Khelani's blood was boiling. She was furious. "Do you know where these bitches live?"

Anya could almost feel the heat radiating off her sister. She knew that when Khelani got like this, there was no talking her down, and Anya didn't care. Camila's ass deserved whatever she had coming her weak-ass way. Jumping her was some coward-ass shit to do. As soon as her face healed, that bitch had to see her. And so would Caresha.

"I've never been to her place. The bitch Caresha works in the same building that Snow does."

"She jumped your ass over a dead nigga, because Kasim and Delante handled that nigga last night. I'll let that bitch grieve for a few days before I get her, but I'm on Camila's ass. Today."

Anya knew she wasn't bullshitting. If it hadn't hurt so bad, she would have smiled knowing Camila was going to get hers. It also made her feel good to know that Caresha was somewhere crying her eyes out. She didn't feel bad because Snow shouldn't have robbed Delante. He did that shit to himself. Anyone who thought Khelani, Kasim, or Delante were sweet would be in for a rude awakening every time they tried one of them.

"Do you have something for pain?" Anya asked her sister.

"I'll check in my room."

Khelani wasn't even going to give Anya any lectures about being smart and leaving bitches' niggas alone. No matter who she had sex with, she didn't deserve to be attacked like that by a coward and her friend. They should have fought straight up. Camila didn't have to involve herself, and now she had to see Khelani. As Khelani passed the pain pills to Anya, her phone rang, and she saw that her father was calling. Her eyes rolled upward. Kemp's third eye was open for sure, because each time Anya got in trouble, Khelani was having doubts about hustling, or anything of that nature, he would call. Too many times she thought about how life would be if she stopped hustling and just gave a relationship with Kyrie a shot. Then she'd think about him playing her or cheating on her, and all bets would be off.

"Hi, Daddy."

"Hey, baby girl. How is everything going?"

"Everything is good." She dared not tell him about Anya's drama. Since he cut her off, he hadn't asked about her, and Khelani hadn't volunteered any information.

"Good. There is a shipment coming in tomorrow. You know the drill. Send Kasim and Delante to retrieve it."

"Got it."

"You sure everything is okay? You need anything?"

"I'm sure. We had the issue with Delante being robbed, but that's been handled. I've secured a new customer. Things are running smoothly."

"I appreciate you, my dear. To show you how much so, I am depositing a check from my company into your account for twenty thousand dollars. On record, it shows as a signing bonus for your promotion in my company. Take the money and buy yourself something nice."

"Thank you. I appreciate that."

"Anything for you, my dear. I love you."

"I love you too."

Khelani and her father ended their conversation, and she leaned against the island in the kitchen. She may as well push her anger to the side and get her work done, because as soon as the sun went down, she was going to bust Camila's ass.

Kyrie walked into Camila's office with an expression on his face that was devoid of emotion. She had called him crying earlier, and he really almost ignored her. When Camila was desperate, she'd go through great lengths to get her way. She could cry at the drop of a hat, yet here he was trying to see what she wanted. Kyrie refused to go back on the tough love he was giving her. Camila sat behind her desk with a puffy face.

"What's wrong with you?" he asked.

"Kyrie, I fucked up bad. I haven't paid the light bill for the past two months, and in order to avoid disconnection, I had to pay $1,625 today. On top of that, the liquor inventory came today, and I had to pay $7,021 for that. I'm dead-ass broke, Kyrie, and the rent on my condo is due in three days. Please just give me some coke to move, and I swear every dollar will be accounted for."

He didn't even blink. "If you don't know how to run a business, I suggest you hire someone to do it for you, or you let this club go. You already owe me money. It's not my job to bail you out."

Camila's mouth fell open from shock. She couldn't believe that Kyrie was treating her like this. Before she could respond, one of her bouncers came through on the walkie-talkie that they used to communicate with.

"Camila, there's a female at the front of the club demanding to see you."

Camila hissed as she stood up. "Who in the fuck is demanding to see me?"

Kyrie followed her to the front of the club because he planned on leaving. Camila wasn't talking about shit. All she wanted to do was beg, and he didn't have shit for her. Kyrie stopped to speak to someone he knew since patrons had begun to enter the club, and by the time he exited the club, he was shocked to hear Khelani yelling in Camila's face.

"Bitch, for what you did to my sister, I'm gon' beat yo' ass." She hit Camila in the face, and by the time her second punch landed, security was grabbing her.

Khelani wasn't the hair-pulling type, but she was furious that the fight was being broken up before she could do what she wanted to do, so anger made her grab Camila's hair. She wouldn't let it go for shit. The bouncer tried to pry her hands off Camila's tracks, but she wasn't budging. She then attempted to hit Camila with an uppercut. Khelani was out for blood. After a good three minutes, she finally let Camila's hair go, and Camila tried to charge her, but security grabbed her, and Kyrie grabbed Khelani.

"Chill! Fuck is you doing? That's my cousin," Kyrie declared.

Khelani's head jerked back. "I don't give a fuck! That whore and her friend jumped my sister, and she has to see me. You can't fuckin' save her."

Kyrie shook his head. He wasn't trying to get in the middle of female business. Camila could be a messy muhfucka, but he couldn't let her be attacked in his presence. "Khelani, ju—"

"Nigga, fuck what you talking about," she spat. No one could save Camila. Not even Kyrie.

Before he could speak, he heard a popping sound, and a look of shock registered on Khelani's face. He heard people scream just as Khelani fell forward. It took him a second to realize that she'd been shot. His eyes scanned her body until his gaze fell on a bloody stain on her shirt near the top of her abdomen. Kyrie's eyes darted out into the sea of people scattering, and as he held Khelani in his arms, he saw the nigga who had robbed his artist of his chain fleeing the scene with a gun in his hand.

Chapter 14

"It's gonna be a'ight." Kyrie looked down into Khelani's face as he waited for the ambulance to come.

He was trying his best to comfort her, but it was hard to do when he was scared. Nah, he was terrified. He had her in his arms cradling her, and he could see her clenching her jaw muscles tight. The shit she was enduring had to hurt, but she was taking it like a G. "I'm sorry," he whispered. Khelani thought he was just saying something, but really, he was apologizing for being sloppy.

He should have never let that nigga go. Suddenly, he remembered that he needed to apply pressure to her wound. He blocked out everyone going crazy around him and focused solely on Khelani and her injury. This was the woman who had come into his life and changed shit up. The way he thought, the way he moved—it was all different now. When he pressed on the spot where the bullet had entered her body, she groaned slightly, and he peered back into her face. "I'm sorry, baby," he apologized again. The thought of hurting her didn't sit well with him, but he was trying to save her.

Fuck being a businessman. All that shit went out the window. He didn't even remember the name of the nigga who shot her, but he had signed his death certificate. Whether Khelani made it or not, that nigga was dead. As sirens wailed in the distance, it hit Kyrie that Khelani might not pull through, and he damn near lost it. His mistake could cost her her life, and that shit was tugging at his heart strings. He closed his eyes to keep the tears at bay as an ambulance raced into the parking lot. He waited for the EMTs to near before he gently pulled his arm from underneath her head and got up off the ground. His clothes were saturated with her blood. It was a crimson-colored reminder that he had fucked up. Kyrie didn't speak a word to anyone. He simply walked to his car, but once inside, he hit his steering wheel and screamed at the top of his lungs.

"Fuck!"

Kyrie angrily started his car and sped out of the parking lot. With flaring nostrils, he grabbed his cell phone with bloody hands. As soon as Montana answered the phone, Kyrie began yelling so aggressively that spit flew from his mouth. "We gotta find that nigga again! The nigga who took Kilo's chain. He just shot at me outside of Camila's club, and he hit Khelani instead."

Montana groaned. "I told you we should have deaded that nigga. Say less. I'm on it."

Kyrie ended the call. He gripped the steering wheel tight and breathed hard through his nose. He was out for blood. The nerve of a nigga to even shoot at him had him pissed, but the fact that Khelani took a bullet meant for him . . . it wasn't sitting well with him.

Kyrie drove home and peeled his bloody clothes off. He took a shower and let the hot water pelt his muscular frame. He closed his eyes but opened them back up abruptly when images of Khelani's face entered his mind. Kyrie quickly showered, then slid the frosted-glass shower door back.

It dawned on him that since he refused to do business with Kasim, he didn't have any of Khelani's people's phone numbers. He wasn't even sure if her sister or anybody had been contacted, and that would mean she was at the hospital all alone. That thought sprang Kyrie into action. He got dressed fast as hell, then hopped back in his car and headed toward the hospital.

When he arrived, he found that she was in surgery. Kyrie sat on pins and needles for what felt like hours. Finally, he could go in. Khelani was still sedated, and she looked angelic. Even with dry, cracked lips, she was still gorgeous. Kyrie knew he had it bad when he reached into his pocket for ChapStick. Gently, he smoothed the balm across her peeling lips. He peered at her beautiful face, and all he could feel was joy. The anger had taken a back burner, and he was ecstatic that she was okay. Now what would really make him feel good was Montana finding the fuck nigga responsible for this.

Kyrie stared at her for the longest time. Never in his life had he just sat and looked at a woman the way that he was admiring Khelani. He even said a silent prayer and thanked God that she was still there.

Kyrie finally tore his gaze away from Khelani long enough to scroll through his phone and check some of his messages. Even being engrossed in his phone, he saw her stir out of his peripheral vision. Kyrie looked anxiously at her, and the first thing he noticed were her tearful eyes. Seeing Khelani vulnerable wasn't common for him. Kyrie got up and stood at her bedside.

"I'm here. I don't know your people's numbers. They don't even know what happened to you. Are you in pain? What's wrong?"

Khelani prided herself on being tough, but this one was hard for her. She lay in Kyrie's arms, scared for her life. For a second, she almost felt she wouldn't make it, and that was a terrifying feeling. Being weak wouldn't help her though, so she reached for the button that would raise her bed, all while blinking back her tears.

"I'm kind of sore, but it will be okay. I'll call Kasim and Anya in a bit. I kind of need the peace right now." She gave him a small smile.

For a moment, all he could do was stare at her. It didn't take him long before he snapped back into the present. "Okay. Do you need anything? Are you hungry?"

Before Khelani could answer, the door opened, and in walked a nurse. The woman was no taller than four foot eleven. She had platinum blond hair that hung down to her behind, and she had skin that looked like it had taken years of abuse from tanning beds or the sun. Kyrie couldn't even begin to guess her age. Maybe 25, maybe 35.

"Hi. I'm glad to see that you're awake. I just need to take your vitals and go over some medical information with you." The nurse looked over at Kyrie, then back at Khelani. "Is this your family, or would you like him to leave the room while we have a brief discussion?"

Khelani hadn't even answered the question, but Kyrie prepared himself to stand and leave the room for a moment.

"Umm, he can be here. I don't mind."

Kyrie looked over at Khelani as if to ask if she was sure, but her eyes remained on the nurse. She got shot. She didn't see the nurse telling her anything that she didn't want Kyrie to hear, so what was the point in him leaving?

The nurse continued in her pleasant voice, "Wonderful. Well, my first question to you is, did you know that you were pregnant?"

Chapter 15

Khelani's eyebrows shot up. "Excuse me?" This lady had to be mistaken, and if she was, Khelani was out of there. There was no way in hell these quacks would look after her for another minute.

"You're very early. Five weeks, so it is completely normal if you didn't know. There was no direct injury to your uterus, and for the moment, the embryo is fine. Since you are so early in the pregnancy, and your body has gone through some trauma, it's almost expected for your body to expel the embryo at some point." It was too soon to even call the baby a fetus. At this point, it was simply an embryo, and she felt that using medical terms would make it less sentimental. She knew it might be a hard pill for any woman to swallow. She was basically telling her to wait to miscarry because of all the trauma she had endured.

Khelani was speechless, and so was Kyrie. His heartbeat quickened, and he rubbed his sweaty palms on his jeans. This was the kind of shit that happened from unprotected sex. Still, he didn't expect it so soon. He'd only had sex with Khelani twice. Did it happen the first time or the second?

"Thank you for letting me know." Khelani's tone was grim. No one in the room could tell if she was upset at the news of being pregnant or the news of the impending miscarriage.

All the other words that the nurse spoke were blocked out, and all she could think was, *I fucked up*. Khelani wasn't heartless, but she was almost relieved that her body would correct the mistake that she made, and she wouldn't look like a villain by getting an abortion. She didn't even know Kyrie, and she had allowed herself to get pregnant by him. Lust was too damn powerful. It made all logic and common sense go out the window. That was why her father was so against love. Find a nigga with a li'l swag who always smells good, has some bomb-ass dick and a handsome face, and women lose their damn minds. Even with all the times Khelani thought about having a normal life, this wasn't that. She had more than enough money to leave the game and go do something normal. She just wasn't sure why she was dragging her feet.

Khelani zoned back in as the nurse was saying that the doctor would be in shortly and that she would bring her something to eat. All Khelani could do was nod her head. The nurse's presence had been the saving grace, because when she left the room, the tension seemed to be thick enough to choke her. Khelani's mouth went dry, and she didn't want to face Kyrie.

"How do you feel?" His deep, masculine voice sliced through the tense fog, and Khelani looked over at him. It was hard for her to read his expression. Concern maybe?

"I feel fine. It will work itself out."

Kyrie's eyebrows furrowed. "What do you mean, it will work itself out?"

"She said I'm going to miscarry. There's nothing to worry about."

Kyrie chuckled lightly. He didn't know Khelani that well, but she still managed to surprise him often. He could be passive, uncaring, cold even, but it shocked him to see a female so much like himself. Damn near scary.

"So that's it? You're waiting to miscarry? What if you don't?"

Khelani's eyes widened slightly as if she hadn't even considered that option. "Ummmm, I mean . . ." Her voice trailed off.

"You don't want the baby?"

Khelani's eyebrows hiked up. "Don't tell me you do."

"What would be the point in you not having it? We both have money. We can afford a child. I know I'd for damn sure be a good father." His voice held a proud tone.

He hadn't really considered kids only because he wasn't in a relationship. Kyrie tried to be careful, and it had worked for most of his life. Last time he wasn't careful, he was 19, and the girl he got pregnant had miscarried. He didn't have nearly as much money back then as he had now, but he was going to take care of that one too had he or she been born. Kyrie had no desire to deal with baby-mama drama, which was why he'd been so careful, but he wasn't going to use that as an excuse to condone abortions. To him, they were for people who truly couldn't take care of kids, absolutely didn't want them, or got pregnant under unfortunate circumstances such as rape. He was perfectly capable of taking care of a child and would be a single father if he had to be.

"Is money the only criteria for having a child? We don't know each other, and I don't exactly have the kind of profession a child needs to be in the midst of."

Kyrie was trying to keep from getting pissed off. "Every reason you just gave was selfish as hell. We have nine months to get to know each other, and if we don't like each other, cool. We can still be adult enough to coparent, and the profession that you're in is a choice. You can stop anytime you want, and if you won't stop for your own child, that says a lot about your character."

Khelani's head jerked back. "Excuse me?" The way her brows dipped and her lips turned up, it was obvious to anyone that she was offended, but Kyrie didn't care.

"You heard me." Kyrie refused to back down. "You have a job at my company. If you need a raise, you got that. I'll double your salary. Fuck that, I'll triple your salary. You never have to sell another pound if you don't want to."

His eyes held a pleading glare. He was begging her to leave the game, but Kyrie didn't know her. It wasn't that easy, and she didn't feel like explaining the shit to him.

Khelani's phone rang, and that saved her from having to respond right away. She saw that Kasim was calling, and that gave her a chance to run down to him everything that transpired. It was when she said she didn't know who shot her or why that Kyrie's anger melted away and guilt returned.

He decided to leave the baby talk for another time, and when she got off the phone, he was ready to confess. "I know who shot you. I have my people looking for him right now. He was trying to shoot me, and he hit you instead." Kyrie's throat tightened as he spoke the words. His skin felt warm as he got mad all over again.

"Trying to shoot you? Why?"

"He stole one of my artist's chains and was bragging about it. I had him snatched up, whooped his ass, and got the chain back. My people wanted to kill him, but I try not to be on that type of time anymore. I let the nigga go, and that proved to be a mistake. I'm sorry."

Khelani could see that he was genuinely sorry, and she had to admit that Kyrie was handsome as hell. Even while they were discussing such a serious and grim matter, she could still appreciate his handsome features. "Sorry for what? You didn't pull the trigger. You better find his ass before I do." Fire blazed in her eyes, and for one brief moment, Kyrie was turned on. He really believed that if she got her hands on the nigga, she'd do him dirty. A woman who could hold her own was sexy. But she could also be bullheaded and stubborn.

The nurse entered the room with a tray of food for Khelani, and by the time she was done eating, Kasim was barging through the door. He looked over at Kyrie and gave him a brief head nod. Khelani sucked the rest of her Pepsi through a straw, and Kyrie bit his tongue. Literally. He wasn't even gon' tell her she didn't need to be drinking that shit while she was pregnant.

"He knows who shot me. Dude was aiming at him," Khelani informed Kasim, and his head whipped in Kyrie's direction.

If he were easily intimidated, Kasim's glare would have scared Kyrie, but he wasn't bothered in the least. Just like Khelani said, he hadn't pulled the trigger. When he found the man who did though, the muhfucka would regret the day that he'd been born. Kyrie could empathize with Kasim because he wanted the fuck nigga to pay too.

"We need to talk outside," Kasim stated in a gruff voice.

Kyrie stood and walked over to the bed as Kasim left the room. "We have a lot to talk about, but I'm going to let you get some rest." He leaned in and kissed her on the forehead.

If Khelani didn't miscarry naturally, then she was going to have to go through him to end the pregnancy, and he really didn't care how she felt about it.

Khelani winced from the pain as she got back in bed. Her pain medication had lasted long enough for her to take a shower, wash her hair, and brush her teeth, but her body was sore as hell. She felt as if she'd been run over. Her stomach was cramping, and in the back of her mind, she wondered if she was about to miscarry. Just as she pressed the button for the nurse, Khelani's door opened, and she wasn't able to stop the groan that left her mouth when her parents stepped into the room.

She had prayed as hard as she could that her parents wouldn't come, but she had obviously prayed in vain. Kemp stepped into the room with a stern look etched on his face. He looked like he was out for blood, but as soon as his eyes locked with Khelani's, his expression softened.

"How are you?" he asked in a concerned tone.

"I'm fine. The doctor said I can go home tomorrow. You really didn't have to come all this way."

"Nonsense. Our daughter was shot. Did you think we weren't coming?" her mother asked as she walked closer to the bed. Khelani peeped that her father was eyeing the vase filled with roses that Kyrie had sent her earlier that morning.

Khelani's eyes were trained on her father for a moment. It wasn't until her mother cleared her throat that Khelani directed her attention toward her. She was usually poised, put together, and unbothered, but she couldn't pass up the chance to be just slightly petty with her mother. "Even if Dad came, I didn't think you would. I didn't know you cared."

Kemp's head turned in his daughter's direction, and his mouth was slightly agape while his wife gasped. It was almost comical how shocked they seemed by her words. After all, Anya was the feisty and unruly one. Khelani rarely ever gave them problems, but as soon as her mother's eyes narrowed, she knew she was about to get it.

"I'm going to assume that the stress and the trauma of this situation has you talking a little out of your head. You and Anya are both my daughters, and I love you both just the same. As grown women, you both need to lay that favoritism line to bed," she chastised her.

Courtney stood tall and proud. She was five foot seven with light skin and almond-shaped eyes. Her long, curly hair was pulled up into a sleek bun, and she wore a red pantsuit. It looked as if she'd just stepped out of a board-room, but she was just a housewife—a housewife who made it her business to be stunning at all times. She even went to bed looking like that bitch. It would be over her dead body if anyone ever caught her slipping. She wore a full face of makeup each time she gave birth, and because she got epidurals, she didn't even sweat the shit off. If Kyrie thought Khelani was passive and uncaring, he'd be in for a treat when meeting her mother. She was the queen of no fucks given, and she rarely showed emotion unless it was anger.

"Where is your sister?" Kemp decided to try to change the subject. For as much as they tried to admit it, they did have favorites, and Khelani was his. It had nothing to do with age, smarts, looks, or anything of the sort. He hated that Anya always defied him, while Khelani made his life as a father easy.

Khelani had just opened her mouth to say she didn't know when Anya entered the room. She had large shades covering her eyes, and the heavy makeup she wore cov-ered the bruises from her fight with Caresha and Camila. "I'm right here."

Her mother rushed over to hug her while her father tried to decide if he was going to give her a piece of his mind. Before he could do so, she spoke and shocked them all.

"I came to check on Khelani, but I also wanted to tell her that I would handle things while she heals. I'm no longer fighting you on this." She looked her father in the eyes. "I'm stepping in for Khelani."

Chapter 16

Kyrie stood patiently by while Kasim slid his black leather gloves over his hands. The man who shot Khelani had been located. It only took three days, and some- one had given him up. Not for free of course, but with the reward money that Kyrie offered, his own homie gave him up. The man was hiding out an hour away from Atlanta, and Kyrie had his exact location. He no longer cared about being a businessman. This fuck nigga should have been handled after he took Kilo's chain, but Kyrie wouldn't make the mistake of letting him go again.

Once Kasim was ready, the men gripped their Glocks and headed up the walkway to the house that their mark was in. Kasim wasn't like Khelani's father. He wanted her to find love and leave the game. He stood by his decision that the game was no place for a woman, but he simply took orders from Kemp. He refrained from telling him how to raise his daughters, plus, Khelani was a grown woman. If she truly wanted out of the game, all she had to do was express that to her father. He wouldn't be happy about it, but as long as she was happy, that was all that mattered. As long as he was alive, however, he would protect her, and he had a feeling that this Kyrie character felt the same way. Kyrie might be just what Khelani needed in her life to soften her ass up and get her away from the madness of the hustle.

He seemed real upset about Khelani being shot, and that was all right with Kasim. Kyrie stood back, waiting patiently as Kasim tampered with the locks on the car that was parked in the driveway. Kasim wasn't interested in the car. He wanted the car alarm to go off. The street was dark, and the men were dressed in all black. Kasim and Kyrie both wanted the person who shot Khelani dead, and they were trying to flush him out of the house. If the car shit didn't work, then they were going in and bodying everything breathing inside the house. Kyrie thought those days were long behind him, but he was willing to do whatever it took to make sure that he was never tested or disrespected by this lame muhfucka again.

The front door opened, and a tall figure appeared in the doorway. Kyrie remained hidden behind a large tree that was in the front yard, and Kasim stopped messing with the car.

"Fuck are you doing?" a male voice barked before he ran down the porch steps, headed in Kasim's direction. All he saw was someone messing with his car, and he forgot all about the fact that he was supposed to be in hiding.

Kasim wasn't immediately sure if it was their man. He had never seen him before, but that didn't stop him from pointing his weapon at the man and sending a bullet flying into his right kneecap.

"Fuuckk," he groaned as he hit the ground.

Kyrie emerged from behind the tree and walked over to the man writhing around on the ground.

"Take the car, man. Just take it." He grimaced from the pain.

"This him?" Kasim asked as he looked over at Kyrie.

The man's eyes widened, and he knew he had messed up. He didn't recognize Kasim, but he knew exactly who Kyrie was, and he had just made the biggest mistake of his life by trying to come outside and stop a carjacking.

"Yeah, this is that muhfucka," Kyrie sneered as he pointed his gun at the man's head.

"No. Please, man, wai—"

Two bullets to the face silenced him forever, and Kyrie and Kasim got the hell out of dodge.

"Is there something you need to tell me?"

Khelani was trying to be respectful, so she wouldn't let the scowl that she was holding back break through. Her father was getting on her last nerve though, and she respectfully wanted him to get back on his private jet and go back to Trinidad. She'd been released from the hospital, and the ever-observant Kemp took notice of the second vase of flowers along with some fruit that had been delivered to her room before she was discharged. He hadn't gone so far as to read the card, but anyone could see that his daughter had a suitor.

"Nope. Nothing that I can think of." Khelani's tone was respectful but flat and devoid of emotion.

"Are you seeing someone?" He decided to come right out and ask it.

"Dad, why does that matter? I mean, I know what you'll say, but you do realize that I'm a human being, right? It's really not logical to think that I want to spend my entire life being focused solely on money and running your empire. Even in your position you still have a wife and kids, yet you want me to die lonely and desolate all for the sake of making you richer than you already are. I know I can't fall in love, get married, have kids, or do any of the normal things that other people do, but can I at least get flowers sent to me without the third degree?" Khelani was still respectful, but she was agitated, and it showed. Her emotions were all over the place and not necessarily from being shot. Finding out she was pregnant had caught her completely off guard.

Even though she was grown as hell and could afford to take care of herself, she was still fearful to have a child simply because she knew her father wouldn't approve, and that made her sick. She was really starting to see why Anya had rebelled so hard, and she felt bad that she gave her sister a hard time for it. In her eyes, she was her father's right hand first and a daughter second. Sometimes, she just wanted a regular father and not one who was the head of a drug cartel.

"If you want out, just say that." Kemp's tone was low and even. He thought he was passing down a legacy that his daughters would appreciate. Power had no gender, and he was grooming them so that they would never need a man, be weak for one, or be dumb for one, but he couldn't hold them forever.

"Once Atlanta is taken care of, I want out. I don't want to move on to the next city or the next state. Someone else can do it." She had money. Maybe not enough to live off of for the rest of her life, but that was the easy part. Khelani could live off what she had comfortably for the next ten or so years. That was more than enough time to figure shit out.

"Very well then. Anya seems eager to take over for you until you heal. Once you have done what you set out to do, you are out. I will make arrangements for Kasim to groom someone else, and they can move on to Dallas. Will you be coming back to Trinidad or staying here?"

Khelani was stunned that her father wasn't fighting her. She almost expected him to cut her off the way he did Anya. Only Khelani didn't depend on him financially, so it wouldn't matter. He was too calm and taking the news too well. Maybe her being shot had affected him more than she thought it did.

"I hadn't really thought about it." The way her eyes shifted down to her comforter made Kemp aware that her statement might not be true.

He wasn't going to push the issue, however. When he got word that his oldest daughter had been shot, he stopped breathing. He didn't even realize he'd been holding his breath until he damn near got lightheaded. Even though her being shot had nothing to do with the fact that she sold drugs, for the first time, it hit him what it would feel like to find out she'd been picked up by the police or robbed or killed, and the fear damn near crippled him. Death was inevitable. Everyone would meet that fate, but he'd never be able to rest knowing the game that he put his child on to cost her her life or her freedom. Before, he felt as long as she had muscle behind her and moved carefully, she'd be good. It took him some time to understand that he was a fool for thinking that shit. No one was invincible. His daughter was far from weak, so his job had been done. If she wanted out, he would give her that.

"All I ever wanted was the best for you and your sister. Maybe I went about it the wrong way. Females are always taught how to be wives, and I never wanted that for my daughters. I wanted you tough. I wanted you to have everything I have and more, and I didn't want to just put it in your hands. I didn't have a son to pass my empire down to, so I gave it to my daughters. If I was wrong for that, I apologize. I only want you and your sister happy. No matter where you choose to live, I will buy your house. It's the least I can do."

Khelani relaxed her facial muscles and let out a small sigh. "You don't have to buy me a house. I'm fine, Dad. I just need a moment to breathe and to figure everything out. I'm irritated about being bedridden, but it's what I needed. My body needed this break."

"Well, this is our first visit in more than a year, and I leave tomorrow. I am going to order takeout, and we can all eat here. Is that okay with you? Your mother and I will be going back to the hotel in a few hours."

"That's fine. You can order me a steak well done, lobster, baked potato, and asparagus." Khelani knew her father well, and she knew that he loved steak, lobster, and lamb chops. Any restaurant that he ordered from would have those items on the menu for sure.

With a nod of his head, Kemp left the room, and Khelani looked down at her flat belly. She was still cramping, but each time she went to the bathroom expecting to see spotting, there was nothing. Every six hours, she took strong pain medication, and she doubted that was good for the baby, but through it all, her unborn child was hanging on, and Khelani didn't know how to feel about that. The longer she stayed pregnant, the more used she would become to being pregnant. She talked big shit, but she wasn't sure she would have an abortion. If she didn't miscarry on her own, then obviously her child was meant to be here, right?

Khelani's phone rang, and she saw that Kyrie was calling. She cleared her throat and answered in a low tone. "Hello?"

"Hey. Did I catch you at a bad time?"

"Not really. My dad is about to order food, and I'm going to eat with my parents. What's up?"

"I just wanted to check on you and see how you were feeling. I won't come by because I know you have company and you're resting, but I miss that pretty-ass face." Kyrie's deep baritone voice was sincere and sexy at the same time. A wave of heat rushed through Khelani's body from his words.

"I don't look that pretty at the moment," she chuckled, making light of the compliment that had her blushing.

"That's cap and you know it. Even when you're asleep with drool on your face, you're gorgeous as hell."

Khelani was instantly mortified. Her mouth fell open, and she tried to recall if she'd ever fallen asleep around him and if he'd ever seen her in such a way. "Um, I guess. Thanks for checking on me though. I'm good."

"Are you still, um . . . Have you . . ." Kyrie didn't know how to ask the question that had been plaguing him since he woke up that morning.

"I'm still pregnant," she stated in a voice just above a whisper.

Kyrie shocked even himself when he breathed a sigh of relief. "When will be a good time for us to talk? In person."

"Maybe tomorrow evening. I guess it depends on how I feel, but my parents are leaving tomorrow. You can text me around six, and I'll give you a good time."

"Bet. Do you need anything? I can send something over."

A small smile formed on her face. "I'm fine, Kyrie. Thank you."

"You're welcome, ma. Rest well."

Khelani ended the call and didn't even realize that she was smiling until her mother walked in the room, and the smile disappeared instantly. Not before her mother saw it, however. "Only a man can make a woman smile like that." She peered at her daughter through the same gray eyes that Khelani and her sister were known for.

"I don't know about all that," Khelani mumbled.

Her mother sat down on the edge of the bed. "It saddens me that you feel you can't talk to me. Whatever I did as a parent to make you feel unloved, I am sorry about it. You and your sister have very different personalities, and that is the only reason you were treated different. It had nothing to do with looks or skin complexion. I complimented Anya more because she received the compliments well. You were always so stubborn and moody. A minia-ture version of your father indeed, and honestly, there were times that I was jealous of how you were with your father. You always preferred him over me, and Anya was the opposite. But I want you to know that I'm very proud of the woman you are, and I would die for you. There is no more love in my heart for Anya than there is you. Got it?" Her mother even smiled, shocking the shit out of Khelani. Damn, maybe she needed to get shot more often.

Her injury had everybody acting different. Even Anya. Khelani felt as if she were in *The Matrix,* but it felt nice. Finally, for once, her parents weren't being demanding, insulting, or dramatic. They doted on her. They had even complimented her condo and were doing everything they could to make her comfortable. It made Khelani feel really good, and being pregnant must have made her emotional, because she and her mother were shocked when tears glistened in her eyes. Courtney hadn't seen Khelani cry since she was a small child. She had always been too stubborn to cry.

Courtney reached over and hugged her daughter tight. Life was too short for the bullshit. Just like her husband, fear had made her almost physically ill when she found out her daughter had been shot. This wasn't a time to be petty or to give tough love. It wasn't even the time to assume that her daughter knew she was loved. To find out that her daughter wanted to leave the game and was possibly smitten with a man made Courtney extremely happy. All she wanted was for her daughters to live nor-mal lives and to settle down and do something safe. She wasn't thrilled when Anya agreed to take over the game for a bit, but even as rebellious as she was, she looked up to Khelani. If Khelani was going to exit the game, it was only a matter of time before Anya did too. Then both her daughters would be safe.

Chapter 17

"How is your sister doing?" Kyrie asked Anya as they met up so he could re-up. He was supposed to go see her at seven p.m., but it was three in the afternoon, and he wanted to know how she was doing at the moment. The fact that Khelani consumed his thoughts as much as she did almost had Kyrie concerned, but he got over it. His uncle always told him that he'd end up finding the woman who made him sit his ass down somewhere, and he had a feeling that Khelani was it.

"When I left home, she was asleep, but she's doing good. You like her, huh?" Anya asked with a sly smile. She was still going to beat the brakes off Camila's junkie ass, but Kyrie didn't have anything to do with his trifling-ass cousin. She and Caresha would both get theirs in due time, and until then, her best revenge was her paper. She didn't need Camila's hole-in-the-wall-ass club when her father was a whole kingpin.

Kyrie chuckled. "She's definitely something special. But about this business . . ." Kyrie always stayed on task when it came to business.

"About that." Anya turned serious too. "There's conditions with this weed."

Kyrie raised one eyebrow. He wasn't up for the games. His money was good, and that was all she needed to be concerned with. He didn't even speak, and she took that as her cue to keep going.

"Mozzy is a bitch-ass nigga. He raped me, and he's going to get what's coming to him. Until I can find him, you can't fuck with him. He's cut off. I'm not serving anybody who deals with him on any level."

Kyrie pinched his bottom lip between his teeth. He was trying to remain calm and professional. She was tripping giving him ultimatums. His actions were the only actions that he should have to atone for. The weed that Anya was serving was good indeed, but he wasn't about to be acting like they had the best shit on earth and none better could be found. On the other hand, he had no respect for men who raped women, and he didn't owe Mozzy shit. He had to give Anya the side-eye though. She was too much like Camila, and that meant she couldn't always be trusted. It was as if Anya read his mind.

"I slept with Mozzy willingly once. The sex was trash, and I started ducking him after that. Because he tricked off a few dollars in the club, he felt like I owed him something. That nigga dead-ass raped me, and for that shit, he gon' die." The coldness in Anya's tone let Kyrie know that she meant exactly what she said. He also believed her.

He didn't have time for dumb shit. Even though he didn't like ultimatums, Mozzy was disposable and not worth putting up a fight for. "He's cut off then. Now can we handle that? I got shit to do."

"No doubt."

Minutes later, Kyrie had his weed, and Anya had her money. He headed to the condo that he kept his weed in and began the process of breaking it down. Most times Tae did it, but sometimes he didn't mind doing the task. He put his phone on DND, and by the time he was done, he had missed calls, missed text messages, and a few emails that needed to be answered. There was always some kind of business with Kyrie, but he was used to it. The more money he made, the more motivated he got. Kyrie really wanted to see just how rich he could get. There was no time for slacking. He was still young, and if he went hard now, he could retire in his late thirties and live like a king until the day he died.

Once the last bit of business was handled, he gave Tae the okay to come pick the weed up and go make the sales. Kyrie had his hands in a little bit of everything, but he didn't do the small tasks. Even in his legal businesses, he had people to do the work for him. Shit, what was the point of having workers if he had to do everything? His record label was worth millions. The weed he sold added to his net worth, but he wasn't about to be actually doing the selling. That would be dumb on his behalf.

Kyrie went home and took a shower. His chef had come through, and he packed up the food that was cooked so he could take Khelani some. When he arrived, he rang the bell, and she answered the door a minute later. Khelani's curls were slicked back into a ponytail. She wore black and red plaid pajama shorts and a black tank top, and on her feet were black socks. She looked tired, and she was walking slightly bent over. Kyrie could tell that she was still in pain, and the fact that she was still pregnant kind of amazed him. That alone told him that any child created by him and Khelani would be strong indeed. A fighter for sure. Stubborn just like the both of them. That thought alone made him smile.

"I brought us food."

"Thank you. It smells good." Her voice was slightly raspy, and he could tell she was just waking up.

"If you were asleep, we could have done this another time. I don't want to interrupt your rest, ma."

"Nah, I've been up for about thirty minutes. All I do is sleep. I'm kind of tired of the shit. I wanted rest, and I've caught up on that. As soon as I can stand up for more than ten minutes without being in pain, it's up and it's stuck."

Kyrie couldn't help himself. Shit, they'd already had sex, so what was the use of pretending? He couldn't get over cradling her in his arms and praying that she survived being shot. There was no need to front about anything. Anytime he was in her presence, he became lost in her beauty and her vibe. He had missed her, and he had no problem showing her. He wrapped his arms around her, careful not to hurt her, and placed a kiss on her forehead.

Khelani inhaled the scent of his cologne as she hugged him back, and she had to admit that being in a man's arms had never felt so good. Kyrie placed one finger underneath her chin and pushed up. As soon as their eyes locked, he placed another kiss on her lips.

"Did you come to talk or push up on me?" She smiled up at him.

"Damnnnn, I can't kiss on you a li'l bit?"

"Yeah, you can." Khelani found herself longing for another kiss, but when he just peered into her eyes, she made the move and kissed him.

That made his eyebrows hike up. "Let me find out you be fronting. You like when I push up on you."

Khelani backed out of his embrace. "Li'l bit. I need to sit down though."

"Damn, my bad." He took her hand and led her over to the couch. "You want me to fix your plate? I have jerk chicken, yellow rice, plantains, and green beans."

"Yes, please. That sounds yummy."

Kyrie rolled up his sleeves and got right down to fixing their plates. As soon as they said grace, Khelani took a bite of her chicken, closed her eyes, and moaned. "Oh, my God, this is so good."

"It is. Damn."

The next ten minutes were silent as they tore into their food. Kyrie broke the silence as he nodded his head toward the cran-lemonade juice he had poured her. "I saw the Pepsi in there. I hope you aren't drinking it every day. It's not good for you, period, but it's really not good for a pregnant woman."

Khelani stopped chewing and glared at him. She wasn't sure how she wanted to answer. For the past two days, it tasted like she had a penny sitting in her mouth. No matter what she ate or drank, the taste came back, and it made water taste absolutely disgusting. In an effort to stay hydrated, she had been drinking more juice, which was better than soda, but she still had at least one Pepsi a day. She wasn't in the mood to explain herself to Kyrie, however. She was grown as fuck. "We're not going to start doing this."

"Doing what? If you think I'm not going to be concerned about my child, then you're bugging. If you haven't mis-carried by now, maybe you won't, and I think you should start making decisions with the child in mind."

Khelani rolled her eyes upward. He hadn't said any-thing wrong, but they hadn't even discussed what they were going to do. Even if she wasn't going to get an abortion, he didn't know that, and he seemed to be under the false impression that he ran some shit.

"What you can do is ask me if I'm drinking sodas. That's how you can start off. But don't start off assuming. Don't start off accusing, and don't act like you're my father. I'm a grown-ass woman, Kyrie. Okay? This is my body. One soda can't be any more dangerous than the strong-ass pain meds I take several times a day."

"You're using pain meds to justify drinking that poison-ous-ass soda?" he asked with a scowl on his face.

"I don't have to justify shit," she said, raising her voice slightly. "Goddamn."

"My sentiments exactly. You think if you make these nine months hell, I won't care? You don't intimidate me, and you can't run me away from my child. I don't have to deal with you, but we will talk about our child. I don't give a damn how much you pout."

"Nigga, you got me fucked up." Khelani was seething. "I never even said I wanted to have your child."

"Well, tough shit. I told you about playing with me. There's safer shit out there for you to do, but don't try me," he stated as his nostrils flared. He was mad as shit, and Khelani could see that she was pushing his buttons. She still wasn't ready to back down.

"I'm sorry, but do I give you the impression that you intimidate me? I feel the same as you about that. This just proves my point that we don't know each other. Having a child is some dumb shit to do."

"Did we know each other when we were fucking? Don't try to take the easy route. Be the grown-ass muhfucaka you are and raise the baby you made."

Khelani stood up to carry her plate in the kitchen. She just needed to be away from him for a few seconds. This wasn't going how she planned. The fastest way for her to calm down was to try to find the good in the situation. He could not give a fuck. He could be telling her to get an abortion, but he was trying to be there. Even if he was working her nerves, she had to give him that. Both of them being stubborn would only make the next nine months hell, and she didn't want that. The longer she stayed pregnant, she was starting to feel that there was something very special about the child she was carrying. Khelani closed her eyes and counted to ten in her head. While her eyes were closed, she felt arms wrap around her from behind.

"You can't run me away, ma." Kyrie placed a kiss on her neck and that sent a chill down her spine.

She turned around to face him. "You gon' have to chill with that trying to check me. I'm not used to it, and I'm gon' get defensive every time."

"Noted."

He went back to hugging her, and Khelani allowed herself to relax in his embrace. That damn Kyrie was going to give her a run for her money. Khelani had finally met her match.

Chapter 18

"Fuck you mean, my services are no longer needed?" Mozzy spat as he stood in Kyrie's office. He'd just been informed that he could go back to Texas, and that was not what he wanted to hear.

"First off, I need you to remember who the fuck you're talking to," Kyrie replied in a low but firm tone. "I never gave you a time frame of how long you'd be here. I simply said I needed your help with something, and that something was accomplished. You came here on my dime. I paid for your room and your rental car and put money in your pocket. It's been some pretty easy money, too. I treated you to a few bottles in the strip club. I've been pretty damn good to you, and your services are no longer needed. End of story."

Mozzy bit the inside of his cheek in an effort to control his emotions. Kyrie was correct when he said it was easy money. It was the easiest money that he'd ever made in his life, and in the short time since he'd come to Atlanta, he had grown accustomed to a certain way of living. He wasn't ready to go back to Texas, especially since he had been blowing more money than he'd been saving, and he would be going back home the same way he left: broke. He decided to calm down and take a more humble approach.

"I'm just saying, I thought things were going good. I was trying to stay in the A for a minute. I know you have several businesses. Put me on with one of them. Please.

I'll even do security for the label. I'll do anything." Mozzy was begging.

Kyrie eyed the man before him. It wasn't his place to tell the man that he just might be safer in Texas, but he didn't have to lie to anybody, beat around the bush, or play games. Time wasn't something that Kyrie liked to waste, and that was what would happen if he allowed to let Mozzy keep groveling. "Keeping it a buck, my connect has an issue with you. I was told that if I had you around me, I couldn't be served, and I chose business over personal shit. Now whatever issue you have going on with Anya is your business, and it doesn't have a damn thing to do with me. I don't lose money for niggas I barely know," Kyrie stated unapologetically.

Mozzy was all the way confused, and the scowl on his face along with the dip of his eyebrows gave that away. Anya was the connect? Since the fuck when? He had raped Kyrie's connect? How was she the connect and she was a stripper? He had fucked up royally. He wasn't scared of a bitch, but he was now out of a job. Mozzy didn't know what in the hell he was going to do. He didn't know anyone in Atlanta, and he didn't have anything to go back home to. Mozzy didn't even have a car in Texas. He probably had enough for a plane ticket and a hotel room back home for one night. That was just how much of his money he fucked off, because he foolishly thought there would be plenty more where that came from. He didn't even know what to say to Kyrie, but he held his head high as if he were proud of every decision that he ever made.

"Thanks for the opportunity to get money with you. I got myself from here." Mozzy left Kyrie's office meaning every word that he said. In order to get back home or even set up a new life in Atlanta without Kyrie's help, he would have to get it out of the mud. It looked like Mozzy was gon' have to rob a nigga.

***

Kyrie was walking out of a business meeting when he felt his phone vibrating in his pocket. He'd just gotten wonderful news. Three of his artists currently had songs on the Billboard Hot 100 chart. Kilo was twenty-four hours away from dropping an album that the streets were fiending for, and Tae needed more weed. Financially, life was lit for him, and so far, Khelani was still pregnant. He wasn't sure how she viewed it, but he viewed it as a good thing. In the meeting, he found that he would be in California for the next four days, and that worried him just a bit. Khelani was still in a fragile state, and even though he had access to a private jet, he would hate for something to happen while he was all the way on the West Coast.

A dejected sigh left Kyrie's mouth when he saw who was calling him. He already had a slight clue what the shit was about. "What up, Unc?"

"What's going on, nephew? I called to check on you because it's been a little over a week since your aunt and I saw your face. Just because you're successful, grown, and rich doesn't mean you can't visit your auntie and put a smile on her face."

"I really have been meaning to come by. Life is hectic at the moment. I'm leaving at five a.m. for Cali, but when I get back, your place will be one of my first stops," he promised as he walked into his office.

"I'm going to hold you to that. Speaking of people who haven't been by a lot, have you seen your cousin?"

Kyrie's jaw muscles tightened at the mention of his cousin. He didn't put anything past anybody, but Camila stealing from him was some ill shit. Of all the people in the world, her doing it hit differently. He knew that people addicted to drugs did outlandish things, and that was the second thing that hurt him. To see his cousin down bad enough off of coke that she would steal from him meant that she no longer had a handle on the shit, and it could only be downhill from there. "No, I haven't seen her either. Like I said, it's been hectic. Both businesses are keeping me on my toes."

"Since things are going so good at the label, why don't you offer Camila a job? I know that strip club was her dream, but the shit has failed. She lost her liquor license because of the shooting that occurred out there. Unless she's able to get it back very soon, she may as well hang it up. Who in the hell patronizes a strip club that they can't drink in?"

"Camila wanted to own a strip club, and that's the only reason she put work in there. With anything else, she's spoiled and lazy. Camila never wanted a job at my label because then she would have to work. I would have paid her lovely just to answer the phone, deliver mail to each office, reply to my emails, et cetera. Simple shit that would have required minimal effort. That's still not something she wanted to do. Having to sit behind a desk for eight hours would have driven her insane. She loved to come hang out sometimes with the hopes of seeing a rapper, but work wasn't what she wanted to do." Kyrie knew that about her and his uncle did too. He just wanted the best for Camila, and he was supposed to. She was his daughter. That's why Kyrie couldn't break his heart by telling him she was on that shit and that she had stolen from him on several occasions.

"We both know Camila has no interest in working. She could have had a job at the label years ago. She's not interested in sitting still and taking orders. Camila likes to run shit."

"Well, she ran that club right in the ground. I just don't want her to get too stressed out behind it. Last time I talked to her, she kept sniffing like she was coming down with a cold. I just want her to rest and take care of herself and give that damn club up."

"Camila is stubborn, and she doesn't give up easy. She fought for as long as she could, but since she lost her liquor license, she just might consider waving the white flag. I will be sure to stop by when I get back from Cali, Unc. I need to do a few more things before I leave the office."

"All right, nephew. Do your thing. I'm proud of you, son."

"Thank you."

Even though Kyrie had work to do, he turned his swivel chair around and stared out at his gorgeous view of the city. Everything had good sides and bad sides, and that rang true for Atlanta. The A could be grimy, it could be tough, and it could be intimidating. But it could also be the best thing that ever happened to a person. Kyrie was rich as hell, and it was all because he put in the work, the time, the effort, and he wouldn't stop until he saw the results that he wanted. Atlanta had made more black people successful than anywhere else, and it felt damn good to be a part of the elite. And the fact that he might have a child on the way had him anxious on a whole other level. Kyrie didn't want to get too excited in case Khelani miscarried, but she had a doctor's appointment coming up.

"Fuck," he mumbled when he realized that he would miss it. Kyrie heard his office door open, and he turned his chair around to see who was rude enough to come up in his shit without knocking. Rebecca. "You forget how to knock?" he asked with knitted brows and a voice full of agitation.

Rebecca smirked as she stepped farther into his office, the soles of her Louboutin heels clacking loudly on the linoleum with every step. "Aren't we grumpy today? I haven't seen or heard from you in a few weeks. What's going on?" She invited herself to sit down. Rebecca crossed her thick caramel-colored thighs and glared at Kyrie with her round, doe-shaped eyes.

She had pretty much answered her own question. Or at least, she should have been able to. If someone went weeks without reaching out, it just might mean that they had no desire to be bothered. All common sense seemed to fly out the window with people who wanted what they wanted. Rather than hurt her feelings with brutal honesty, he decided to be as polite as he knew how to be. "I've been busy." His tone was flat and indifferent. He showed no remorse for his absence and offered no apologies.

"Okay. You're always busy. But you also make time for the things that you want to make time for."

Kyrie was baffled. Again, lack of common sense. If she knew that about him, then she very well should have been able to put two and two together. "That I do." He left the answer short and sweet.

He smirked when Rebecca drew back. She was getting it. He wasn't about to offer up lame excuses for why he hadn't been around and tell her that he would make it up to her. She was becoming irritated, and he didn't care because he felt the same way. "Sooo you haven't made time for me because you haven't wanted to?" she asked with a scowl on her face. The skepticism that laced her voice made him aware that she had never once considered that to be an option.

"That is correct."

"Wow." Rebecca chuckled sarcastically and clicked her tongue. "Fucking wow. You can really be an asshole, Kyrie. You know that?"

"How am I an asshole for honestly answering your questions? I've never given you the impression that you were a priority of mine. Don't get me wrong. We've hung out, and we've had some great times. All those times were spontaneous with no strings attached. I don't owe you time or anything else, just like you don't owe those things to me either. I've been busy. I answered your question honestly. I haven't thought about reaching out, but you shouldn't take that personally. We aren't in a relationship. I told you a minute ago that I don't appreciate the way you get all extra and territorial when another woman is around. You do too damn much, and despite me telling you to stop, you never did. That shit was a turnoff, and I'm done with it. Did that answer all of your questions?"

Rebecca shot up out of her seat like there was a rocket attached to her ass. She was there for a meeting with Swag and had decided to pop in on Kyrie and make arrangements to link up later, but the shit had gone way left. She was embarrassed, but she could only blame herself. In the past, Rebecca had encountered men who liked that "crazy shit." They liked toxic females. One of her exes always used to joke that it was always the girls with good pussy who were crazy. No matter what she did, he wouldn't leave her alone, and foolishly, she thought she'd have the same luck with Kyrie. She stormed out of his office without replying. What could she really say?

Kyrie chuckled and shook his head. Hopefully, that was the last of her. He wasn't sure where in the hell he and Khelani were going, but she wasn't the type to deal with the bullshit. She was already fighting him, so all she would need was any excuse to run away, and he didn't plan on giving her any. Kyrie had slept with some of the most beautiful women from Atlanta to Honduras. The shit was getting old to him. Coming home to a woman who had the personality to match her looks and a kid or two might not be the worst thing. He just had to get Khelani's ass on board.

Chapter 19

Khelani was making her bed when Anya came into her room. "You don't have to do that. I could have done it for you."

"No, thank you. I am so tired of resting and not doing anything that it is driving me insane. I feel better actually. I don't even need the strong stuff anymore. I can be fine with two Tylenol. You headed to meet Kasim?"

Khelani couldn't believe how Anya had stepped up to the plate and taken things over for her while she was sick. And the most shocking part was she hadn't fucked up once. Khelani knew she had it in her all along.

"Yep. I have to meet Kyrie's friend Tae. Then I have like six more people to meet. You need me to bring you anything back?"

"Nope. I just ordered groceries, and I'm having them delivered. Even though it's two p.m., I'm about to shower and get dressed for the day, then cook. If I don't get back into the swing of things soon, I'm going to scream. Speaking of which, I should be ready to jump back in next week. You can still help out if you want. I already told Dad that once everything is running smoothly here, I'm out. Atlanta is my last city."

Anya's eyes widened in shock. "Seriously? You're out?" Before Khelani could even answer, a thought registered in her mind, and a grin spread across her face. "It's Kyrie, isn't it?" she asked in a gleeful voice.

Khelani had to chuckle at her sister's excitement. If she was acting like this now, she'd really blow her shit when she found out her sister was pregnant. If she found out. Khelani didn't plan on telling anyone until she felt it was safe to do so, and that would be many more weeks from now. "I need you to slow down. It has nothing to do with Kyrie. I'm just tired. I was tired of running and doing everything alone, but even now that you're helping, just the thought of another state, another city, new clientele, it's draining. I'm over it. I finally want to live a nice, normal, boring, quiet life. I really didn't support you when you said you didn't want to do this shit, but now I totally see where you were coming from. My advantage was getting shot. When I told Dad I want out, he didn't even fight me."

"What are you going to do once you're out of the game?" Anya leaned onto the counter. She wouldn't feel right moving on to another city and running things without her sister. She had always been a confident person, but she wasn't that confident. Khelani was a hustler. She'd pulled all of the weight since they had been in the States, and Anya was sure that she had a lovely stash. She, on the other hand, didn't have a dollar to her name before she took over for Khelani.

Their father sent them pounds every month. The girls would move the work and keep a percentage of everything that they moved. Once all the weed was gone, they then sent their father his cut. Once the pipeline was made, the hustlers would begin to deal with his traffickers directly, and the girls and Kasim would move on to the next city. That way, they all saw a piece of the pie, and being that they were his daughters, their father took the bare minimum from them. He was already rich, and once they went out and got him new clientele, he would grow richer in time. Others had to pay way more for pounds than

Khelani did. She got them so cheap that Kemp barely saw a profit, but he was fine with that. He had no problem with his daughters making the bulk of the money to get things set up in various cities across the country.

Khelani shrugged. "I don't really know yet. You know I have a thing for putting pieces together. Kyrie has suggested before that I become a stylist. It doesn't really sound like a bad idea. I mean, who wouldn't want to get paid just to pick out fly clothes for people?"

Anya didn't reply as she chewed nervously on her bottom lip. She didn't even make the usual comment about Khelani liking Kyrie. She could see it. Hell, a blind man could see it, but what would she do? It was crazy that she fought selling weed for so long, and as soon as she got comfortable with the idea, it would be over in a matter of months. Then what? She'd go back to stripping? She didn't want to be a bartender. Kemp's riches were plentiful, and if she wanted to start a business, he would help her, but what would she do? What Anya was good at was partying, bullshitting, and being a fly bitch.

"I'm sure you'll figure something out. You always do," Khelani assured her. It was as if her sister could read her mind, and that was one of the reasons that Anya would be scared to be away from her. If Khelani moved on to another city, would she follow her there? Would she stay in the A if Khelani stayed in the A?

Anya stood upright. "I guess."

Khelani had never seen her sister appear unsure about anything. "What made you want to all of a sudden get on board? I know it wasn't me getting shot."

"Dealing with Camila's stupid ass." Anya rolled her eyes upward. "At first, I was just like, damn, this is a real boss-ass bitch. Then she just switched shit up and became a total bitch. I had to really tell myself like, this chick thinks she's above you and that she can treat you any kind of way, and meanwhile your father's money could build a hundred strip clubs that look way better than the roach trap she was running. I really had to remind myself of who the hell I was. I'm praising her for being a boss bitch when I could have been one all along, but I was playing. Anyway, I have to go and meet Tae. Call me if you need me."

"Will do."

Khelani ran a piping hot bath and immersed herself in the water. She had to do so slowly. The water wasn't so hot that it burned, but she for sure had to ease into it. She was stiff and sore, but once her entire body was in the tub, she leaned her head back, closed her eyes, and exhaled a sigh of relief. The water felt so good that she was on the verge of falling asleep in the tub.

She had almost drifted off when her phone rang. Khelani opened her eyes and saw Kyrie's name on her phone screen. She almost smiled, but she caught herself. Things were happening super fast, and she wasn't about to let herself get so caught up that she lost all common sense. Whether she remained pregnant or not, she needed to slow down and not fall so fast and hard for Kyrie, who still seemed too good to be true.

"Hello?"

"Hey. Were you asleep?"

She chuckled. "Almost. I'm in the tub, and it feels so good that I was almost gone, which is weird because I'm tired of sleeping. I'm about to wash and get out though. I have an Instacart delivery coming, and I'm going to cook."

"You don't have to do that. I can order something and have it delivered."

"I never thought I would be tired of fast food, but I am. I've had food from the finest restaurants, and I'm still over it. I want some of my own cooking."

"Okay. What are you cooking?"

"Spaghetti. Very simple, but it's my favorite, and it tastes better than any restaurant."

"Can I get an invite to dinner, or are you tired of looking at me for a while?"

That time, Khelani allowed herself to smile. "Sure. You can come by for dinner."

"Bet. I need to head home and pack because I leave in the morning. I'm flying to Cali, and I'll be out there for four days. I hate that I'm going to miss your doctor's appointment, but I'll for sure make the next one."

Khelani hadn't put much thought into him going. She was still too nervous to be excited, and she was expecting bad news at the doctor's. For some reason, she didn't mind going alone, but it was cool that he offered. "Oh, that's okay."

"If you didn't have to go to the doctor, I'd invite you out. What if you come tomorrow, and I'll send you back on the jet in time for your appointment?"

"What?" she laughed. Because her father was who he was, she was no stranger to private jets and luxurious lifestyles. Her father once flew them to Paris so they could go to the Hermès store and get Birkin bags. They literally got the bags, ate dinner, and flew back home. She was just shocked that he wanted her with him. "I don't know. . . ." Her voice trailed off.

"Why not? You can rest on the jet. You can rest at the hotel, and if you feel like getting out, you can. I just want to spend time with you. Make sure you're good."

He was trying. He was trying something serious, and that was all she could ask for. Plus, next week, she'd be back in the swing of things with the weed and she'd be running nonstop. "I guess I can fly out for a day or two, yes." She sounded skeptical, but Kyrie didn't care. All he heard was the word yes.

"Bet. I'll be there in a few hours."

Khelani washed her body, then got out of the tub, dried off, and put lotion everywhere that she could reach. She freshened up her bun and dressed in a pair of multi-colored Calvin Klein yoga shorts and a matching sports bra. Her Instacart delivery was right on time, because as soon as she placed her dirty clothes in the laundry room, her doorbell rang. After putting her AirPods in, Khelani busied herself with putting away the groceries, except what she was going to cook, and she started her food.

While the sauce was simmering and the pasta was cooking, she went into her bedroom and grabbed a few outfits, some clothes to sleep in, and toiletries. She wasn't going to be gone long, but she was going to be with Kyrie. His ass was a mogul, and she couldn't dare be caught looking any kind of way. After she was done packing, she placed her suitcase by the bedroom door and went to make a salad and finish the spaghetti.

Just as she was pulling garlic bread from the oven, Kyrie was ringing the bell. Khelani was glad the food was done because all of the day's activities had tired her out. For as tired of the bed as she thought she was, she was ready to eat and climb back in it. She prayed that her body was just healing from being shot, and it wasn't the baby tiring her out after a few hours. Khelani couldn't spend nine months sleeping.

She opened the door to find him standing there look-ing handsome as ever with flowers in his hand. He was dressed in what a lot of women considered ho attire. The gray sweats that he donned had his dick print visible to anyone with good vision. The white tee that he wore clung to his muscular frame, and his Versace slides com-pleted the comfy look. Khelani grinned from ear to ear as she took the flowers from him. She'd never really been a flowers type of girl, but the gesture was nice. "Thank you. You have a thing for sending flowers, huh?"

"I have a thing for putting a smile on your face, whether I gotta send flowers or diamonds. Whatever it is that makes you happy."

The grin returned. Khelani's entire body grew warm, and she shook her head lightly. She couldn't ever remember a time when a man made her smile and blush as much as Kyrie did. He stepped into her personal space, and she lifted her gaze to meet his. The light scent of the oil that was moisturizing his beard wafted into her nostrils and instantly became one of her favorite scents without her even knowing what it was.

Being that Kyrie was much taller than her, he had to dip his head low to place his lips on hers. The kiss was soft and juicy, and one peck wasn't enough. He placed his mouth back on hers and parted her lips with his tongue. As his tongue probed her mouth, his dick stiffened, and he felt her nipples harden through her bra. Kyrie wanted her. He picked her up and placed her on the island in the kitchen. After he removed the flowers from her hand, he placed them on the counter and placed his face in the crook of her neck.

Khelani moaned and pinched her bottom lip between her teeth as he devoured the flesh on her neck. Her chest heaved up and down as his tongue assaulted her spot, and her clit began to throb for him. They both knew there was a chance that Anya could come in since she lived there, but they didn't care. Kyrie removed his mouth from her neck and pulled her to the end of the island, where he pulled her shorts and panties off, swooped his head low, spread her flower, and admired her pink glistening pussy for five seconds before he began to probe her slit with his tongue.

Khelani's body jerked at the sensation of his tongue going up, then down, inside just a bit, then circling her clit. He sucked softly on her clit, and a low whimper fell from her throat. Khelani leaned back on her elbows and looked up at the ceiling as Kyrie performed tricks with his tongue that had her letting out all kinds of deep, guttural moans. When he went back to sucking on her clit and her vagina began pulsating, Khelani grabbed the back of his head with one hand and locked her thighs around his head.

That only inspired Kyrie to go harder, and he locked his hands on her thighs as he moaned into her pussy and slurped at her like she was ice cream melting off a cone. She came and their moans filled the kitchen in unison. She had never felt anything so good, and he had never tasted anything so sweet. Her body jerked a few times, and Khelani breathlessly fell back onto the counter. Kyrie came up for air and multitasked as he unbuttoned his jeans while engaging in a sloppy and passionate tongue kiss that had her tasting her juices off his tongue.

Khelani cupped the sides of his face as their tongues swirled, and he pushed into her. She felt so good that he groaned. Kyrie had never been one for lovemaking. He felt that one had to be in love to engage in such an act. He never did the eye contact or any of that during sex. He barely even kissed, but he found himself staring into Khelani's eyes and attempting to show her everything that she didn't hear from the words he spoke. She had encountered a fuck boy or two, and she was skeptical. That was to be expected. He wasn't the most trusting person either, but something was telling him that Khelani was different. What could he provide her with that she couldn't get for herself? So he didn't have to worry about her using him.

His strokes were borderline aggressive, but his glare made the moment sensual. Khelani became lost in his eyes, and she wasn't able to look away until he hit a spot that made her eyes roll back in her head. Kyrie used that opportunity to gently bite and suck on her neck, and then he pulled her bra up and swirled his tongue over her nipple. He pulled out of her and placed a trail of kisses from the bottom of her breasts down her stomach. The kisses that he placed on her stomach were deliberate. They were precise. When he dipped his head back between her thighs, Khelani thought she was going to lose her mind. The things that Kyrie was doing to her body should have been against the law. He plunged back into her after she had her second orgasm, and Khelani was borderline delirious. Not long after he entered her again, he came, and he lay on top of her while they both tried to catch their breath and process the pleasure they had just experienced.

Khelani finally found her voice. Her throat was dry as fuck, and her voice came out scratchy. "Okay, we have to get up because this is not how I want Anya to see me if she walks in this condo."

Kyrie pulled out of her and picked her up. After placing her on the floor, he kissed her lips, and she headed to the bathroom to clean up on wobbly legs. When he acted like he couldn't get enough of her, when he kissed her multiple times or played with her curls, it made her feel like he was genuinely into her. Nightmares about her murdering Malachi had stopped, but what happened would linger in the back of her mind forever.

Kyrie, of course, had no reason to steal from her, but that didn't mean he wasn't capable of betraying her. As she cleaned up, she decided to stop stressing. There wasn't anything she couldn't bounce back from. Khelani was a tough girl. If he did fuck up, she'd live. She'd get over it, and she'd go on with life. She was tired of the overthinking and expecting the worst. Khelani was just going to let shit be. The cards could fall where they may.

When she left the master bathroom, she heard him in the guest bathroom, and she decided to go ahead and fix their plates. By the time he entered the kitchen, she had perched on one of the red stools at the island. Kyrie stopped behind her and nuzzled his face in her neck. Khelani hunched her shoulders and giggled. It amazed her at how affectionate he was. She had never been that person. Khelani didn't think she had a romantic bone in her body.

"That food looks good, and it smells delicious. Thank you for cooking."

"You're welcome."

Malachi was nothing like Kyrie. He was cocky. Borderline arrogant. Khelani rarely ever cooked for him, but if she did, he for sure didn't thank her for cooking. When they first met, he acted like she should be honored to have the attention of a man like him. She kept her profession hidden, but the more he got to know her, when he saw the car she was pushing and the house she was renting, the clothes she wore, and the bags she carried, he shut that cocky shit up. Khelani adopted a different identity, so to speak, in every new place she lived. She told Malachi that she'd been a successful real estate broker in Trinidad, but since she didn't have her license in North Carolina, she was chilling and living off her savings.

Malachi was impressed. With the way she lived, he surmised that her savings must be long. He wasn't a slouch. That was before he fell off, but when he first met her, he was getting bread himself. He still doubted that he was getting more than her, and that cocky shit died down. He was cool. He had to be because she was starting to like him, but being around Kyrie had her wondering what in the hell she'd even seen in Malachi besides looks. He loved to fuck and floss. He wanted to show her off, but that was because she was a bad bitch and had her own. In his mind, being seen with a woman like Khelani would give him more clout than he already had.

"Damn, this is good. You're fine as hell, you know how to get money, you can cook, and your pussy is perfection. Goddamn, you should have been married by now."

Khelani shook her head and chuckled. "Those qualities have nothing to do with me not being married. I haven't found a man worth marrying." Kyrie's eyebrows hiked up, and she smiled bashfully. "Prior to meeting you, I didn't know a man I would consider worth marrying. I still don't know if you're worth it," she joked.

"Time will tell."

Khelani drank water, and they got through their meal without arguing. He had his bag in the car, and since she was flying out with him, he spent the night with her. Him in bed behind her with her butt on his dick and his hand resting flat on her belly made Khelani feel some type of way. It was almost scary, but it was nice at the same time. It was something that she could for sure get used to.

Chapter 20

Tae eyed Anya as she entered the condo that Kyrie kept his weed in. The place was sparsely furnished, and he only housed his weed there. Maintenance came in from time to time to do routine work, and he didn't want to seem suspicious by requesting that no one ever come in. There was a living room set, a TV mounted on the wall, and a game system. The master bedroom had one bed and a dresser. The walk-in closet had a few clothes, some shoes, and two large safes. Each safe contained pounds of weed that had been broken down and placed into large glass jars to contain the smell. Even when the weed was wrapped in bubble wrap and plastic, all the pounds he purchased were still enough to smell up the entire floor of his building. The weed that he purchased was that loud indeed, and he had to be careful when storing it.

There was food in the fridge, and either Kyrie, Ghalen, or Tae came by the condo at least four times a week. Sometimes, Kyrie would leave the gym and go there, shower, change clothes, eat, and relax for three or four hours before leaving again. No one suspected that the $1,700-a-month one-bedroom condo was nothing more than a glamorous place for Kyrie to keep his drugs.

Tae had seen her when she used to dance at Camila's club. Those eyes were hypnotizing, as well as that ass. Tae knew it was always business first, but he was far from blind, and looking never hurt anyone.

"Hello," she greeted him in an even tone before placing the duffel bag in her hand down on the couch.

"What's good? We got fifteen," Tae clarified.

"Yep."

He passed her the bag of money while unzipping the duffel bag and taking in all the pounds of weed. When Khelani first came to town and started taking Kyrie's clientele, Tae never fathomed the plug would be someone as fine as Khelani, and her sister was just as impressive. Since the product and the money had exchanged hands, Tae decided to get a tad bit personal.

"I remember you from the club. Whole time you were dancing, you were really on some queen-pin-type shit."

Anya smirked at the handsome man. He was fine as hell for sure. He looked ten times better than Mozzy's weird ass. He, unlike Mozzy, really was Kyrie's right-hand man, and he was holding some serious paper. The old Anya would have fucked the hell out of him, sucked him dry, and let him trick on her a li'l bit, but being wild and impulsive in the A had already gotten her into enough shit. She needed to stack her money so that when her sister left the game, she wouldn't be stressing money. There was no way she was hustling without Khelani. That wasn't even an option for her. Maybe, once she was comfortable with the amount of money that she had saved, she'd go back to digging in niggas' shit.

"I was tripping back then. Just on some rebellious shit. Having fun and getting paid for it while my sister was getting the real bread. My ass was asleep, but I'm up now."

Tae's eyes slid down her thick frame, and he could appreciate the way her nude sundress hugged her curves. Shorty was delivering pounds of weed with Yves Saint Laurent heels on her feet. That shit was high-key sexy as fuck to him. Tae loved a boss chick. "I feel you on that. Get ya bread, mama."

"I know the A can seem small when it comes to certain circles. You know a nigga named Tuson?"

Tae's brows hiked up. "There could be a million niggas named Tuson in the A."

"I'm assuming this one sells weed. Kasim did business with him once. I'm meeting him out in Buckhead. Kasim wants me to wait until he's done with business so I don't have to go alone. But I don't want to wait. Once I meet Tuson, I'll be done for the day. So I said all that to say, if you know him, do you think he's a standup guy, or should I wait for Kasim?"

Tae shrugged one shoulder. "I mean, I've heard of the nigga, but I can't in any way vouch for that man. What I will say is you're not from here. Your trust for people should be at a negative zero, especially when you're carrying around pounds of this potent-ass shit. Niggas have killed for way less. And niggas don't hesitate to kill niggas, so what you think they'll do to a sexy-ass chick approaching them in heels and shit? You look like an easy-ass lick."

Frustrated, Anya breathed hard through her nose. "A'ight. I guess I'll wait for Kasim," she mumbled. "Thanks."

"Listen, I know you said you don't want to wait, but if you can give me an hour, I'll ride with you. Niggas will be less likely to try some shit if they see you didn't come alone. You got a gun?"

Anya nodded.

"Bet. Choice is yours. You can wait for me or Kasim, but don't go alone."

"Kasim quoted me two hours, so I guess I'll go with whoever can assist me first."

Tae nodded. Anya made herself comfortable while he proceeded to pull the weed from the bags and open them so he could break them down. He already had the glass jars lined up in the living room. Tae pulled out a scale and went to work. He was always focused when it came to this shit, so there wasn't much small talk.

Tae started hustling at the age of 17, but three years ago, Kyrie changed his life. The man put him on as security when it was time to do shows or when his artists simply wanted to go to the mall or some shit. The average person wearing millions of dollars' worth of jewelry and carrying bags of cash didn't go out alone. Tae stood six foot one with a slightly muscular build, but his physique didn't scream security.

Kyrie knew looks could be deceiving, and Tae was a beast with his hands and a gun. He mostly only put him on just to put money in his pocket. Kyrie was *rich* rich, and he would put on as many of his niggas as he could. Kyrie would pay Tae $2,500 just to accompany Kilo or Swag somewhere. When Tae wasn't working for Kyrie, he was hustling, so Kyrie eventually upped the pay and put Tae on his team. He had too much at stake to sell weed himself, but he rewarded Tae handsomely for taking the risk for him. Now years later, Tae was only 25 and owned a million-dollar condo. He had everything he ever wanted in life except a yacht, and he was working on that shit. He knew he would be a multimillionaire well before the age of 30, and he was going to retire and live life on some real boss shit.

Anya scrolled through her phone, but every so often, she would glance up and discreetly glance at Tae. The more she observed him, it seemed as if he got finer. His rich dark skin had her imagining what their offspring would look like, and that was when Anya knew she was tripping because she hated kids. She didn't hate them necessarily, but she never wanted any of her own. She couldn't see herself dealing with a screaming infant all day or constantly changing shitty diapers or being thrown up on. That wasn't her idea of a fun time. The moment she decided it was time for a break, she would definitely see what was up with him. Anya bit her bottom lip and wondered what that stroke game was like.

She was serious about getting money, but Anya didn't think she'd ever be as serious as Khelani was. Not to the point that she swore off men and rarely got dick. Had Kyrie not come along and gotten her smitten, Anya knew there was a chance that Khelani would go years without a man just because of what went down with Malachi. Anya wanted her own money for a rainy day, a plan B, a cushion, but she would never stop fucking or running niggas' pockets. Ever. Tae just might be someone she could add to the team.

"So you from Trinidad, huh? I've never been." Tae broke the silence after about twenty minutes.

He looked up, and Anya's kitty began to purr. *Yeah, he could get the pussy for sure.*

He took a break from what he was doing and pulled his own personal glass jar of weed from behind the leather ottoman in front of him. Tae grabbed a cigar off the top of the ottoman and began the process of rolling a blunt. He always kept his personal weed that he paid for separate from Kyrie's shit. He had never even crossed Kyrie for so much as a gram. Tae was loyal as hell to those he fucked with.

"It's a beautiful place. Living there isn't really fun when you have a very powerful father and people watch your every move and report it to him. I had to get the hell away from there."

"I can dig it. Maybe I'll make it before the end of the year. Most times, I go hard as fuck until I feel myself about to crash, and then I'll take a vacation. Last time I went to Punta Cana, a nigga was so tired I slept the entire first day. Seven days later, though, I came back rejuvenated as hell and in beast mode. I might hit Trinidad up for about a week. They got some beautiful-ass women over there." He peered at Anya when he spoke, and she wasn't sure if that compliment was geared toward her, but she smiled anyway.

"Yeah, they do."

Tae went back to quiet mode, and they silently passed the blunt back and forth until he finished what he was doing. By that time, Kasim still hadn't hit her, so he rode with her to meet Tuson. Anya had been with plenty of men. Getting fine men, rich men, the men everyone wanted, none of those things were new to her. So she wasn't sure why she felt nervous having Tae riding shotgun in her car. Like most men, he immediately laid the seat back and got comfortable. She headed toward the address that Tuson had given her while Yo Gotti played from her radio. They were both high as hell, and for most of the trip, Tae scrolled through his phone.

When she pulled up to meet Tuson at a small brick house, she grabbed her gun, and Tae grabbed his as well. He got in the back seat and placed the gun in his lap with his finger caressing the trigger. Anya didn't even try to hide hers. She placed it in her lap as well. She texted Tuson, and he came out to the car. He was a very large dark-skinned man with a scruffy beard, but he was dressed nicely. Anya could tell that when he cleaned up, he was probably a decent-looking guy, but she would never fuck him. He looked to be over 300 pounds, but she was sure she was in the minority. If he had money, his list of women was probably long despite his weight.

As he neared the car, Tuson peeped Tae in the back seat. He wasn't alarmed nor did he care. He wasn't trying to rob shorty, and his paper was legit. "What up, nigga?" he spoke to Tae first when he got into the car. He didn't really know him on a personal level, but he knew of him.

"What's good?"

"What's up, ma'am?" He held his hands up in surrender. "I got your bread, and I'm not strapped. No problems out of me," he assured her as he eyed the Glock in her lap.

Anya gave a small nod, and when he passed her the money, she checked it, and when she didn't say anything, Tae passed the bag of weed from the back seat. Tuson peeked inside and was satisfied with what he saw. "'Preciate you." He tipped his head at Anya and got out of the car. Tae got back in the front.

"That was easy enough," she stated.

"Yeah, but it don't always go like that."

Anya knew he was right, because grimy shit was the reason that Snow was dead. Anya knew she had to be careful because drug dealers got robbed every day.

Tae's phone rang, and he engaged in conversation with who she surmised was Kyrie. After their ten-minute phone call, as soon as the call ended, his phone rang again. Anya could tell by that conversation that he was talking to a female.

"Word? What you cook? You bugged out. Why you even call me if you got pork on the menu? Oh, word, porkchop for you and steak for me? That's what's up, but I can't even fuck you when I know you just ate some swine," he chuckled.

Anya made a slight face at his comment, and she didn't know why. She didn't even know him. His conversation continued all the way until she dropped him back off at Kyrie's condo. Before he got out of the car, he told whoever he was speaking to to hold on. "Be safe out here, li'l mama."

"For sure. Thanks for coming with me."

"No problem."

He got out of the car, and Anya drove off. Yeah, he might just be her next addition to operation "Show Anya a Good Time."

Chapter 21

Camila tossed items into a cardboard box aggressively as she cleaned out her office. She didn't want to accept defeat. Without a liquor license, she was forced to close her doors. Patrons weren't going to patronize a club they couldn't drink in, and strippers weren't going to dance in a club that no one was patronizing. Deep down, she knew that, had she not stolen money from Kyrie, he could have possibly saved her. He had the money and the power to make things right. She could even low-key let niggas bring their own shit in as long as they would come to the club, but her shit was washed. All Kyrie had to do was send one of his artists up there or come himself and people would flock to the club in droves, but he wasn't fucking with her.

She didn't know what in the hell she was going to do for money, and she was tired of her parents suggesting that Kyrie give her a job. Camila couldn't tell them the real reason why Kyrie wasn't fucking with her. She was just glad that he hadn't sold her out. If her parents knew she started sniffing coke, they would be devastated. Camila was *broke* broke. Like, she had less than $300 to her name. She had just paid her bills for the month and had no clue how she would pay for the upcoming month.

Caresha grabbed tape from Camila's desk and taped up the box that she had filled. She had been mourning Snow's death for the past week, but she decided that she would get out of the house and help Camila. She needed

some fresh air anyway. Being in her home was beginning to suffocate her. The kids who were old enough to
understand were sad and asking for their father. Even
though Caresha and Snow had their ups and downs, she
loved him, and she couldn't believe he was gone. No one
knew who had murdered him, and Caresha wasn't going
to waste her time trying to figure it out. The truth of the
matter was, his grills business was pretty successful, but
Snow wasn't rich. He was always looking for a come-up,
and sometimes the "quick licks" that he engaged in
meant him doing someone else dirty. Caresha could only
assume that one of those times had caught up with him.
Atlanta was notorious for its scammers, and Snow was a
scammer indeed. He once used a cracked credit card for
pay for an elaborate hotel suite for her birthday, and they
went to a five-star restaurant and ordered $400 worth
of food and drinks. They lived it up that night. All on
someone else's dime.

"It seems crazy as hell that you're just letting this club
go after all the hard work you put into it. What's the
point of having a rich cousin if he can't or won't help you?
Kyrie could have this club packed every night."

Caresha and Camila were close. Caresha even knew
that Camila dabbled in coke sometimes. But she didn't
know how bad it had gotten. Camila wasn't going to
confess her sins to anyone but God. So of course it didn't
make sense that Kyrie wasn't helping her with the club.
With all that Caresha was going through, Camila appreciated her assistance, so she was going to try very hard not
to spazz on her, but she wasn't in the mood for twenty
questions. "You see me packing up this club, right? That
means it's gone, and I'm over it. I really don't want to talk
about it either."

Caresha wasn't letting up. "You love this club, Camila."

She didn't have the chance to say anything else because someone walked in the office. He was short and light-skinned and had beady eyes. His face also held an expression that gave away the fact that he wasn't pleased. His gaze bounced from Caresha to Camila. When their eyes locked, he rushed up on Camila and wrapped his hand around her neck. Caresha's eyes widened, and she gasped. Normally, she and her friend helped each other during physical altercations. Camila came to bat for her with Anya and a few times while she was fighting Snow, but this nigga looked deranged. Caresha just stood by helpless while her friend was being assaulted.

"Where is my fuckin' money? You think I'm playing with you, bitch? I told you that you had three days, and I gave you four. You still don't have my money." He shook her body roughly before he finally let her go.

Camila was gasping for air, and tears were streaming down her face. It felt as if her windpipe had been crushed, and for a moment, she couldn't speak. Her attacker used that opportunity to continue his verbal assault. "You asked me to front you an ounce claiming you were going to sell it in the club, and the club is closing. So where the fuck is my eleven hundred dollars?" he seethed.

"The club closing is beyond my control," Camila cried in a hoarse voice. "I was desperate to keep the club afloat. I swear I will have your money by tomorrow. I swear, Boogie."

"If you can't sell the coke because the club is closed, then you would have my coke. You don't have my coke or my money, and that's a problem. If your junkie ass snorted up a whole ounce, you might be better off dead anyway. And dead is where you'll be if you don't have my money by tomorrow, and I put that on my kids." Boogie turned and walked away, and Camila was embarrassed as hell.

Caresha knew she had to be embarrassed, so she didn't even speak on what she had just seen. Camila had bigger problems than she could help her with, so she just minded her business and continued packing up the office.

"Here you are." Kyrie walked out through the sliding glass doors of the Airbnb that he had rented and found Khelani sitting out by the pool.

She looked up at him and smiled. "It's gorgeous out here. I had to wait until the sun went down though. This damn Cali heat makes me sick," she stated with a frown on her face.

Kyrie smiled and sat down beside her. He still couldn't get over the fact that Khelani was pregnant by him. He did manage to have brunch with her, but he'd been in meetings all day. A total of four meetings had taken six hours out of his day, but they were necessary. The luxurious Airbnb that he was renting for $1,700 a night was fit for a king. It had five bedrooms, six bathrooms, and a fenced-in backyard that had a pool in it, and the water was blue and pretty. It mimicked some shit you'd see on a tropical island. Khelani had been enjoying the view for the past hour.

"You want to get in?" Kyrie was tired, but he wanted to get some time in with Khelani. He had spent a lot of years giving all of his time to the hustle. Now he wanted to learn how to balance the two.

She looked over at him. "I didn't bring a bathing suit."

"How you come to Cali with no swimsuit? It doesn't matter. Get in in your bra and panties."

Khelani chuckled. "What?"

To show her he was serious, Kyrie stood up and stripped down to his boxer briefs. He jumped in the pool, and she laughed at him. "You are nuts."

"Get in."

A grin spread slowly across her face, and she decided, *what the hell?* Khelani stood up and pulled her gray dress over her head. Kyrie eyed her petite frame that was only covered in a green bra and green lace panties. Kyrie felt his member start to stiffen as she walked slowly toward the edge of the pool. He took in everything about her, from the healing bullet wound to her pretty yellow manicured toes. Khelani lowered her body into the water and moved steadily toward him. When she was up on him, Kyrie wrapped his arms around her body.

"I want to take you everywhere with me," he confessed while staring deeply into her orbs.

Khelani cocked her head slightly to the left. "Why? Why do you want to take me everywhere with you?"

Kyrie didn't miss a beat. She couldn't trip him up because he wasn't running game. He meant everything he said to her. "Because I never met another woman like you. You are indeed one of a kind, and I'd be a fool to let you go. I want to know everything about you. I want our bond to be one that no one or nothing can ever break. I want you to know that you can trust me and that you're safe with me. I want to protect you."

Her breath caught in her throat, and she wrapped her arms around his neck. She had to stand on the tips of her toes to kiss him. He had a way with words. The way he spoke to her, the way he handled her, the way he sexed her. Kyrie appeared to be one of a kind his damn self. His hands found their way to her ass, and he massaged it as their tongues probed each other's mouths.

"Can I have you?" he whispered as the pace of her heart quickened.

Khelani wasn't sure why the question scared her so much, but she almost felt as if she couldn't breathe. "Literally or figuratively?" she said, deciding to buy some time.

Kyrie stared into her eyes without missing a beat. "Both. Me and you. No other niggas, no other bitches. Us in a relationship learning how to trust and communicate and all that shit. I want that."

He appeared so sincere that she would have felt like shit telling him no. She was already carrying his child, so what did she really have to lose?

Kyrie sensed her hesitation, and he refused to get irritated. He wasn't going to get tired of proving himself so long as she proved to be worth it. She was scared. He knew that much, so he just had to be patient with her. Khelani finally nodded, and he felt a sense of relief but not enough. "I need to hear you say it."

A half-smile graced her face. He always had to give her a hard-ass time. Wanting to be stubborn, she simply stared at him, but she decided to stop her shit. He just said they had to learn to communicate, to trust, and all that. She had to learn to let her guard down. Khelani needed to learn how to be soft, ladylike, and submissive.

"You can have me," she stated in a voice just above a whisper, and that was all he needed to hear.

Kyrie picked her up so that her legs were locked around his waist, and he emerged from the pool carefully, leaving a trail of water on the pavement as he carried her into the house. He kissed her all the way to the couch, and then he lay her down and peeled her wet panties and bra off. Kyrie was determined to prove to Khelani that he wasn't playing with her. Each time their bodies connected, they made magic. It was nothing short of amazing. Khelani had to fight back tears as Kyrie sexed her slowly. She had never had feelings so strong for a man, and they were scary but exhilarating at the same time. Khelani finally felt soft. She felt feminine. She felt like a woman. If only for a little bit, she just wanted to let her guard down and allow an alpha male to lead her.

Kyrie couldn't get enough of Khelani. As he stroked her, his lips never left her. Whether they were French kissing, sharing small pecks, or he was simply sucking on her neck, his mouth on her skin was a constant. To top it all off, they came together. When they were done, Kyrie lay on top of Khelani, heart racing and breathing hard. This was how he wanted to end every night. He hated that she would be leaving the next evening for her upcoming doctor's appointment in two days. Kyrie knew that as long as Khelani was happy, it would make her less likely to fight him on the things that he wanted.

He lifted his head and peered down at her. "You happy?"

"Yes. I'm happy."

He just had to make sure that she stayed that way.

Chapter 22

Khelani lay anxiously on the table as the doctor moved the ultrasound device around inside of her. Vaginal ultrasounds weren't exactly comfortable, but there was no pain. Khelani was so nervous that her palms were sweaty. The silence was deafening, and even though it only lasted a minute or two, it seemed much longer. A whooshing sound filled the room, and Khelani's eyes flew over to the ultrasound screen.

"There goes the baby's heartbeat." The doctor smiled, and Khelani was amazed.

Even after she'd taken a bullet and spent days on extremely strong pain medication, her baby had a strong heartbeat. The moment was so surreal and overwhelming that tears filled her eyes and rolled over her eyelids. Whether she was blindsided by this pregnancy or whether she was ready for a baby, how could she ever abort such a miracle? Her child was a fighter already, and that was nothing short of amazing.

Khelani peered at the screen, and even with the doctor explaining everything as she pointed at certain spots, Khelani couldn't really tell what she was looking at, but it didn't matter. She had expected the doctor to give her bad news, but it was anything but that. A shaky sigh of relief left her lips as the doctor pulled the device from inside of her. She gave Khelani the regular prenatal advice and suggestions and asked her if she had any questions. Khelani didn't, so she headed to the front desk to schedule her next appointment. She was still very early in the pregnancy, and Khelani tried to tell herself that she wasn't all the way out of the woods. However, she was choosing to be optimistic.

Kyrie made her promise to call him as soon as she was done at the doctor, and she kept her word. Khelani got into her car and pulled her cell phone from her purse. The phone rang three times before Kyrie answered in a hushed voice. "Everything good?"

"Yeah, um, did I catch you at a bad time? I can call back."

"No. No, I was in a meeting, but I told them they had to excuse me for a minute. This is important. What did the doctor say?" His anxiousness was sexy.

"Everything looks good. I gained two pounds, and I heard the baby's heartbeat."

"Word?" His tone rose slightly and went from anxious to excited. "Damn, I hate I missed it. Two pounds? That's it? I gotta feed you some more."

Khelani laughed. "I have a little more than seven months to go. I have plenty of time to gain weight, and I'm not rushing it. Next appointment is four weeks from today at two p.m."

"I'm putting it in my calendar right now. I have to get back to this meeting, but I will call you later, okay?"

"Okay."

Kyrie was the only other person who knew she was pregnant, and she was going to keep it that way at least for another month. Even though she had plenty of money, Khelani would give three more months to the game. By the time she started showing, she was going to be out. That would give her enough time to research and to get into being a stylist. Kyrie had a lot of connections, and he could even hire her to style his artists, but she wanted to put work in and prove herself. She didn't want it to be handed to her. Khelani had no problem working up until the day she gave birth. She was a hustler, and that was what hustlers did. Once her baby was born though, she would dedicate at least six months solely to being a mother. Her bank account could afford her the luxury of staying at home with her child and not having to depend on day cares or a nanny. She knew that Kyrie would take care of his child, and child support never once crossed her mind. Damn near every hour of the day was spent plotting. One thing that Kemp had embedded into her mind was to always have a plan, several plans, and to go over them as many times as it took for the plan to become perfectly orchestrated. He always stressed to her that she should dot every i and cross every t.

Of course, she wanted Kyrie around. She wanted him around because there were already too many children out here without fathers. She wanted him around so he could be either his daughter's first love or her son's first coach. It had nothing to do with money. If it was only about money, she was more than good. Even without Kyrie's money, her child was already rich. Once Kemp got past her falling in love and being regular, if the child was a boy, he'd have the world handed to him simply for having a penis. Kemp had always wanted a son more than anything. After Courtney almost died birthing Anya, she refused to have more kids, so he never got his heir to the throne. That was why he passed it down to Khelani.

Khelani started her car and headed home. It was hard for even her to believe, but she was almost excited about becoming a mother—something that she had started to believe would never be in the cards for her.

Anya zipped the duffel bag that she was carrying and headed down to the parking garage of her building. She was a little excited that she was going to see sexy-ass Tae. Kyrie might have been a millionaire from his record label, but the money he made from weed was a nice-ass addition to what he already had. He moved the product fast as hell because he was plugged into the industry. Rappers did all kinds of drugs, but they would always remain true to weed. Kyrie could move ten pounds in less than ten hours simply from letting all the rappers, producers, and employees of his label know that he had product. Other rappers from other labels hit him up as well. Kyrie was the industry plug. One of Yo Gotti's artists had just requested two pounds of weed.

Kyrie had to re-up often, and it kept Tae on his toes. It also kept money in Anya's and Khelani's pockets. Not even just from Kyrie, but business in the A was booming. Khelani wasn't back at work yet, and Anya, Kasim, and Delante stayed on the move. Kasim and Delante rarely let her move alone, but they felt Tae was cool people. He was copping on behalf of Kyrie, and he wasn't dumb enough to try any dumb shit.

Anya had just made it to her car when she felt a blow to the back of her head so forceful that she was knocked into her car. She had never been hit that hard in her life, and though her eyes were open, all she saw was black.

Despite the pain of the blow, the strap of her duffel bag was still clutched tightly in her hand, and she felt it being jerked away from her. Her vision was slowly coming back, but the throbbing in her head had her teary-eyed, and that further clouded her vision. Despite her life being in danger, it was a reflex for her to resist. Anya kept a tight hold on the bag, and her attacker wrapped his hand around her neck and squeezed.

"Don't make me kill you for this shit, bitch."

A tear spilled over her eyelid, and she stared into a pair of cold, dark eyes. His face was covered with a ski mask.

The pain in her head and the fear of her windpipe being crushed made Anya let go of the bag. As soon as she did, her attacker ran off, and she fell back against her car, sobbing. Her head was hurting so bad that it was making her nauseated. She had never had a concussion before, but if it felt worse than what she was going through, the only relief would be death. Anya was shaken up and discombobulated.

Anya figured that since he got what he came for she was pretty much out of harm's way, but she still didn't think she needed to close her eyes. The shit hurt so bad though. A sob escaped her throat as she pulled her cell phone from the pocket of the thin jacket she was wearing. Anya wasn't even in the position to drive herself to the hospital. She almost dialed 911, but then she remembered that Tae was waiting for her. Not only was he waiting for her, but he was waiting for her to bring him fifteen pounds of weed. A whole hell of a lot of money had just been taken from Anya.

She moaned slightly before calling Tae. His phone rang four times before he answered. "What's goodie?"

With her eyes closed and her head laid back on her headrest, Anya spoke in a low, strained voice. "I was robbed. I'm in the parking garage of my building. The nigga hit me in the back of the head, choked me, and snatched the bag from my hand. I think I have a fuckin' concussion." Her voice cracked. "I need to go to the hospital, but I can't even drive. I just wanted to let you know that the shit isn't coming. I'm sure I can get you more, but it won't be tonight."

She couldn't even focus on the financial loss she just took. Their pounds were plentiful, and Tae could still get his shit. But no way were her sister, Kemp, or Kasim going to let this shit fly.

"Yo, text me your address. I'll come drive you to the hospital."

Kyrie wouldn't like having to wait, but he wasn't that heartless. Shit, without any weed on him, Tae had free time on his hands anyway. The least he could do was to make sure that she got to the hospital okay. Anya agreed, and after they ended their call, she texted Tae. She prayed he was close because she couldn't keep taking the throbbing that was going on in her head. It was excruciating. She needed some strong-ass pain medication to get her through this shit. Anya was trembling. That was how bad her body was reacting to the blow to her head, and it wasn't fear. What was going on in her head was agonizing.

A minute seemed like an hour, but finally Tae pulled up on Anya. She had tears streaming down her face as she slowly got out of the driver's seat so Tae could take her place. One look at her and he could tell what she was going through.

"Let me see," he said as he gently placed his hand on the back of her head. "Goddamn." He winced when he felt the golf ball–sized lump that had formed. "Yeah, let me get you to the ER ASAP."

She got in the car, and he pulled off. "There's no drugs in here, right?" He decided to check before he broke the speed limit.

"No," she groaned.

The wheels in his head began to turn. "If that nigga was in the parking garage, he was waiting on your ass. I told you these Atlanta niggas are savage as fuck. They like to sit back and watch, and whoever is out here getting it, they just take their shit. Was his face covered? If so, you might not ever find out who did that shit."

Anya's eyes remained closed. "His face was covered, but I know who did the shit. The same nigga who was going to die anyway because he raped me, but for this shit right now, I'm gon' do that nigga dirty as fuck," she stated between clenched teeth.

Tae's head whipped in her direction. "Who?"

"That lame-ass fuck nigga, Mozzy. I'd know his bitch-ass voice anywhere."

Chapter 23

Khelani rushed into the room that Anya was in. Her sister had texted her and told her what happened. She also let Khelani know that they wanted to give her a CAT scan to make sure there was no internal bleeding or swelling of her brain. Khelani's heart felt as if it dropped into the pit of her stomach, and she got there as fast as she could. On the way there, she was so nervous and preoccupied that she almost rear-ended someone twice. One thing Khelani wouldn't miss about the drug game was annoying-ass niggas always trying to take some shit that didn't belong to them. Like flies on shit, they were more worrisome than the police.

The first person she saw was Tae. Anya's eyes were closed, and she appeared to be asleep. Tae tipped his head in Khelani's direction. "She was in a lot of pain, so they gave her the good shit. Nurse said she was going to be discharged in an hour or two. They want to watch her a little longer before they release her."

Khelani breathed a sigh of relief. "Thank you. I haven't even had a chance to call Kyrie, but let him know that Kasim can meet you in the morning. Sorry about the delay."

"It's all good. Shit happens." He tipped his head at her once again before glancing over at Anya and then leaving the room.

He had never seen such sexy plugs in his life. He could see why his mans was so gone over Khelani. She was sexy for sure, and her sister was right behind her. Tae didn't feel one way or the other about Mozzy. When Kyrie introduced them, he said, "What up?" and kept it moving. They were rarely around each other, but if he had to give a quick opinion, the nigga did look like a lame. He had no reason to give it too much thought though. It was news to him that Mozzy had raped Anya, but he wasn't shocked. That was some shit that lame niggas did. Last he heard from Kyrie, he sent the nigga back to Texas, but Mozzy obviously didn't go. When Tae texted Kyrie and told him that shit didn't go as planned and that Anya was in the hospital, Kyrie told him to come by the crib. He had just gotten back from California thirty minutes before. That wasn't what he wanted to hear, but he didn't ask for details over the phone.

Tae went straight to Kyrie's house, making sure he wasn't being followed the entire way. Not many people got invited to Kyrie's home, and not only that, but he wasn't sure if Mozzy was still on his jack-boy shit. Tae rode with his pistol in his lap ready for whatever.

Kyrie lived way out past Buckhead. It seemed like he drove for hours, but finally he pulled into the long, winding driveway. Once he approached the door, he rang the bell, and Kyrie let him in, looking concerned. "What happened?"

Tae could look at Kyrie and tell he was exhausted. That was the life of a boss. The man hardly ever slept. His phones were always ringing. He had three of them, and they all went off constantly. Even with assistants and plenty of people working for him, Kyrie was always on go mode.

"Anya got robbed. Nigga was in the parking garage of her condo waiting for her. So not only does he know where she lives, but he knows that she's moving that work. He hit her in the back of the head, and she has a concussion. Khelani came to the hospital, so I left. She told me to tell you that Kasim can meet me in the morning with the pounds."

Kyrie blew out a frustrated breath. "Khelani does not need this shit. With Anya out of commission for a while, I know she's gon' jump back headfirst into this shit. And niggas know where she lives?"

Kyrie paced back and forth, and Tae could tell he was pissed. "Bro, I know you really like this chick, but she was doing this way before she met you. I can get you wanting her to stop, but you think it will be that easy?"

"It should be when her ass is fucking pregnant. We found out after she got shot, and the nurse basically told her to wait to miscarry because the baby probably wouldn't survive the trauma. But she's still pregnant. She went to the doctor and heard the heartbeat. That should be enough for her to hang all this shit up. But if I try to tell her that, she's gon' get defensive and shit. That's one hardheaded-ass female."

"Damn, my nigga, congratulations. I feel where you're coming from. I told Anya she needed to be careful. Niggas are out here getting robbed left and right, so I knew they would eventually try her or Khelani. I think Kasim knows I'm good people, so he let her meet me alone, but he shouldn't even do that. They shouldn't be moving weight alone, period. Shorty said she knows who did it though."

"Who?"

"Yo' nigga Mozzy. She said she knows that voice anywhere. I guess he's not back in Texas."

Kyrie ran one hand over his waves. "This ho-ass nigga. She already told me that he raped her, and as long as he was working for me, she wouldn't serve me. That's why I cut him off."

Tae shook his head in disbelief. "If he's smart, he better take that weed and haul ass back to Texas because they're on his ass."

Kyrie sat down in his recliner, stressed out. He had the money to give Khelani to replace the fifteen pounds that she lost, but he knew that wasn't what she wanted. It was the principle of the situation. She would want to have a hand in helping Anya and Kasim get at Mozzy if they found him. Khelani was going to be the reason that he had gray hair, but he knew the only thing that would stop her was if he found Mozzy first.

Kyrie's body was tired, and he couldn't keep fighting the shit. The next morning, he slept in for the first time in months. There was no getting up at five, six, or even seven a.m. He slept until noon, and it felt damn good. He texted his chef to see if he could come over around two to make him a late lunch, and he ate cereal while he waited for a reply. Kyrie had to know when to turn it off, and today he was turning it off. There would be no going to the office. He was going to work out and simply relax. After he smoked his morning blunt and took a shower, Khelani was on his mind, but he called Tae first.

"What up, boss?"

"Did you get that?"

"Yep. I met Kasim about two hours ago, and five of them are already gone."

"My man. I definitely appreciate you. I'm doing something today that I rarely do, and that's staying my ass in the house. If you need me, just call."

"Go ahead and rest up, my G. You deserve that shit."

They ended the call, and Kyrie called Khelani. He texted her briefly the night before after she got home from the hospital. He was going to let her rest and calm down, so he decided to wait to try to talk to her about the situation. Hopefully, she woke up in an okay mood, and their conversation wouldn't lead to an argument.

"Hey."

"What you doing, gorgeous?"

"Just left from making a run with Kasim. I'm about to head back to get some more."

Kyrie closed his eyes to remain calm. As he predicted, she was right back in the streets as if she weren't pregnant and as if she hadn't been shot a few weeks ago. Keeping in mind that he didn't want her to get defensive, he didn't express his feelings to her just yet.

"I decided to take the day off. My body is tired as hell, and I need some rest. I'm not leaving the house, and my chef is coming through. Come eat with me."

"I can be there in an hour. No longer than an hour and a half if that's cool."

"That's not a problem. I'll see you when you get here."

They ended the call, and he walked over to his bar. Kyrie was going to need a blunt and a few stiff drinks for this shit. He already knew that Khelani didn't like being told what to do. She wasn't naturally submissive. A nigga had to earn that shit. As long as she was carrying his child, however, he felt he had a say in what she did. Kyrie couldn't control her, but he could let her know that she needed to fall back with what she was out there doing. She wasn't broke, and what if she had been the one hit in the back of the head instead of Anya? Kyrie knew his baby was a soldier for real, but he didn't want to keep testing shit. There was no way Khelani could successfully carry a child with all kinds of painful shit happening to her on a regular basis. And had she been the one Mozzy hit, he'd die a slow and painful death for real, and that wasn't good. Being that Kyrie sold weed, he was still technically in the streets, but he was 98 percent a legit businessman. He couldn't keep bodying niggas and putting his freedom at stake because Khelani wanted to be a queen pin. It was time for her to gracefully bow out of the game and leave the hustling to the men. This was one time that Kyrie didn't mind being sexist.

He poured a double shot of cognac and carried the glass back over to his favorite recliner. Things don't have to be super expensive to be nice to look at or of a good quality, but the way his Italian leather recliners and sofas felt, he would never have any other kind of chairs in his home. It literally felt like his ass was sitting on a cloud. Kyrie pulled from his blunt with thoughts of his future heavy on his mind. His days of clubbing five to six times a week and having sex with a different woman every night were over. That shit didn't excite him anymore. There truly was a time for everything, and his time had come. The good thing about it was that he didn't meet Khelani before that time. Letting her get away would have been a huge mistake on his part, but had she caught him three years ago, no matter how fine she was or how good the pussy was, Kyrie seriously doubted he would have been ready to settle down and have a kid. He probably would have offered to pay for the abortion without even waiting to see if she would miscarry.

The doorbell rang, and he drained the cognac from his glass. Kyrie knew it had to be his chef because he doubted Khelani was there that fast. His assumption was correct, and the chef carried two large bags into the house. "What's on the menu?" Unless Kyrie had a specific taste for something, he always let the chef choose, and he'd never been disappointed.

"I'm going to start with calamari, and then you'll have lobster bisque. Next will be a chopped salad and then spinach and shrimp fettucine."

"Goddamn that sounds good as hell." Kyrie licked his lips, and the chef headed for the kitchen with a chuckle. He'd be for sure tipping his ass lovely for coming through with that. Kyrie thought it was dope as hell that he knew a black chef who could cook his ass off. His food was always on point, and he always made sure to pay him very well. In fact, he was so good at what he did that he only had five regular clients. That was one of the reasons why Kyrie was often able to hit him on short notice. He cooked a guaranteed three meals a week for Kyrie if he was in town, and any other time, if Kyrie needed him on the spur of the moment and he was free, he would slide through. He also cooked for Swag and three other celebrities. He did catering every now and then, but just off the regular five clients, he was able to live very well. Homie drove a Porsche truck. Kyrie usually tipped him anywhere from $150 to $300 on top of what he charged.

As soon as Kyrie got comfortable in his chair, the doorbell rang again. He was looking forward to seeing Khelani so bad that a nigga didn't even get frustrated that he had to get right back up. When Kyrie opened his black frosted-glass front door, his face fell immediately. He wasn't expecting to see Camila standing on his porch looking sad as fuck, and he didn't mean she looked regretful. Her ass had lost a few pounds. He didn't know the exact number, but it was noticeable. She had a long, silky sew-in, but her edges were frizzy and threw the entire hairstyle off. Her skin looked dull, and it hurt Kyrie to see his people like that. He never thought he'd see the day that prissy-ass bougie Camila looked like shit. It was clear that she had a monkey on her back. A part of Kyrie wanted to hug her and offer to pay for rehab. His love for her was bigger than the money she stole from him. Kyrie knew enough to know, however, that appearing soft would make him a victim. Camila was a finesser before she got a coke habit. He would have to move really careful with her because the moment he felt she was trying to play him, he would have no mercy.

"Why you at my crib unannounced?"

Camila's eyes darted here, there, and everywhere. It was hard for her to look him in the eyes, and he didn't know if she was high or if she was ashamed. Maybe it was a combination of both. "I'm not even gon' bullshit you. I owe somebody some money. It's serious enough that he's gon' kill my ass. I was supposed to have his bread three days ago, and I've been hiding from him. If I don't give him his money, I'm going to die." Her voice held a pleading tone. Camila actually looked fearful, but she was an addict. Nothing was bigger than her devotion to coke.

Kyrie kissed his teeth and shook his head at the predicament that she'd found herself in. "I give you the money and then what? You go buy more coke and continue to hide from this nigga? The only way I'll clear your debt is if you agree to go to rehab, and I don't mean kicking no bullshit game to me. I mean, let me drive you to a facility tonight and watch you go in. Then, whoever you owe, I'll hand him the money myself."

He watched as her weight shifted from one leg to the other. She didn't want to go, but if she didn't, he wouldn't help her.

"Kyrie—"

"Save the bullshit, Camila. I'm not playing with you. You already stole from me, and you won't finesse another dime out of me. It's rehab or nothing."

"You got all this fuckin' money," she snapped. "You're rich as hell, and you wouldn't even save my club. You automatically assume that I owe someone money for drugs. What if I was trying to save my club? I know you want to think the worst of me, but drugs aren't always the case."

Kyrie's nostrils flared angrily. "Just for you coming with that stupid shit, I should slam the door in your face. Drugs are the reason you were stealing from me in the first place. I've never been green or lame, so you can take

that shit somewhere else. I don't owe you shit, and I'm
not giving you shit that you don't deserve. Now let's pick
out a rehab facility or you can get the fuck off my porch."
If she chose not to go to rehab, not only was he going to
continue to act as if she didn't exist, but he would have
to tell his uncle that Camila was out there. It would break
his heart, but if he had eyes to see, then he should know
anyway.

A car pulled up in his driveway, and he noticed that
it was Khelani. With all that had gone on, Kyrie had
honestly forgotten about Khelani's beef with Camila.
He didn't feel like she'd still be harping on the fact that
Camila jumped Anya, but he was wrong.

Khelani never gave out fake threats. If she said some
shit, she meant it, and when she saw Camila, all common
sense went out the window. She didn't think about being
pregnant or about being at Kyrie's home. All she saw
were flashbacks of her sister's battered and bruised face
after Camila and Caresha jumped her. She didn't say one
word. She just balled her fist up and punched Camila
square in the face.

Kyrie's jaw fell open in shock as she hit Camila again
and again. He finally came to his senses and jumped in
between the women, but Khelani was on go. She just
wouldn't stop, and he had to grab her roughly and carry
her in the house. Once she was secured, that gave Camila
balls, and she hit Khelani in the head twice. Kyrie damn
near threw Khelani in the living room and closed the
door behind him. He was breathing hard and furious
when he faced Camila.

"If you're not talking about rehab, then you need to
leave."

"Fuck you, Kyrie. You really choosing that lame-ass ho
over me? She and her whore-ass sister are going to get
it. Watch." Tears glistened in her eyes as she turned to

walk away. Kyrie was her last resort. She couldn't go to her parents for the money, so she was fucked. Camila had no idea what she was going to do because Boogie wasn't playing with her.

Fuming, Kyrie walked back into the house, and he saw Khelani's face contorted into a frown, and her hand was flat on her tummy. She looked to be in pain, and that set Kyrie all the way off. "You really don't give a fuck, do you? You're already a high-risk pregnancy, and you really just jumped on my people? You out here selling drugs and moving like a nigga when you don't even have to be. On God, you a selfish-ass bitch, and if you miscarry, you might do us both a favor. You don't even need to be anybody's mother with your dumb ass."

Khelani drew back and eyed Kyrie with a face full of contempt. No one had ever spoken to her in such a manner, especially not him. He had called her out of her name not once but twice. She wanted to curse him out so bad, but her feelings were hurt. Khelani didn't even know what to say. Maybe she shouldn't have fought Camila, but in her opinion, he hit a little below the belt with the insults. Her stomach was cramping, and she was scared. Khelani was already beating herself up, but to have him doing it in such a callous manner put her into defense mode.

"Tell me how you really feel. That's the last time in your life that you will ever talk to me crazy. Fuck you, Kyrie, and I mean that from the bottom of my heart. As of today, we have no ties." She stormed past him, mad enough to spit nails.

Tears rolled down her cheeks as cramps ripped through her midsection. Getting ahold of Camila wasn't worth her child's life, but she snapped. For just a few seconds, Khelani blacked out. She regretted it, and despite that she was in the wrong, she hated how Kyrie had spoken to her. If she did miscarry, she would carry that guilt for the rest of her life.

Back in the house, Kyrie was so pissed that he picked his glass up and hurled it across the room.

Chapter 24

Khelani left the emergency room feeling exhausted. After two hours and an ultrasound, the doctor told her that her baby was okay, and she had never been more relieved in her life. The doctor suggested bed rest for a week, and Khelani was going to comply. She was done with being stubborn, and she would have to tell Anya about the baby. Kyrie could kiss her ass. Maybe he wanted to be there during her pregnancy, but for the moment, she wanted nothing to do with him. She had the chance to calm down, and Khelani knew that no matter how mad she was with him, he would still have to be in his child's life. She wasn't that petty to keep him away, but he didn't have to be in her life. It would be nice for him to experience hearing the heartbeat and all that, but she wasn't there yet. Khelani didn't have anything to say to him at the moment.

When she got home, she found Anya in the kitchen fixing something to eat. Since her concussion, she'd been doing a lot of resting. Kasim, Khelani, and Delante were handling things. Now Khelani was going to have to tell her sister that she was out of the game sooner than she expected to be.

"Hey, how are you feeling?" she asked Anya.

"I'm okay. Tired of random and intense-ass headaches. I want Mozzy so bad I'm putting a bounty on that nigga's head." Anya peered over her shoulder. "You okay? You look like shit."

Khelani rolled her eyes. "Thanks for not sugarcoating facts." She blew out a hard breath and sat down on one of their stools. "I'm out. As of today. I can't hustle anymore. When I was in the hospital from being shot, I found out that I was pregnant."

Anya whirled around fast as hell to face her sister. Her eyes were wide from shock. "Khelani, are you serious?"

"I am. The nurse told me that because of the trauma that I went through, I would more than likely miscarry. I was completely caught off guard, and I wanted an abortion. Kyrie wasn't really having it though. I decided to just wait and see what would happen, and I'm still pregnant. It just seems that after my kid survived all this shit, I'd be fucked up to go lie on a table and end his or her life."

Anya squealed. "You're going to have a baby? I can't believe I'm excited. I don't even like kids like that," she chuckled.

"Yeah, well, don't get too excited. It's still very early, and I just messed up big time. I went to Kyrie's house, and Camila was there. I snapped and whooped her ass. As soon as Kyrie broke the fight up, I started cramping really badly, and he got so mad. He called me a selfish bitch and said that if I miscarry, I'd be doing us a favor because I don't deserve to be a mother."

Anya's eyebrows hiked up. Those were pretty harsh words. Normally, anyone who disrespected Khelani would have her furious, but she didn't look mad. She looked hurt. Anya was surprised she didn't shoot that nigga.

"He's right. I am selfish, and maybe I don't need to be anyone's mother. For so long, being all about me and only caring about money was all I knew. I conditioned myself not to let people get close to me. Those aren't exactly motherly instincts. I never should have jeopardized my child's life for Camila's zombie-looking ass."

"First of all, you've been pregnant for two seconds. It's going to take some time to adjust and get used to it. You aren't even showing, and I know you didn't feel like Camila could beat you. I'm not excusing what you did, but I'm not going to be cruel about it either. You're human, and you go hard for the ones you love and let in. You fought her for me. And you don't think you'd slit a ho's neck behind your own child? You are going to be a great mother. I like Kyrie and all, but he can go to hell with that one. Are you still cramping?"

"No, I just left the ER. They gave me Tylenol while I was there. The doctor did suggest bed rest for a week. That's why I'm out. As of today, I no longer sell weed." The words sounded funny coming out of her mouth.

"That's cool. Kasim, Delante, and I can handle it. Hopefully, I'll be able to help them out tomorrow. My headaches are becoming less intense."

"So you're not scared to keep going?"

"Nope. I'm just not going to meet people alone anymore. I need to stack my paper up since this was your last city. Once Dad sends Kasim and Delante to another state, that's it for me. I'm gonna be out too because I'm not going to a new place without you. Speaking of that, I know you're mad with Kyrie and all, but are you staying here now? Since you two are going to have a baby?"

Khelani snorted. "We are going to have to figure out how to coparent from a distance because I am not staying in Atlanta." There was a frown on her face, and her voice was thick with conviction. "North Carolina wasn't bad. I might even try Los Angeles since I want to be a stylist. I don't think I want to go to New York. Mr. Private Jet will have to fly to see his child."

Anya decided not to give her opinion since it wasn't asked for. She was always the hotheaded, impulsive one, and it stayed getting her into trouble. She rarely gave her actions much thought before doing them. Khelani was the complete opposite of her. She didn't have to stay in Atlanta just because she was pregnant, but it would be kind of nice if she did. If she wanted to be a stylist, she could do so in the A. She could probably get on without Kyrie's help. Khelani had the freedom to live anywhere in the world that she wanted to, and she was choosing to leave Atlanta out of spite. Even if Kyrie did have a jet and could visit his child, Anya was pretty sure he wanted his child in the same city or at least the same state as him. She was going to mind her business though. Khelani was still mad and making decisions based on being in her feelings.

"When do you think Daddy will tell Kasim and Delante that it's time to move on?" Anya was so focused on saving that she hadn't been spending any money aside from buying food and putting gas in her car. She still needed at least another month or two to get her money right. She also had to figure out if she would stay in the A once Kasim and Delante did move on. Unless she wanted to be an actress, stylist, or some kind of health-food nut, she didn't see how going to L.A. would benefit her. It still might not be so bad to go wherever Khelani went. After all, she'd need help with the baby.

"I think it will be a while. We signed our lease for a year. Daddy didn't tell me to do month to month, so I'm sure you have the time to figure out what it is that you want to do."

"If you go to North Carolina or L.A., who will help you with the baby?"

Khelani shrugged. "I like working, but if I want to, I can stay home with my child for three years and still be okay. I don't have to be in a rush, but I do know that I can't be with my child every second of every day. I'd be willing to hire a nanny in case I need to run out for an hour or two.

She would go through an extensive background check, and I will have cameras in every room of my house."

Khelani seemed to have it all figured out. She was tough. She was smart, and she was resilient. Anya had no doubt that Khelani could take care of herself, but moving to a city where she knew no one and having a brand-new baby would be hard for anyone. If her sister was really determined, however, she knew there was nothing that could be done to stop her.

Kyrie sat in his office trying to go over some papers that his lawyer needed him to sign, but no matter how many times he read the words on the paper, the meaning of them refused to sink in. He was preoccupied. It had been two days since his argument with Khelani, and he had no idea if she was still pregnant. Did she miscarry? Did she decide to terminate the pregnancy? He could see her doing something like that, and Kyrie was pissed. God really had a sense of humor, because of all the people in the world he could have fallen for, he chose a stubborn-ass woman who didn't take kindly to any kind of advice even if it was for her own good. Trying to prove yourself to people was for the birds. It would be much easier for him to settle down and have kids with someone who was on the exact same page as him. There were hundreds of women, maybe even thousands, who would kill to be carrying his baby. Kyrie was frustrated. It wasn't like he had wasted years with Khelani, and the child she was carrying was still in the very early stages, so why couldn't he just cut his losses and move on?

He wanted to not give a damn about her, but thoughts of her still crept into his mind every hour on the hour. Even though he had calmed down, he still didn't quite regret the things that he had said to her. Somebody had to call Khelani out on her bullshit. She was selfish, and she wasn't acting like a mother. Just like she didn't kiss ass, he didn't either. They just couldn't be, and he was going to have to learn how to be okay with that.

Along with thoughts of Khelani and his unborn child, something else was plaguing Kyrie. He also kept having visions of Camila. Not the Camila that he had known all of his life, but the coked-out Camila who looked bad as hell. Maybe he should have asked her who she owed money to. He could pay them directly and make sure that they spared his cousin's life. Even if she didn't go to rehab, he could make sure that she was safe.

That was what he would do. Kyrie picked his phone up off his desk so he could call Camila and find out who she owed money to. It would piss him off all over again if he ended up finding out that she didn't owe anyone. It could have simply been her objective to try to get him to put some money in her hands. Camila's phone rang and rang, and eventually the voicemail clicked on. Kyrie wasn't one for leaving messages, so he decided that if she really wanted the money, she would simply return his call.

As soon as he ended the call and laid the phone back down, it rang, and he figured it was Camila. Upon looking at the screen, he saw that it wasn't her and that it was actually his uncle. An inexplicable chill ran from the base of his spine all the way up his back and into his neck. The chill had such a sting to it that Kyrie damn near dropped his phone. He had never in his life felt such an eerie emotion. It had him almost afraid to answer the phone, but he did.

"What's up, Unc?"

The first thing he heard was wailing in the background, and his heart sank. It was a female's voice, and if he had to guess, he would assume it was his aunt. Kyrie's breath caught in his throat as he waited for his uncle to speak.

When Mario finally spoke, his words came out choppy. His voice was strained, and Kyrie could tell that the man was fighting back tears.

It was taking every ounce of strength that he had not to break down in front of his wife. He had to be strong for her because she was falling apart in front of his eyes, and that only contributed to his already-broken heart breaking some more.

"They, um . . . The police found . . ." Mario paused. It was hard for him to get the words out of his mouth. They weren't words that he ever saw himself having to speak. "The police found Camila dead in her car about an hour ago."

Kyrie's heart sank. It felt as if he were suffocating. The air in his office became thick. Kyrie was choking. He pictured his cousin's body riddled with gunshots. He was too damn late. He should have offered to pay off her debt before it ever even got to this. Just like his uncle's, Kyrie's voice gave away the fact that he was on the verge of tears.

"What happened?" he asked in a tone so low that he wasn't sure if his uncle heard him.

"They say there was no evidence of foul play. They found, um . . ." Mario sucked in a sharp breath. "They found cocaine in the car, and they think it was an overdose. We won't know until the toxicology report comes back."

Kyrie sat back down. He put his head in his hands, and he broke down.

Chapter 25

"How is your head feeling?" Tae asked Anya when she ran into him at the gas station. She hadn't seen him since she left the hospital, although she had texted him and thanked him for accompanying her to the ER. She had been hoping that he would hit her on some personal shit, but he never did. Anya then began to realize that she didn't know anything about him. Maybe he had a girl and he was one of the rare ones who was faithful.

"I feel much better now. It took a few days of sleeping a lot and taking pain medication every four to six hours. That big-ass knot finally went down, too. I could barely even comb my hair. I felt like if you cared though, you would have called or texted me and asked," she flirted just a bit.

Tae licked his lips as he recognized what she was doing. "My bad. A nigga been busy. I was busy anyway, but I'm gon' be super busy now. I gotta take over for Kyrie in a few different areas. He lost his cousin yesterday, and he's gonna be outta commission for a minute."

"Oh."

Tae didn't miss the bored expression on Anya's face, and because he knew Camila's character, it didn't take a genius to guess that Anya probably didn't care for the girl. "You used to dance at her club, right? I thought you and her were cool."

"We were, but she's a bitch. I mean, I normally don't disrespect the dead, but I can't even be fake. I don't know if she started doing drugs too heavy or what, but she just started switching up. First, she talked to me crazy, and then her and Caresha's bum ass jumped me. My sister just saw her at Kyrie's house the other day and whooped her for that shit. Now they beefing."

"Damn." Tae shook his head. "That's why that nigga was in a bad-ass mood even before Camila died. Shit is crazy. Anyway, I'm glad you feeling better though."

"Thank you. I know you said you're going to be busy and all, but you can't find the time to get a few drinks? You got a girl?"

"You were supposed to ask me if I had a girl first."

"Oops."

Tae chuckled. "You something else, ma." He briefly contemplated her question. Tae wasn't usually scared of a challenge, but Anya seemed like she came with a lot. He could tell she was way wilder than Khelani. Did he even want the problems that came with that? She was sexy as hell though. And thick. Of course, Tae started out thinking with the big head, but the final decision was made with the little head. "Yeah, we can link up tonight around ten if that's not too late."

"That's fine, and could you do me a favor?"

"What's that?" Tae peered into her sexy-ass eyes. They were hypnotizing indeed, but he refused to get caught up over her the way Kyrie was so gone over Khelani.

"Could you let your people know that I have five thousand dollars for anybody who can point me in the direction of that fuck nigga Mozzy?" Anya smiled like she hadn't just told him she had a hit out on a nigga and walked off, leaving Tae staring after her.

"Muhfuckin' trouble," he mumbled.

Khelani felt bad as hell when she learned that Camila was dead. She didn't care for the woman at all, but she didn't wish death on her. She knew that Kyrie was probably taking it hard, and she felt it would be petty not to hit him up. Then she thought about the fact that the last time she saw him she beat his cousin's ass, and she decided that reaching out might not be a good idea. She was low-key salty that he hadn't attempted to check on her and see how she was doing. Khelani was snapped out of her thoughts when Anya came in the condo with a big smile on her face.

"It's done. I told Tae to spread the word that I have five stacks for whoever can tell me where Mozzy is."

"I want him to pay too, but be careful with that. We need to let Kasim and Delante take the lead. We might only be selling weed, but niggas are thirsty for that shit. I never really stopped to think about how dangerous it really is. Malachi could have done more than wait until I was in the shower to try to rob me. He could have killed me for the weed. Mozzy could have killed you. This shit isn't worth our lives."

Anya grinned. "Look at you getting all soft and shit. That baby is finally making your mean ass fold a li'l bit."

Khelani rolled her eyes upward. "It has nothing to do with that. I just have time to finally sit down and reflect. That's all I do lately is sit and think. I was playing a dangerous-ass game."

"Living, period, is dangerous, Khelani. I could get up every day and go to a job that pays me big bucks and get jacked and killed for my car or my jewelry. It happens every day. People don't discriminate. I will agree that I need to move carefully, but I just can't stop this shit until I'm sitting on at least a hundred thousand dollars. I'm hoping that since I'm stepping up and making Dad proud, he'll get back to feeling generous. If I can stack a hunnid K, get a nigga or two on my team, and get enough from Dad to pay my rent up for a year or some shit, I'll be in there. I still won't be doing as good as you, but that's my fault for being out here playing."

"I guess. You know, Dad will really take care of you if you move back to Trinidad," Khelani teased, and Anya groaned.

"Yeah, right. I'm too damn old for Dad to be watching every move I make. I'll have unlimited access to his money and no privacy. I'd rather meet a rich-ass nigga and get wifed up. The A is full of rappers, producers, actors, and hustlers. I'll even take a scammer as long as his money is long."

Khelani shook her head. "There goes the Anya I know."

"I wish you'd make up with Kyrie. Then maybe I could get close to some rappers. He's not a rapper, but I'm meeting Tae for drinks later. He is one sexy-ass man, and I'm due for a little tune-up."

"TMI. I don't know Tae like that, but he seems like cool people. Be safe and have fun."

Yeah, he was cool people, but Anya was thinking about what that dick did. "I will. I'm about to take a shower and get dressed. Oh, did you hear about Camila?"

"I saw it on the news. My bed-rest ass alternates between reading, the TV, and my cell phone. The police said they don't suspect foul play."

"Her coked-out ass probably overdosed. I fell back from popping E pills and shit because a lot of these drugs now are laced with fentanyl. One shot will stop a person's heart just like that. I know for sure that some people lace their heroin with it, so I wouldn't be surprised if they do the same with coke."

"I thought about hitting Kyrie up, but I decided against it. Will it even matter to him if he knows I didn't like the girl?"

"There's only one way to find out."

Khelani bit her bottom lip as she contemplated calling him. "Nah. He's already said enough foul shit to me. If I call and he says something crazy, it'll be a wrap for real."

"I'll be glad when you two make up," Anya stated before walking off.

Khelani got up from the couch to make herself a snack. Little did Anya know that this time felt different to her. Of all the times she had been irritated with Kyrie, there was something in Khelani's gut that told her they might not be able to come back from this one.

Chapter 26

Tae looked at Anya in awe as she threw back a double shot of tequila and didn't even flinch. "You just might be part nigga, yo."

Anya kissed her teeth. "Whatever. There isn't shit manly about me. I'm just a big girl, and I can handle my liquor." She bit her bottom lip and eyed Tae seductively. There was no doubt in his mind that he'd be fucking her before the night was over.

"Is that right?"

"You better know it. So, Mr. Tae, you don't have a girl?" She waved the bartender over to order another drink while Tae downed his shot.

"I don't. If I had a girl, I wouldn't be out in public with you."

Her brows hiked up. "You wouldn't be out in public with me, or you wouldn't be with me period?" she asked for clarity.

"I wouldn't be out in public. I won't say I never cheated, but I won't make getting caught easy. Plus, that shit OD disrespectful."

"Cheating, period, is disrespectful."

"Yeah, but I'm just saying, most men are going to stray. That's just life. Especially if he's been with the same woman for a long time. Show me a man who's been with the same woman for five or six years who has never slipped up not even once. That shit is highly unlikely even if it was just a one-night stand with a coworker or an ex. My thing is, if she's my woman and people knows she's my woman, I won't be flaunting my indiscretions for the world to see. I'll keep it low and hope she never finds out."

"I guess that's how it goes. We'd be here all night arguing about the double standard. Even when I'm single and not attached to any man, I'm considered a ho if I'm free and out here doing me. I would be considered run through and somebody not worth wifing. But a man can have a good woman at home. She can be the wifey type and he'll cheat on her with someone like me. If I'm not good enough to wife, why risk a relationship for me? It's dumb as fuck, but oh well."

Tae smirked as the bartender placed their drinks in front of them. "You one of them free chicks, huh?"

"When I want to be. That an issue?"

"Hell nah. Do what you want, and unlike a lot of men, I don't judge. Now I can't see me wifing a chick who's out here going straight bananas getting trains run on her, fucking whole crews and shit, that's a bit much, but I don't really care about a woman's past if I'm feeling her. As long as she hasn't had sex with my closest homies or my family members and if she can show me that she's disease free, it is what it is. I've never been the type of nigga to care what people think about me or who I rock with. No one but me should be concerned with where I stick my dick."

It was rare that Anya was speechless, but at the moment, she was. Tae was a real one. That was easy for her to see. It took a real secure man to be that way. Even though she wasn't well-known in Atlanta, Anya knew for sure that her past behavior with men would be considered ho shit. She only dealt with men who had money, and she was always looking for a man with a bigger bag than the last. *What does being with a broke man get you? Not a damn thing*. She loved sex, but she would never choose good sex over comfort. Her man could have the best stroke game in the world, but if he couldn't provide, then he may as well have been a little-dick nigga because the sex would become irrelevant. At least to her it would. Not to mention, Kemp would have a fit if Anya ever ended up with a broke man. She challenged her father on a lot of things, but that wasn't one of them.

Tae was the one to break the silence. "So what's the story with you and Mozzy? That's if you want to talk about it."

Anya shifted on her stool and picked up her drink. Not much traumatized her or made her feel some type of way, but being raped did. She thought about it often, and she wanted Mozzy dead. She liked sex, and she could have it as much as she wanted with whomever she wanted. Being sexually free never made her feel dirty, but being raped made her feel absolutely disgusting. There were times she wished she could crawl out of her own skin. Some days were better than others, but it was a memory that replayed over in her mind every day, and she hated it.

"I met him when I was dancing at the club. I saw him with Kyrie, and he was okay. I mean, I don't know. I can admit that all I saw was dollar signs. And I wasn't even seeing correctly because he really didn't have shit. Anyway, I left the club with him one night, and the sex was horrible. Worst I've ever had." She frowned at the memory. "I was new in town and horny, so I thought why not, but the experience left me wanting to vomit. It was something I knew I'd never do again regardless of if he had money or not, and I found out the hard way that Mozzy isn't the type to take rejection well. The rest is history."

"Most lames can't handle rejection. There is nothing on this earth that would ever make me take a woman's pussy.

That shit is foul. That being said, I put a few people on to what you said. Be careful with that though. I keep telling you that you can't trust niggas. Anybody cruddy enough will make you think they have info for you just to rob you for that five bands. That's not even no real money, but to a thirsty nigga, five stacks could make his day, and he would kill for it. I've seen niggas kill for less. Not all robbers will leave you with your life."

A chill ran down her spine at his words. "I know. From here on out, I'm not making any more moves without Kasim or Delante. My sister thinks I should fall back altogether, but I need this money. Soon, my dad will be sending Kasim and Delante to another city, and anyone getting weed in the A will deal directly with him. If my sister is out, then I'm out too, so as far as weed, Atlanta is my last stop. There isn't a job out here that I can get that will pay me what I make moving pounds for my dad, so I need to stack my bread."

Tae nodded. "I can dig it. I never thought I'd work a legit job until Kyrie put me on. He pays me more than he'd pay on average 'cause that's my man, but I still don't make what I make with this drug shit, so I feel you. Stacking is the key because no matter how carefully one moves, this shit can't be done forever."

"I agree." Anya threw back her second double shot, and it put her right where she needed to be.

A warm, fuzzy feeling took over her, and she eyed Tae's handsome face before her eyes slid down to his crotch area. He was dressed in black jeans, so she couldn't see a dick print, but Anya still licked her lips at what she envisioned it to be. A sexy-ass nigga with a stance and an attitude like Tae had to be able to put it down in the bedroom. Just the thought of seeing his toned chocolate body shirtless made her kitty moist. She had never been shy, and she wouldn't choose tonight to start being that way.

"You gon' take me to your crib or what?"

Tae chuckled. Anya was just as wild as he assumed she was. He normally didn't take females he didn't know to his crib, but she was the plug. His boss copped his weight from her, so what could she do, rob him? She was connected enough and had her own money, so he wasn't even worried about anything crazy. These other Atlanta females though, bitches would have their brothers and baby daddies coming straight to your shit to clean it out. Tae didn't even play those kinds of games.

"We can do that," he answered in a low baritone that turned her on further.

"Let me get one more drink and some wings," she giggled.

Ten minutes later, Anya was following Tae to his condo. She hadn't had any good sex since Snow, and she was ready. Anya hoped Tae didn't live far because those shots had her seeing double. After fifteen minutes of driving, he pulled into a parking garage, and she was right behind him. Anya grabbed one of her wings and demolished it before getting out of the car with the tray in hand. She was ready to get straight to the D, but she'd put a lot of alcohol in her system. Nothing would ruin the night more than her getting sick, so she needed to put something on her stomach.

Tae waited for her by his car, then he led her into his building. They got on the elevator, and she pulled another wing from the Styrofoam tray. The elevator stopped on the sixth floor, and she followed Tae off the elevator. Anya eyed his sexy, thuggish walk, and she couldn't wait to pounce on him. Inside his condo, she looked around in appreciation. It was hard to impress a woman who was raised by Kemp, but Tae was doing very well for himself. Anya loved the winding black staircase that led up to the second level of the condo. His shit was spotless, was decorated nicely, and smelled good.

"I see someone has good taste," she complimented him before sitting on the couch.

"I do a li'l something. You want something to drink?"

"Yes, please. These wings are spicy as hell."

Tae went to the kitchen and got a plastic cup and filled it with crushed ice. "Ohhhhh," Anya squealed, and Tae looked over his shoulder with dipped eyebrows. She laughed at his facial expression. "You have the same crushed-ice maker that Khelani has. That girl is obsessed with ice, and she has me hooked on it now." Khelani loved ice so much that she ordered the $500 ice maker with no hesitation.

"You have to be a female getting that excited about ice. Sprite good?"

"Yes."

He took Anya her drink, pulled his shirt over his head, then sat down to roll a blunt. He wasn't interested in anything on TV, so he turned to YouTube and put on a playlist. A Da Baby video began to play on the seventy-inch television he had mounted to his wall. She finished off her food just as he was done with the blunt. Tae lit it and took a few pulls. He was even sexy when he smoked. Anya almost felt like a creep watching him, but there was just something about him. When she was in his presence, she could never keep her eyes off him for long. She loved all of his features from his sharp nose to his thick brows and even the slight gap between his two front teeth. Anya knew she had it bad when she was salivating over a nigga's gap. He passed her the blunt, and she plucked it from between his fingers. The weed heightened the high that she was already on, and when a video by Megan Thee Stallion began to play, Anya stood up and began to dance. She used to get on stage and dance topless in a roomful of strangers, so it was nothing to put on a show for Tae. She wasn't doing a lot just twerking and having a good time. She loved the way Megan popped her shit.

Tae eyed Anya through hooded lids. If the saying about dancing and fucking was true, he knew he was in for a treat, because Anya was tossing her ass perfectly with the beat of the music. She could dance, and it was making his dick hard. After a few more pulls of the sticky, Anya placed the blunt in an ashtray. She walked over to Tae and placed her hands flat on each of the armrests of his chair. She leaned in and placed soft kisses on his neck before using her tongue to trace a line up to his earlobe, which she gently bit. Anya placed a trail of kisses along his jawline and placed the last one on the corner of his mouth. She then turned her back to him, sat on his lap, and began giving him a lap dance. She could feel his hard dick poking her through his jeans, and she could feel enough to know that she would be pleased with his size. Damn, he was paid, fine, and had a big dick. If he knew how to use it, then this dude was something like a unicorn because she could rarely find a man who possessed all four qualities. Some of the richest men she knew had the most trash sex.

Tae locked one arm around her waist. "All this teasing shit a dub. Let's go." She stood up, and he was right behind her.

Anya waited for him to take the lead, and she followed him up the winding staircase. His bedroom was as nice as the rest of the condo, and as soon as her feet crossed the threshold, she took her heels off. As soon as she pulled her shirt over her head, Tae was on her. He appreciated the fact that her perky breasts were bra free, and he cupped one in his hand before flicking his tongue over her nipple. He alternated between sucking and licking, and Anya's pearl began to throb. She reached down and unbuttoned his jeans so she could place her hand inside his underwear and feel his tool.

She moaned from pleasure and anticipation as she stroked his thick pipe. Ready for it, she pushed his jeans and boxer briefs down. Tae took his mouth off her breast. "Oh, you ready? Bend over that dresser. I want to see all that ass from the back."

Anya undressed while Tae did the same and grabbed some protection. She gripped his dresser and spread her legs like she was waiting on a police officer to pat her down. Tae took in her thick frame with a lustful gleam in his eyes. Walking up behind Anya, he pressed his mushroom tip into her opening and pushed inside of her.

"Yesssss, baby, I need that shit," she groaned, and a broad grin spread across Tae's face. He was about to have some fun.

Anya spread her legs farther and put her chest flat on his dresser. With her ass tooted up, she took the dick like a pro and had Tae grunting behind her. Her shit was the truth. It was good while she was just taking the D, but when she started twerking on the dick, Tae was in heaven. Her shit was tight, and it was so wet that her essence was running down her thighs. Tae smacked her ass cheek so hard that his hand stung, and Anya came instantly.

"Goddamn," he stated between clenched teeth as she got even wetter.

Anya backed up a little and grabbed her ankles. The visual alone turned Tae on like a muhfucka. Anya was definitely someone he could sex on a regular basis. He could already tell that she had the kind of box a nigga would never grow tired of. She was a true freak, and she seemed to really enjoy sex. Those were the best kind, not the women who did it just to be close to the man or to get money or gifts from a man. The women who craved sex and loved busting nuts were great in bed because they had perfected the art of pleasing and being pleased.

It was only about a nut with them. Not saying that they wouldn't use sex for money or gifts, but Tae knew that Anya was having the time of her life while he was beating her back in.

Next, they ended up with her flat on her back and her legs on Tae's shoulders. She stared him straight in the eyes and rubbed her clit while he stroked her walls, and that had her hitting orgasm number two in no time. She moaned loudly, and her body convulsed as she came all over the condom.

"Fuuuckkkk." All Tae could do was groan.

Anya sat up, and Tae figured she wanted to switch positions, so he eased out of her. Anya shocked him when she squatted in front of him, pulled the condom off, and took him into her mouth. He threw back his head and sucked in a sharp breath as she deep throated him into an orgasm. When he came, that shit made his knees buckle. Anya was a keeper for sure.

She knew some men had a "no spending the night" policy, and she didn't care one way or the other. She just needed to know what type of time he was on.

"You got a 'no spending the night' rule in place, or can I wash my ass and get comfortable?"

"You can for sure wash that ass and get comfortable because after I smoke the rest of my blunt, I'm gon' be ready for round two."

Chapter 27

Kyrie couldn't take it. He was trying to remain strong, but he was at the last place that he wanted to be. He had just sat in a church for over an hour listening to a pastor preach, a choir sing, and various people say a few words about Camila. They spoke about how she was always the life of the party and how she was a dope person. Kyrie knew that to be true. Before she got hooked on coke, they used to have some fun times together. She truly was like his sister. The most painful part about the service was his aunt and the way she wailed and cried on her husband's shoulder. Kyrie's heart truly broke for her. Even though she always said he was like a son to her, Camila was her only child.

He was at the gravesite, and it was too much to take in. A prayer was being said, and he stared at the ground the entire time. Kyrie refused to watch them lower the casket into the ground. That would make it final, and he wasn't ready for that. Camila was so much more than the past few months she spent indulging in drugs. Her life had been more than that, and that was what he was going to choose to remember. Though Kyrie wasn't looking, he knew the exact moment that Camila was being lowered into the ground because his aunt collapsed. He ran over and helped his uncle pick her up. At that point, the service was over, and Kyrie had to get out of there. He walked to his car and drove off without saying goodbye to anyone.

If asked, Kyrie wouldn't even have been able to explain how he got home because he didn't remember it. He was sitting in the car, staring out the window, when his phone rang. Kyrie had been ignoring people for the past few days, but something made him look at his phone. It was Taina. He hadn't seen her since the night of their date when he pulled up at the warehouse and got Kilo's chain back. For some reason, he decided to entertain her. He didn't know what she wanted, but she was the distraction that he needed. Kyrie had entirely too much on his mind, and he felt like he might end up losing it.

"Hello?"

"Hi." Taina sounded unsure, and it was understandable. They hadn't spoken in a few months. "I just wanted to call and say hello and that I'm sorry for your loss."

"Appreciate that," he mumbled. Kyrie didn't care to talk about his loss. He wanted to fuck. "What you doing right now?"

"I'm at home. I was off today so I ca—"

"I'm 'bout to come scoop you." He cut her off mid-sentence because he didn't really care what she was about to say. "Send me your address and let me see how far you are."

Taina jumped up off the couch and ran into her bathroom to plug in her flat iron. She had been lounging around the house all day, and in her mind, she didn't look good enough to be in the presence of a rich nigga. She had to fix that fast. She grabbed her face cleanser and her makeup bag. "Okay."

Her fingers moved swiftly as she texted him. Then she put him on speakerphone so her hands would be free to wash and moisturize her face. After a few seconds of silence, Kyrie spoke. "My GPS says you're nineteen miles away."

Taina figured she could work with that. "Okay. I'll be ready when you get here."

Taina wasn't dirty, but she wanted to be super fresh, so she hopped in the shower and washed her body quicker than she ever had before. After putting on scented lotion and panties, she chose not to wear a bra. She dressed in a peach sundress and began on her hair. Taina was tired as hell from moving so fast, but she couldn't let Kyrie catch her slipping. Thank God her lashes were already done. She ironed her hair, laid her edges, and was patting on her foundation when Kyrie texted her that he was five minutes away.

"This is going to have to do," she mumbled as she squirted on perfume.

Little did she know, Kyrie didn't give a damn how she looked. He just wanted to get drunk, have sex with her, then send her home in an Uber. He wouldn't have noticed if she came out wearing a ball gown. He pulled up in the driveway, texted her, and waited for her to come out. She got in the car and greeted him with a wide smile, but he barely looked at her.

"Hi."

"What's up?"

"I didn't expect to see you today. Guess I'm glad I bit the bullet and hit you up. I was starting to think you weren't feeling me like that."

Kyrie gave a slight head nod to let her know that he heard her, but he didn't acknowledge her with words. He had to remind himself that she was there for a reason and not to get too annoyed by her. Of course, she was happy to see him, but he was indifferent. Taina picked up on Kyrie's mood, and she decided to stop talking. She was elated to be going to his home, and she didn't want to do anything to mess it up. He did just leave a funeral, so she couldn't expect him to be in a good mood.

When Kyrie pulled up at his house, Taina almost pissed herself. She was at his house, and it was gorgeous! She had never in her life been to such a nice house. Kyrie pretty much lived in a mansion, and Taina would damn near be willing to sacrifice her firstborn child to be able to live like this. In fact, she needed to get pregnant by his ass! She had to put it on Kyrie. She had to do everything in her power to ensure that, this time, he kept her around. He was living too damn large for her not to get a piece of the pie, and she needed more than dick. She needed to be with a man like Kyrie full-time.

They stepped inside the foyer, and she almost had an orgasm. "You want something to drink?" he asked while she was taking in every intricate detail of his home.

"Yes. I'll take Henny if you have some."

Kyrie loosened his tie and headed for his bar. It felt as if he were choking. He wanted out of that damn suit, and he was never wearing it again. He had to get some liquor in his system first though. He was walking a fine line between sanity and insanity, and alcohol would keep him from going over the edge. Kyrie stood at the bar and downed a shot of cognac before pouring himself and Taina drinks. He took a large sip before taking her drink over to her.

"Make yourself comfortable. I'm going upstairs to change my clothes."

Kyrie made his way up the stairs, and he headed into his large bedroom. He went straight to the walk-in closet that looked like something out of a department store. He had shelves for his shoes that had glass doors to each cubicle so he could see the shoes that sat inside. There were more than 200 pairs of shoes lining the walls. He needed a stool to reach the shoes on the very top row of each shelf. In the middle of the closet sat drawers that contained tees, boxer briefs, and socks. On top sat cases for his watches, chains, rings, and bracelets. Lining the opposite wall were all of his jeans, sweats, shirts, hoodies, jackets, and coats. Kyrie had so many clothes that he could go two years without repeating an outfit. He was aware that he had taken up the entire closet, but should he ever marry, there was a whole extra room next door that his wife could use as her closet. He wasn't sure it would happen anytime soon, but maybe one day. The fact that he didn't even know if Khelani was still pregnant was absurd to him, but he refused to dwell on it. He didn't let the streets take a toll on him, so he damn sure wasn't going to let a female run him crazy. In due time, he would get over her.

Kyrie drained the liquor from his glass and stripped down to his boxer briefs. He wanted to be faded but not so faded that he passed out after fucking Taina. He needed to stay alert long enough to wait for her ride to show up. Kyrie changed into basketball shorts and a tank top and headed downstairs to fix himself another drink. He was going to drink, smoke, and fuck until he felt no more pain.

Anya was sleeping so hard in Tae's bed that she had drool on her cheek. They had two rounds of amazing sex, and the sleep she was getting was heaven. When her phone rang, she wanted to groan. Mad that her sleep was interrupted, she opened her eyes with a scowl on her face and snatched her phone off Tae's nightstand. She saw that Kasim was calling, so she knew she had to answer. Anya attempted to clear the sleep from her voice, but when she answered the call, she still sounded part nigga.

"Hello?"

Tae stirred beside her.

"We got the drop on that nigga Mozzy. I'll text you the location. I need you to come ASAP."

Forgetting all about her sleep being interrupted, Anya sat up fast as hell. This was wonderful news to wake up to. Camila's dog ass was dead, and Mozzy was about to be joining her in hell. Anya was pleased that all of her adversaries seemed to be getting what they deserved. "Say less. I'm on the way."

Anya stood up and began to get dressed. Tae sat up and eyed her thick frame. "Everything good?"

"It will be. Kasim got the drop on Mozzy. Do you have an extra toothbrush I can use?" She wasn't sure how often Tae had overnight guests, but she hoped that he had an extra one lying around. Even if he didn't, she would still go to Kasim. She would kill Mozzy, bad breath and all.

"Yeah, I do." Tae got out of bed with a smirk on his face. "You gon' really go watch them kill that nigga?"

Anya drew back and looked at Tae with a confused expression on her face. "Watch them kill him? No. I'm going to kill that fuck nigga. His ass is gon' suffer, too."

Tae shook his head. "You a real live gangsta, huh?"

"That man violated me not once but twice. He raped me, gave me a concussion, choked me, and robbed me. I'll spend the rest of my life trying to make this right with God, but he gotta go."

Tae respected her gangsta. High-key, he was even turned on. He wished he had time to fuck her again because the way she spoke with conviction about handling Mozzy and the way she looked sexy as hell when she was angry had his dick hard. He knew that had to wait though, so he got her a toothbrush. Anya peed, brushed her teeth, and washed her face. That was as fresh as she was gon' get until she made it home. When Kasim texted her, she saw that he was at the bus station, and that was twelve minutes away from her. This nigga must have been trying to leave town.

"Last night was fun. We should do it again," she said to Tae before letting herself out.

Tae simply looked after her with one eyebrow raised. He'd been with a lot of women, but he'd never encountered any like Anya. She was amusing, relatable, sexy, and a hustler. He couldn't leave out that her body was sick and her pussy was good as hell. She got her own money, and she liked to have fun. There wasn't one damn thing not to like about her unless you considered that she might be too much for the average nigga to handle, but if there was one thing about Tae, it was that he was far from average.

In the car, Anya was excited to be finally headed to where Mozzy was. She didn't want to risk being pulled over for speeding, so she made it to her destination while doing the speed limit. When she pulled up at the bus station, Kasim and Delante were getting out of Kasim's SUV.

"We've been watching his bus. He's up there, and it leaves in ten minutes. We're about to go up there and get him off."

Anya nodded. They were in a public place, but she trusted that Kasim and Delante could get the job done without bringing any unwanted attention to themselves. She didn't care what they had to do. Mozzy couldn't take off on that bus. If he left Atlanta, she knew she would never see him again. She chewed the inside of her cheek anxiously as they headed for the bus.

Once they were on, Kasim's eyes darted back and forth from each row. He found Mozzy at the very back of the bus, and he was glad that the seat next to Mozzy was empty. Kasim sat down while Delante remained standing.

Mozzy didn't know who this big nigga was, but something told him it was trouble.

When Kasim spoke, his voice was low, but Mozzy heard every word that he said. "Your mother lives at 833 Asteria Lane in Houston, Texas. She drives a white Honda Accord, and she works at Target. I have a nigga outside of her house right now ready to send her to meet God if you don't walk yo' ass off this bus and come with me, and I won't stop with her. You'll never be able to outrun me, so I suggest you not even try. You'll just be prolonging the inevitable and making me angrier."

Mozzy's heart felt like it was about to explode in his chest. He could refuse to get off the bus. Maybe this nigga was bold enough to kill him on the bus, and maybe he wasn't. It was a chance that he'd be willing to take if they weren't threatening his mother's life. That shit came with power. No one knew him in the A like that, so this nigga had to be highly connected. Then it hit him that this nigga had to be affiliated with Anya. It would make sense for the plug to have that much reach. He knew he should have rented a car and left town as soon as he robbed her, but his dumb ass waited until all the weed was gone, and he was going to take the bus back to Texas with a bag full of money. Money that he would never get to spend.

Feeling like he was about to shit himself, Mozzy reluctantly stood up. He contemplated taking off running once he was outside. Shit, his mother had lived fifty-plus years. Would it be so bad if . . . He had to shake his head at his damn self. He truly wasn't shit for that. Mozzy was afraid to die, but he didn't consider that when he robbed Anya.

He was down on his luck and pissed that Anya made Kyrie cut him off. One day, he followed Tae from Kyrie's office building, and he led him back to the condo that Kyrie broke down weed in. He was thinking about hitting Tae when Anya pulled up, and then he decided to just follow her home since her bitch ass was who he had beef with.

He watched her for a few days, and when he saw her leaving the building with a bag, he assumed she had weed in it, and he had assumed correctly. Mozzy was geeked when he thought he hit the jackpot, but his life was about to end for that very same jackpot.

Once they were off the bus, Kasim and Delante walked on each side of him. Mozzy felt sick when he saw Anya glaring at him with a sadistic grin on her face. He wanted to spit on her, but he decided not to do that.

In Kasim's SUV, Delante got in the back with him and kept a gun trained on him. There was an eerie silence in the car, and the tension was so thick you could cut it with a knife. The oddest thoughts occurred to Mozzy as he waited for his fate. He thought about the breakfast sandwich he'd just eaten not even knowing that might be his last meal. In the car, he looked up at the sky, the trees. He wished he had a blunt to smoke. All kinds of things ran through his mind. It had been six days since he got some pussy. Four days since he talked to his mother. Fear was starting to grip him like a vise, and he felt like he was suffocating.

To make matters worse, they were in the car for more than an hour. His impending doom had him on the verge of vomiting, and it was taking forever to meet his fate. Mozzy started seeing cows and horses and shit, and he knew they were taking him deep in the country. Finally, Kasim turned on a narrow dirt path that had fields on both sides. They were cotton fields. For miles there was nothing but fields of cotton. Kasim drove down the path, going farther and farther away from the main street. This was for sure an area where no one would hear him scream. Kasim put his gear in park and got out of the car.

"Please don't do this. Whatever I did, I can make it right," Mozzy begged as they dragged him from the car. His heart was pounding like an African drum in his chest.

"Please don't do this. Please." Tears rolled down his cheeks, and Anya laughed at him.

"This nigga is really crying." She watched him as Kasim put tape over his mouth. "You weren't crying and begging when you raped me, or how about when you robbed me?" Anger flashed in her eyes, and she sprayed pepper spray in his face. "Bitch," she spat through gritted teeth while his muffled cries floated to her eardrums. "Yeah, cry like the li'l bitch you are."

Anya went to her bag of goodies as the pepper spray burned Mozzy's eyes. She was gon' torture his ass for sure. Kasim and Delante looked on as she used both hands to plunge a hunting knife into his thigh. Mozzy attempted to scream, and he writhed in pain on the dusty ground. When Anya pulled the knife from his leg, blood gushed out. She cleaned the knife with a Clorox wipe, then poured rubbing alcohol in the wound. Mozzy was rolling on the ground something serious at that point, and tears streamed down his face. Snot poured from his nose, and he wished she would just kill him and get it over with. Anya hummed a tune as she pulled a gun from her bag and casually shot him in the left knee, then the right knee. By that time, Mozzy was in so much pain that he couldn't even move anymore. He lay on the ground praying for death to come to him.

Anya, Delante, and Kasim just stared down at him for a good five minutes, watching him bleed. His body began to tremble, and he pissed on himself. A smile eased across her face as she shot him again in the left arm. Then the right arm. "I'm gon' let your ass lay here and think about all the fuck shit you did while you bleed out. We're so far out that even if someone does find you, by the time the ambulance arrives, you'll be dead. Have fun in hell, fuck boy."

She got in her car, and Kasim and Delante followed suit. Anya pulled off with a smile on her face while Mozzy lay bleeding to death in the middle of nowhere, thinking about how he'd never see his mother again. He thought coming to Atlanta was the best thing that ever happened to him, but that ended up being the furthest thing from the truth.

Chapter 28

With nothing but time on her hands, Khelani decided to go hard as hell with trying to get her name out there as a stylist. She knew it wouldn't be easy, but she wasn't broke. Even if it took a minute to build a brand, she could deal with that. She spent hours putting together outfits and taking pictures for Instagram. She also got in her creative bag and made TikTok videos. She was glad that people from Kyrie's label still showed her love, and by them liking and sharing her stuff, it was getting attention. When Swag shared one of her TikTok videos, her followers went up by over 1,000 people in one day. Khelani was having fun, and it didn't even feel like work. Most of her day was spent on social media, building her website, and researching the business side of being a stylist.

When she wasn't doing that, she was sleeping or reading books about pregnancy. Khelani's body was going through some weird-ass changes, and despite being super tired all the time, she had to thank God that morning sickness didn't really kick her ass. Some days she felt sick, but she rarely threw up. On the days she did feel nauseated, she would eat light food like salad and fruit, and she learned that sucking on sour candy helped.

Khelani thought about Kyrie more often than she would care to admit. Every time she thought about the way that he had spoken to her, she became pissed off. But did she deserve it? She had acted selfishly and impulsively, but she couldn't take it back. She made one mistake, and he attacked her character and basically said she didn't deserve kids. Khelani hated that things ended the way they did, but she had no desire to be with or around someone who thought so little of her.

She was simply being the Khelani she had always been, and she couldn't change overnight. His cousin should have never jumped her sister. But what was done was done. None of it could be taken back, and they had to move forward.

Khelani got a DM, and she raised one eyebrow when she saw who it was from: Jet Malone. He was the very popular owner of a record label that had almost as many successful artists signed to it as Kyrie's. Anxiously, she opened the message and saw that he was inviting her to a party he was having in a week. He told her that he'd been checking her page out, his party would be full of people, and some of them may be interested in her services.

"Wow," Khelani chuckled to herself. Hours of creating content, using a million hashtags, and following the right people had actually paid off. Her fingers moved furiously as she accepted the invitation, and he messaged her back with the details.

Jet wasn't the cutest guy in the world, and he had a huge, round belly. Khelani didn't really have anything against big guys, but Jet wasn't her type looks-wise or body-wise. She was in the minority, however, because he had four kids by four different women. Khelani really hoped that he was inviting her on legit business and not because he wanted to holla at her. Even if she weren't pregnant by Kyrie, she would pass on Jet's advances. Khelani had attempted to put her walls down and give love a try, and it lasted all of a hot minute. She was leaving with a consolation prize, however, and if she never found her soul mate or got serious with another man, it would be fine with her. Khelani would continue being the boss she was, and she would be the best mother she could be.

She was scrolling through social media when she came across a popular blog site. And of course, she had to see a picture of Kyrie. He was at a popular strip club in the A, and he was walking out with a pretty light-skinned female who had a huge ass. In the second picture, he and that same female were boarding his private jet the next day. Khelani wasn't surprised at all by how fast he moved on. It was what it was. She refused to stress it, but she also refused to remain in Atlanta, where she could bump into him at any given time. Khelani logged out of social media and began looking for places to live in Los Angeles. She had decided that would be her next move.

"Nigga, you good?" Tae asked Kyrie with his brows raised, and he was concerned for good reason. Kyrie's private jet had just brought him back from Vegas, and he went straight to the condo designated for keeping weed in. Tae was there, and his boss's appearance was slightly alarming.

Kyrie's eyes were red and low, but it wasn't just from weed. He looked weary. Exhausted. Defeated. Alcohol wafted from his pores and floated directly into Tae's nostrils. Not even the damn near $1,000 track suit he wore made him look like the rich successful man he was. Kyrie looked like life had been beating him down. He flopped down in a chair.

"I feel like a fuckin' zombie. All I do is smoke and drink, and I still can't really sleep. If I close my eyes, I'm only out for an hour or two, and then I'm right back up. Shit is just crazy right now. I feel foul for not being there more for my aunt and uncle, but being around them kills me. I knew that Camila was going too hard with the coke. I knew she was out there, and I didn't want to disappoint them. I should have made my uncle take her ass kicking and screaming to rehab."

"Come on, man, don't even start that. You know like I know that Camila was grown, and no one could have made her do anything. They wouldn't have kept her in rehab against her will, and she would have been able to leave at any time. You and I both know that you can't simply ask an addict to stop doing drugs. That's not how it works."

Kyrie shook his head. "I should have never had that shit around her. I should have never let her start selling it in her club. I fucked up."

Tae remained calm and patient with his friend, but he refused to sugarcoat anything. "We gon' do this all night, my guy? You can come up with every reason in the book to blame yourself, and I'm gon' let you know with every one of them that this wasn't your fault. Camila was far from a kid. She was into street shit and street niggas whether you wanted her to be or not. You didn't make her do anything. She experimented on her own and got hooked. It can happen to anybody. You tried to help her the best way that you knew how. She was just fighting a big-ass demon. It's okay for you to grieve her, but that blaming yourself, you gotta let that shit go."

Kyrie knew that Tae was right, but it just seemed like Camila's death was haunting him. He couldn't close his eyes without seeing her face. The shit was driving him insane. Not even trying to distract himself with drugs, alcohol, and women was working. In the past few days, Kyrie had sex many times, and he didn't really enjoy any of it. He felt numb and detached from life.

"Everything been good with the weed?" he said, deciding to change the subject.

"Yep. Niggas still thirsty for that shit. I been on go mode all day."

"That's what's up. He doesn't really like doing the shit, but next week, I might let Ghalen handle the weed shit for me. I want you to fly out to Paris with me. I have a meeting out there, and I want you to come. You're always here handling things for me, and I want to start finding more shit for you to do that doesn't put your freedom at risk. The extra money is nice, but when I think about it, even though I don't make the transactions, I'm still putting myself at risk. I'm too rich for that shit. I called Khelani selfish, but when I knew I had a baby on the way, I didn't make any moves to leave the game either. I don't even know if her ass is still pregnant, but I'm feeling like it's almost time to wrap this shit up."

Tae nodded. He appreciated the fact that when Kyrie decided to leave the streets, he was going to take him with him. That was some real nigga shit. Tae didn't have any kind of degrees or work experience, but Kyrie would always find something for him to do. "You still haven't spoken to Khelani?" Tae knew that Camila's death was bothering Kyrie, but he also knew that him being on the outs with Khelani played a part, too.

"Nah, I'm not messing with that. If she's still pregnant, I'll find out when the baby is born. I don't have the patience to deal with Khelani right now. I might snap and break her neck or some shit, and I don't even put my hands on females."

Tae let out a small chuckle. "That's how I know you're feeling her. Y'all are both stubborn as hell, and trying to get along might be hard for both of you, but if she is still pregnant, one of y'all gon' have to put your pride to the side and make the first move. Space might be what you need for the moment though." Tae stood up. "I'm about to go to the strip club and look at some ass and titties.

You need to take a shower and go to bed. Rest, my G. I don't care what you have to do to get it. You need some sleep."

Kyrie let out a deep sigh as Tae left the condo. He made it sound so easy, but little did Tae know that, physically, one couldn't rest when their soul was so disturbed.

Chapter 29

Tae had just gotten out of the shower when he saw Anya calling his phone. "What up?" He removed the towel from his waist and put on some black Versace boxer briefs.

"Too bad for you I don't have friends here, so I gotta bug you. Come with me to get a tattoo please. You're my only friend aside from Khelani."

Tae chuckled. Most times, if he dealt with a female strictly on some fucking-type shit, he didn't do the hanging out and going on dates with them. That would have made it too easy for them to get things confused. Anya was cool though, and she had a way of asking him to do things with her, but she wasn't clingy with it. She was a busy woman herself, so she didn't expect to see Tae on a daily basis. Though she would have liked to sex him on a daily basis, she didn't want to wear out her welcome.

"When you going to get tatted?"

"In about an hour. I'm about to stop by a bar and take some shots first."

That made Tae chuckle harder. "Damn, ma, it's four in the afternoon."

"So that means it's almost happy hour. I'm about to get a tattoo. Those things hurt."

"Ohhhh, let me find out you a punk and shit. Where you getting it at?" Tae continued getting dressed.

"I'm far from a punk, but like I said, getting a tattoo hurts. I have four of them, so I'm familiar with the process, and I'm getting it on my thigh."

Tae's dick jumped just from the thought. "Bet. Text me the address of the shop, and I'll meet your drunk ass there in an hour."

Anya giggled. "Okay."

Tae finished getting dressed. His doorbell rang, and he looked at the app on his phone to see who was at his door. He kissed his teeth when he found out it was his mother. He hated that she knew the code to get into his building. Tae was tempted to ignore her, but he didn't.

"What I tell you about coming here without calling and asking first?" he asked when he opened the door and his eyes fell on the rail-thin woman.

"Why you gotta be like that, Tae?"

He backed up to let her in. He knew the right words to say to Kyrie because he'd been dealing with a mother who had been battling addiction for most of his life. The longest she ever stayed clean for was thirteen months when he was 16. Tae had been so proud, and the moment he found out she relapsed, he felt like he had died. It was then that he conditioned himself not to let her actions affect him so much. She was a grown-ass woman, and if she wanted to slowly kill herself, he had no choice but to let her.

"You live a good thirty miles from me. How did you get here? Why are you here? Your rent is paid for the month, and so is your cell phone bill and your light bill. You already know what it is. I'm not putting no money in your hands. You won't get high off my dime."

Sometimes, he gave in to her because he hated the thought of her selling her body to get money for drugs. It might sound bad, but he didn't really care if she stole. In a way, he wanted her to get locked up, and if she did, he wouldn't bail her out. Since she wouldn't go to rehab, she would only get clean in jail. Once she sat in jail for three months, and when she came home damn near fifteen pounds heavier, Tae wondered how long it would last. He got her a place that wasn't in the hood, and he suggested that she get a job so that it would keep her busy. She got a job a waitress, and that time she only stayed clean for six months. That was a year ago. Tae still paid her rent and her utilities, but he wouldn't give her money. One thing about it, even though Sarah was a junkie, she never stole from Tae. He could have a $100 bill on a coffee table, and if he left the room, she wouldn't take it. That alone let Tae know that she loved and respected him. The drugs just had a hold over her.

"I walked. I was at a hotel about three miles from here."

His stomach turned. She'd been out selling her body. Even though she barely weighed a hundred pounds and had dull caramel-colored skin, there were still men willing to pay for her body. Tae often bought her clothes, so she dressed nicer than a lot of other fiends. He didn't even buy her name-brand stuff, but it was nice stuff. The yellow floral print dress that she was currently wearing came from Target. She had even painted her fingernails red. Her naturally curly hair was brushed back in a ponytail. When she was healthy, she looked so good. When she was cracked out, it barely bothered Tae anymore, but he used to shed tears behind it.

"What you want?" he asked with a blank expression on his face.

"Just a ride back home. I need to save the money I have for laundry. Can you take me and get me something to eat?"

Tae grabbed his keys off the table by his front door. "Yeah. Come on."

He knew that she had gotten more money from tricking than just enough to do her laundry. She was going to buy drugs, too, but that was her business. Tae stopped by Wendy's, and his mom ordered $17 worth of food. By the time he pulled up at her house, she had killed the nuggets and the French fries and was guzzling down the strawberry-lemonade.

"Thank you," she panted. She was drinking so fast it damn near had her out of breath. He wondered when she'd last eaten.

Tae sympathized with Kyrie so much because, for years, he'd been waiting to get that same call, the call that his mother was dead, be it from overdosing or being murdered from going off with strange men. He watched as she got out of his car and headed inside. His mother was probably headed inside to call her dealer. There was nothing he could do about that.

Tae drove off, headed to meet Anya at the tattoo shop. He pulled up two minutes before she did. Anya hopped out of her car with a smile on her face, and that shit was contagious. There was just something about her fine ass.

He got out of the car and hit the lock button on his key fob. "You look like you feel nice."

"I only took three shots. Not too much. Just something to take the edge off. I didn't want to ride and smoke, so I ate an edible, too. Yoooo, my dad sent some shits that are like that! I have all kinds of edibles from candy to cookies and even some butter you can cook with."

"Word? I might check that out. There's just something about smoking that I like, but I'm not against edibles. I might need to give my lungs a break for a few days."

They entered the shop, and he spotted his man Cliff who had done a few of his tats in the past. They spoke to each other and gave each other dap. Tae alternated between looking in his phone and watching Anya. She was getting a huge tattoo on her left thigh. She was getting two big-ass flowers and a trail of butterflies. It didn't take Cliff long to draw it, and once he placed the stencil on her thick thigh, Tae had to admit that shit was gon' be fire. She already looked good naked, but that tat was gon' take it to another level. He loved tattoos on women. That shit was sexy as hell to him.

As soon as Cliff started on the tattoo, Anya winced and extended her hand toward Tae. "I didn't invite you here to look at me. I need you to hold my hand."

He shook his head at her, but he walked over and grabbed her hand. Each time Cliff hit a painful spot, Anya would squeeze her eyes shut and squeeze his hand harder. Tae found himself gazing down at her, and she was even sexy when she was frowning.

"Fuckkkk you, Cliff," she moaned after he hit an extra-sensitive spot, and Cliff and Tae both laughed.

It took her two hours to get the tattoo, and there were times that she talked and joked to keep her mind off the pain, but most times, she was just quiet. Cliff had music playing, and there was a chill vibe in the shop. Tae had to admit that any time he was in Anya's presence, he had a good time even when they weren't really doing anything. When Cliff was done, Anya admired her tattoo in the mirror, and it was making Tae's dick hard. He didn't have any plans for the night, and he knew she'd be down to fuck.

"What you about to get into?" he asked her after she paid Cliff, and they walked outside.

"Nothing. What's up?"

"You trying to smoke?"

"You gon' let me fuck after?" she asked him with a coy smile, and Tae erupted into laughter.

"Why the fuck you so bugged out?"

Anya shrugged, and his eyes roamed the length of her body.

"Yeah, ma. You can get this dick fa sho'. Follow me."

"You look cuteee," Anya sang when Khelani walked into the room. When the sisters were getting along, Anya had always been her biggest hype man. Khelani still didn't really know what had caused the big change in Anya, but she was loving it.

Khelani had invited her sister with her to Jet's party. She still wasn't showing, but a lot of her clothes no longer fit due to her weight gain. Khelani was three months pregnant and only looked slightly bloated. She deterred attention from her midsection with a cute-ass white floral-print shirt that hung off her shoulders, and it wasn't meant to fit tight. The shirt was made from silk, and it was bold and cute. On her bottom half were simple black leather pants that hugged her thick thighs and showcased just how much her ass had grown. Pregnancy had her already-thick hair thicker, and it was growing like crazy. Her curls touched the middle of her back.

Anya, in true Anya fashion, was showing way more skin than her sister. She dressed in black leather shorts and a matching bra. Her straight weave hung past her ass, and she had spent an hour on makeup. She looked like a straight video vixen. The women left the condo, leaving a trail of expensive-smelling perfume behind them. The venue where the party was being held wasn't far from them at all, and since Khelani couldn't smoke or drink, she was the designated driver.

When they arrived, Khelani left the car with the valet, and they headed into the star-studded party. There were rappers everywhere and rapper's baby mamas, Instagram influencers, and viral sensations. The event was packed, and Khelani was glad that she had business cards made. A waitress came over with a tray of champagne. Anya grabbed one while Khelani politely declined. She didn't know anyone there but Anya, and even though she brought business cards, she was reluctant to just pass them out to strangers. People would probably look at her like she was crazy.

Luckily, Anya had her back. A popular female rapper walked up to Khelani and complimented her shirt. Out of maybe 300 people, there were only about one hundred "regular" people there. Khelani couldn't believe that a famous person walked up to her and complimented her top. "Thank you."

"My sis is a stylist. She can get some super dope and unique pieces for you." Anya nudged her sister. "Give her a card, crazy."

Khelani smiled at the woman and pulled a card from her purse. "Forgive me. All of this is new to me. I'm just getting started as a stylist. If you know of anyone who can benefit from the service, I would love to help."

She took the card and put it in her Dior bag. "I sure will. Keep killin' it." The woman winked at Khelani and walked off.

"Watch. By the time you have that baby, you're going to be killing the game."

Khelani wasn't sure why she picked the party to open up to her sister, but she couldn't keep her in the dark. "I've been looking at places in L.A. I'm flying out in a few days to look at some places in person before I make a decision. You're free to come with me if you'd like."

Anya looked at her sister in awe. "You really gon' leave?"

"I really am. I'm not a stranger to new places. I'll be fine. I think you would do well in either place. You can stay here at the condo, or you can come with me. You have a month or so to decide."

Anya simply nodded and grabbed another glass of champagne. Khelani was really serious. Anya liked the A. L.A. was cool, but Atlanta was more her speed. She could probably luck out and find some thorough-ass Compton niggas or something, but the classy, rich part of L.A. wouldn't have anything for her but skinny white broads and mad people who didn't eat meat. Khelani was cool with that kind of shit, but L.A. wouldn't be lit enough for Anya. The thought of living without her sister made her sad, however. She still had some time to figure it out. Anya wasn't in love or anything, but she doubted she would find a nigga half as dope as Tae in L.A. Anya wasn't going to make a rash decision. She would think about it before making up her mind. As long as Kasim and Delante were in Atlanta, she wouldn't be completely alone.

A few more people complimented Khelani's shirt, and after being at the party for an hour, she had given out five business cards. Jet finally recognized her and came over and spoke.

"You look dope as hell as always. I've never met you in person, but your posts on the Gram are like that," he complimented her.

"Thank you. Thank you for inviting me."

"No problem. I saw Swag share yo' shit. How you know him?" Khelani didn't look like the typical groupie, but he'd seen all kinds. Women about their business and who appeared to have their own money could be groupies, too.

"I used to work at the label he's signed to."

"Ohh, okay, so you know my man Kyrie. Here his ass is now. That cue was right on time like some shit out of a movie," Jet chuckled, and Khelani felt like she was going to vomit.

Kyrie and Ghalen walked over to the small group, and Khelani didn't miss that he didn't look too pleased to see her. She wanted to walk off, but she didn't. She had to remember that she was trying to get her foot in the door with some heavy players of the game. She ignored Kyrie staring a hole into her and gave Ghalen a small smile. He hugged her, then spoke to Anya.

"Kyrie, what's up, homie? I been seeing Khelani doing her thing on the Gram with the styling and shit, and she told me she used to work for you." Jet was a dog that wanted to hump on anything with a vagina, so he was low-key trying to make sure that the two hadn't fucked. He really didn't care if they did. He would still hit.

Kyrie took Khelani in. He couldn't really tell if she was still pregnant. Her boobs looked big as hell, and that ass was fatter than he remembered. If she just lost a child, would she be out partying? Khelani just might with her coldhearted ass. Kyrie knew that Jet more than likely wanted to holla, and he was on some petty-type shit. He didn't even care about the information getting out to blogs. Shit, it might not even be true, but he was about to say it anyway.

"Yeah, she used to work for me. Now we have a kid on the way."

Anya damn near choked on her drink, and Khelani's eyes darted over to his face so fast it wasn't even funny. Her eyes narrowed, and she wanted to punch him in the throat. He hadn't even called to check on her, but he wanted to mark his territory in front of Jet. That was some real fuck-boy shit.

"Oh, damn, congratulations," Jet stated.

Khelani couldn't be fake anymore. She walked off furiously. Hopefully, the few cards she gave out would get her somewhere, because she was out. Anya could stay if she wanted.

Kyrie was right behind her. "Khelani, wait!"

She ignored him and walked even faster, but she was wearing heels, and he caught up with her. Kyrie grabbed her gently by the arm, and she jerked away from him. "Get your fuckin' hands off me. You haven't shown one ounce of concern for me or your baby. You haven't even texted to see how I'm doing, but you want to claim me in front of Jet? Boy, fuck you. We don't have anything to discuss ever again in life until this baby is born."

She was still pregnant. That softened him just a bit, but he was still angry, too. "The phone works both ways. I just lost a family member who was like a sister to me, and you're too stubborn and full of yourself to even tell a nigga that you're sorry for his loss. Everything is always somebody else's fault. You never take accountability for shit."

"And you don't know how to talk to people," she hissed. "You get your panties in a bunch and start hitting below the belt. I've never claimed to be perfect, but if you can't point out my flaws without belittling me, then I don't have a desire to speak to you. We were careless. We had unprotected sex without knowing each other, and now a baby is being brought into the situation. We have to find a way to deal with that, but we gave us a try, and it doesn't work. We're not good together, and I don't do toxic. I'll be sure to hit you up when I go into labor. Until then, keep doing you with these women out here, and leave me alone."

She stormed off, leaving Kyrie staring after her. He had never met a more difficult female than Khelani, and he was over the shit.

Chapter 30

"You trying to come through? I can send my driver to come scoop you up."

Anya had been on the phone with Brent Sawyer for two seconds, and he was already trying to get her to come to his home. He was a football player for the Atlanta Falcons she'd met at Jet's party. "Dang. You just get straight to it, huh? You're not even gon' ask me out on a date? You just want me to come to your house so we can have sex?"

"Date? Nah, I don't do dates like that. As soon as someone sees me out with a female, they'll take pictures and send it to the blogs. I don't have time for nosy folks in my business, and I'm too old for games. We're both grown. You know you would love to come to my house and fuck with me. You don't have to play the good-girl role with me."

Anya laughed. "You are funny as shit. I've never fronted to anyone like I was a good girl. I tell people quick that I'm with the shits, but I really can't stand a cocky nigga. Like, you're overly cocky, and according to Google, you're barely worth five M's. My father has more money than you," Anya stated with a scowl on her face. "You be easy though." She ended the call, disgusted.

The crazy thing about it was that Anya, six months ago, would have fucked him just because he was a pro football player. She almost loved dick as much as she loved money, and though she tried to get money out of niggas, she would have fucked him just because. She had sex with Tae quite a few times, and she had never asked him for a dime. The sex was so good she didn't even care about trying to run his pockets. Also, the fact that she bossed up helped her a lot. With the kind of money that Anya was making, she felt like a bad bitch. She didn't have to ask niggas for shit. Anything she wanted she could purchase herself. It sounded cliché, but getting her own money really did make her feel empowered. She no longer had to deal with cocky niggas like Brent with the hopes of getting a few hundred dollars or a bag or some shoes. It felt good hanging up on him. He wasn't even all that cute.

It was a little after ten, and Anya was nowhere near ready to go to bed. Khelani being pregnant made her super boring, and at times like this, Anya almost missed Camila's ho ass. Almost. She could have fun by her damn self. She didn't need wishy-washy females. Anya hopped in the shower and decided she would go to the strip club for some drinks, hookah, and fire-ass wings. An hour later, she was dressed and ready to hit the town. These days, it wasn't super safe for a female to go out alone, but Anya had pepper spray on her keychain, a Taser in her purse, and a .22 in her car. A nigga could try her if he wanted to.

It was a weeknight, so the club wasn't super packed. Anya found a table and ordered her drinks and hookah. She also had $100 in ones. She was far from gay, but she didn't mind showing the strippers some love. After all, she used to be one. Anya even did something she never did when going out: she wore jeans. They were ripped and looked painted on, but she still never wore jeans to go out. She just didn't feel like doing the most on this night. She had on tight-ass jeans, a red corset top, and red Valentino flip-flops. Anya was on some super chill shit.

She ate an edible before she left the condo, and by the time she took her second shot, Anya was feeling lovely. She danced in her seat and stood up every now and then to toss money on the stage. She was a vibe all by herself. A few guys flirted, but Anya didn't like any of them. She and Tae spotted each other and locked eyes. There was a drink in his hand and a bad-ass dark-skinned female in his lap. She had thick, wild, curly hair like Khelani, but hers was a weave. Anya smiled, nodded her head at Tae, and kept dancing. She wasn't mad in the least. Tae was single and could do what he wanted. If she could meet another him, she would have another nigga on the team, too. It seemed, though, that Tae was the only decent man she met in the A so far. Her skin crawled every time she thought about how she had sex with Mozzy. She played herself with that one. Snow was cool, but he was lame, and Brent was so corny he couldn't even smell the pussy.

By her third shot, Anya was feeling good, and she decided to go ahead and order her food so she could head out. Once she ate, she would be ready for bed. It would be nice if she had some dick to go home to, but she didn't. There wasn't even anyone in the club she was interested in having a one-night stand with. Anya figured that just maybe she was growing up. She had just ordered her food when Tae came over to her.

"I see you out here turning up by yourself."

"Yeah. I was bored, and I wasn't ready to go to bed. I'm good now. I'm gon' eat my wings and turn in. Bust a nut for me tonight with that sexy-ass chick who was all on you." She smiled a genuine smile that made Tae laugh. He had never in his life met a woman with a vibe like Anya's.

He swiped his tongue over his bottom lip. "If you can't bust a nut tonight, it's damn sure not for lack of these niggas trying. I see how they on you."

Anya kissed her teeth. "And none of them are worth me taking my panties off for. Just don't give ol' girl your best moves. Save some for me." She winked at him, and Tae laughed.

"You could join us, you know." He was joking, but if she was with it, then so was he.

"Nigga, I don't do fish." Anya twisted her lips. "I don't know. Maybe I should think about it. She do got a fat ass, but you can just hit me later. Go home and enjoy that," she laughed.

"I got you, mama. You be safe. Text me and let me know you made it home."

"Will do." Anya got her food and left the club truly unbothered. It would take more than Tae fucking some random chick to piss her off. Anya was getting money, and life was good. She didn't need a thing to be sad or mad over.

Inside the club, Dessi walked over to Tae with an attitude. "You finished flirting in my face?" She snaked her neck, causing Tae to frown.

That was the shit he was talking about. He had only had sex with Dessi once. He had sexed Anya way more times than he had Dessi, and Anya wasn't even tripping. She had a whole vibe that he had never found in another woman. He appreciated her knowing her place and not questioning him about anything.

"I was speaking to my homegirl. I don't call that flirting. She was talking about how pretty you are and shit, and you over here bitching. I'm not yo' nigga. If I want to flirt with every bitch in here, I can do that. So I can walk up outta here and leave you standing there, or you can fix yo' muhfuckin' attitude and bring yo' ass on here."

Dessi knew she had crossed a line. Tae was clearly pissed. Dessi hadn't meant to make him mad, so she simmered down. Little did she know the damage had already been done. Tae found himself wishing he had sent her on her way and just let Anya come through.

Kyrie and Tae were boarding his private jet when Tae hit him with some news. They had a cool four days in Paris, and Khelani had randomly texted him earlier that day. She made him aware that she was in L.A. and when he got back to the A, he would have to get his re-up from Kasim. In casual conversation, she mentioned that Khelani was over there looking at condos. He wondered if he should tell Kyrie or just mind his black-ass business. For some reason, on the jet he decided to tell Kyrie.

"You know I'm not a gossiping-ass nigga or a nigga who concerns himself with what other people have going on, but did you know that Khelani was moving to L.A.?" He knew she was still pregnant because when they were shopping the other day, Kyrie was looking at baby clothes and talking about how much drip his child was gon' have.

Kyrie whipped his head in Tae's direction. "Fuck you mean?"

"She and Anya are over there now looking at condos. Anya told me when we touch down I gotta get that from Kasim. They won't be back until tomorrow."

Kyrie's body grew warm with anger. No one tested his gangster more than Khelani. He didn't know what in the hell to do. Kyrie had never been lame, and he didn't have the desire to fight for a person who wasn't fighting for him. But there was a child involved. He didn't have to be in the same state as his child to be a good father, but it would damn sure make life easier. He could let Kim, Ghalen, Tae, and all of his other employees handle business at the label while he spent one to two weeks out of the month in L.A. He could even buy a house out there and be bicoastal. Even knowing all of that, Khelani moving didn't sit well with him. It bothered him so much that he found himself standing up and going to have a conversation with the pilot. There was a change of plans, and he was no longer going back to Atlanta. It was his money and his jet, so if he wanted the pilot to fly that muhfucka to hell, that was what he'd better do.

Chapter 31

Anya and Khelani followed their tour guide into the third condo of the day. "This is niiceeee," Anya stated. The condos in L.A. were five times more expensive than the condo they were living in in Atlanta, but Khelani could afford it. She knew out of the gate that L.A. wasn't cheap.

They were way more expensive, but they were very nice. Luxurious for real. Khelani knew that a condo wouldn't be her forever home, not with a baby. She wanted her child to have a huge yard to run around in, but she had time for that. This was just something for the moment. She didn't know if Anya was coming with her, but she was looking at three-bedrooms just in case. After the tour, Khelani told the guide that she was almost certain that this was the place she wanted. She had one more condo to look at the next day and would make up her mind after that.

Back in the Uber, Anya looked over at Khelani. "It's really pretty out here. You getting excited?"

Khelani felt a lot of emotions, but excited wasn't one of them. "More like nervous. I'm not strange to coming to a new place, but this time will be a little different. I won't have you or Kasim. What if I suck at being a mother? I'll be alone in this big city with a baby." Khelani's nerves were getting the best of her.

"You don't have to move, Khelani. I mean, you do know that, right? I haven't decided if I'm coming with you, but even if I don't, the first month after you have the baby, I'll come out and stay with you. I don't know about kids either though. That damn baby might pack its own shit and leave, messing with us."

Khelani giggled. She was so happy at the woman that her sister was becoming. The immature, bratty Anya was gone. Khelani hated to say it, but maybe Camila and Caresha had beaten some sense into her.

The Uber dropped them off at the hotel, and the sisters were talking about what they wanted to eat. As soon as the glass doors slid open and Khelani entered the hotel lobby, it felt as if her heart fell into her stomach. Time seemed to stand still, and her heart pounded heavily in her chest. She looked over at her sister, and Anya had a sheepish look on her face. She speed walked toward the elevator, and Tae followed her. Khelani wanted to walk right past Kyrie. She wanted to act like he wasn't standing there, but her feet wouldn't move. Khelani stood paralyzed.

Since she wasn't moving, he walked toward her. Kyrie wasn't confrontational. He stepped into Khelani's personal space and wrapped his arms around her. "Don't do this to me." His tone was gentle. "I need you and my baby in the A with me. The things I said to you were fucked up. I need to work on my communication skills. I can own that. You can hate me. You can never speak to me again, but don't take my baby away from me."

Khelani nervously stepped away from him. "Maybe we should have this conversation elsewhere." She headed toward the elevator, and he was right behind her. "Do you have a room here? I'm sure that traitor—I mean, my sister—is in our room."

"Don't be mad at her." Kyrie stared at her with a pleading look, and she had to look away. She spent so many days mad at him, and now that sad, puppy-dog face was going to make her give in.

Kyrie pressed the penthouse button. The short elevator ride was awkward, and once the doors slid open, Khelani sucked in a deep breath and followed Kyrie off. In his room, she didn't even have a chance to speak. He placed his lips on hers and parted them with his tongue. Kyrie had missed her, and he kissed her like he did. His fingers clutched a handful of her curls as his mouth found its way over to her neck. He sucked hard as her breathing became labored, and her pussy became moist. Not able to wait another minute to be inside of her, Kyrie was glad that she had on a simple black dress. He picked her up, and with her legs locked around his waist, he pinned her body against the door. Their lips connected again as he unbuckled his belt. They kissed feverishly, and when he pushed himself into her, Khelani moaned into his mouth.

Kyrie buried his face in the crook of her neck and stroked her intensely. Her smell. The familiarity of her walls. The way she moaned. It was all nostalgic. He wasn't lying when he said he needed her. Kyrie had missed her more than he'd been willing to admit.

"Khelani, fuck," he growled as he nipped at her bottom lip.

She stared into his eyes on the verge of an orgasm. Khelani could keep being stubborn, or she could admit just how good Kyrie made her feel. His words only had such an effect on her because she feared they were true. She held the power to make them be untrue. "I am selfish," she whispered. "I never should have done what I did."

Kyrie didn't want to talk about the past. It couldn't be undone. He was caught up in the present moment. Kyrie carried Khelani over to the bed, and by the time he took her mound into his mouth, she came almost immediately. She gripped the back of his head and locked her legs around his head as she had the most powerful orgasm she'd had in a long time. It left her gasping, but he wasn't done. Kyrie came up for air and stroked her into several more orgasms that had tears running down her face. He did what he set out to do, because after he fucked her like that, Khelani wasn't moving anywhere.

"You really thinking about moving out here?" Tae asked Anya. While they gave Kyrie and Khelani privacy, they had gone and had dinner, smoked, and had drinks. That ended up with them in bed. Once they were done, they lay there and smoked.

"Depending on what Kyrie says to my sister, her ass might not be moving out here." The weed smoke in her lungs made Anya's words come out choppy. "She is a stubborn one though, so I don't know. It's pretty out here, but the A is more my speed. If I'm lonely in the A, I know I'll be lonely out here because I doubt these chicks would be my thing. Only time will tell."

Tae was stuck on Anya's beauty. He was stuck on the way that he felt when they were around each other. If she moved, it wasn't like he'd be devastated, but he wouldn't even front and say he wouldn't be happy if she stayed in Atlanta.

"Well, if you stay in the A, I promise to make time for you at least once a week. That might not be a lot, but I don't want you feeling lonely. You a li'l vibe and shit. A nigga like hanging out with you."

Anya smiled. "Awwww, let me find out Tae wants me to stay in the A."

His expression remained serious. "I do. I like being around you. Like this though. I don't want that complicated shit. The insecurity and the arguments. The nagging. I don't want none of that shit, but as long as you stay like this, I'll always make time for you. Regardless of whatever. I'll take you anywhere you want to go, and we can do anything you want to do."

His words melted Anya's heart. She had never been pressed for relationships. Only dick and money. She liked having fun, too. All that arguing and shit was for the birds. She wasn't really the jealous type. Anya had to really like a nigga to get jealous over him and be acting all crazy. Other than that, she had no issue keeping it light.

"That's really the only way I know how to be. I told myself a long time ago that I would never let a man drive me crazy. All that being sad and heartbroken and shit, I don't have the energy for that. Only things a nigga could ever do for me were fuck me and run me that scrilla. I have got to like you, 'cause I done gave you this top-notch, grade A, Super Soaker 1000 on several occasions, and I've never asked you for shit."

Tae chuckled as he climbed in between Anya's legs. He peered into her eyes as he placed himself inside her tight opening. "I got you. We can go shopping in the morning."

Anya gasped and arched her back. "You trying to make me fall in love?"

Tae didn't respond. He just snaked his tongue into her mouth and fucked Anya like he had never fucked her before.

Chapter 32

Khelani was staring out the window of the private jet that her father had sent for her, and she hadn't said a word in almost an hour.

"You nervous?" Kyrie asked, breaking the silence.

Khelani turned to face him. "Hell yes. I have never taken a man to meet my father."

Kyrie grabbed her hand and gave it a light squeeze. "There's no need to be nervous. What's gon' happen if he doesn't like me? You're still going to be pregnant with my son, and I'm still going to be in your life. Case closed. You're grown. I will respect your father, but I'm not a child. If he doesn't like me, I never have to see his face again." He kissed Khelani, and she relaxed immediately.

It had been four weeks since she got back from Los Angeles, and they had been inseparable. Out of nowhere, Khelani's pregnancy hormones went into overdrive, and she turned into a nymphomaniac. Kyrie was loving it. Khelani wanted to have sex no less than twice a day, and if she didn't get it, she cried. He had a business meeting in New York, and he was gone for a day and a half. Khelani called him in tears because she was horny, and Kyrie laughed until his stomach hurt. Pregnant women were something else. Kyrie had fallen in love with Khelani, and it didn't matter to him if Kemp liked him.

A week ago, an ultrasound had revealed that Khelani was having a boy. She finally broke the news to her parents, and she couldn't tell how Kemp felt one way or another. He did make it clear, however, that he wanted to meet Kyrie, and he sent a jet for them. He couldn't have been too pissed, however, because upon hearing her news, he wired $1 million into her bank account, and he gave Anya $1 million as well. He made it clear that Kasim and Delante were to handle the weed business from then on out, and that his daughters were no longer hustlers.

Khelani gave Kyrie a small smile. "I love you."

It shocked the both of them. Kyrie had been feeling like he loved her for a few days, but he couldn't believe she said it first. Even with her hormones raging and the mood swings and changes to her body, Kyrie took note of how hard Khelani was working on her flaws. In an effort to appease him, she only drank soda twice a week, and it was caffeine free. She didn't fight him when he made suggestions that he thought were best for her, and what really took the cake was him hiring her to style his artists. He just wanted Khelani happy. She could see that, and she decided to submit and let him lead. It wasn't so bad after all.

The words that she spoke to Kyrie made his face light up like a Christmas tree. "I love you too." He kissed her again, and for the rest of the flight they talked about anything and everything. They were staying in Trinidad for two days, and then they were going to Hawaii for three days.

Once the baby came, Kyrie was going to take three weeks off work, but that was so he could bond with his son. In the meantime, he was balancing work and getting to really know Khelani. They needed all the alone time they could get before the baby came. He admired her hustle and the fact that she wanted to work, but he wanted her to relax as well. She was a millionaire. He was a multimillionaire. If he had anything to do with it, they were going to play way harder than they worked.

His aunt and uncle were still having a hard time coping with Camila's death, and Kyrie went to visit them at least once a week. He also called them every other day. He knew that losing their only child couldn't be easy. He wished that things could have turned out differently.

When Kyrie and Khelani got off the jet, there was a black Tahoe waiting to take them to Khelani's parents' house. They rode for about thirty minutes before they reached their destination. Kyrie had traveled to a lot of places, but he had never been to Trinidad. It was beautiful, and he made a mental note to come back. When the driver pulled up to the house, Kyrie's eyes stretched wide. He was rich as fuck and not easily impressed. The last time he was this awed by a home, he had been to Jay-Z's house. Kemp's shit was next level. The two-story nude-colored house looked like a resort.

Kyrie looked over at Khelani. "How many rooms are in this house?"

"The family room, den, movie room, kitchen, study, seven bedrooms, and six bathrooms. There is also a separate wing for guests that has two bedrooms, a kitchen, and two bathrooms. We'll stay on that end. My parents also have three maids and two chefs."

"Well, goddamn."

Kyrie hoped Khelani's father would act like he had good sense, because even without meeting him, Kyrie had a lot of respect for this self-made boss. If Kyrie wanted a home like this, he could go get one today. He'd never been in the spirit of trying to keep up with anyone. He could give props where they were due. Plus, he lived alone. A house this size didn't make sense for just him, but if he and Khelani remained together and she gave him more babies, he needed something like this built for sure.

The driver opened the door for Khelani and Kyrie, and she led them up to the house. Before they reached the door, Courtney emerged from the house with a wide smile on her face, and Kyrie immediately saw where Khelani got her looks from.

Courtney was elated that Khelani was pregnant, and her eyes fell on Khelani's small protruding belly. Her oldest child was glowing. She'd never seen her look so happy, and she had made Kemp promise to behave.

"Hello. Welcome home." Courtney hugged Khelani, and Khelani surprised herself by not tensing up. Affection from her mother was rare, but oddly, hugs from her felt nice.

"This is Kyrie. Kyrie, this is my mother."

Kyrie extended his hand toward Courtney. "Hello. It's very nice to meet you."

"Likewise. You have to be the reason for my daughter's glow."

Khelani shook her head bashfully, and they followed Courtney inside the house. Kemp was in the family room drinking whiskey and smoking a Cuban cigar. He stood and hugged his daughter. Then he shook Kyrie's hand, and introductions were made. The maid led them to the kitchen, where there was a spread of crab and dumplings, pelau, jerk fish, jerk chicken, plantains, acras, curried goat, and yellow rice. The food was foreign to Kyrie, but it smelled delicious. Khelani was in heaven, and she began digging in as soon as grace was said. Kemp was the first one to speak.

"Kyrie, tell me about yourself."

"I own a record label. It's very successful. One of the most popular labels in the world with some very successful artists signed to it. I've been selling weed for many years, which is how I ended up getting my weight from your daughter. I plan to back away from weed before my son is born and just focus on the label. I might start a few more businesses just because a person can never have too much money. I'm trying to set it up so that, by the time I'm forty, I'll never have to work another day in my life but the money will continue to roll in."

Kemp nodded. He liked Kyrie's drive. The man was wealthy, and Kemp was secure in knowing that he didn't need anything from Khelani. Kemp didn't care how much money she had. Her money was irrelevant. She needed to be with a man on her level, one who could provide, and Kyrie could certainly do that. That alone didn't make him good enough for Khelani, however. Kemp needed to make sure this man loved and respected his daughter. Kemp didn't even care about Khelani having a child out of wedlock. If Kyrie didn't prove to be worthy of her, he would never be anything more than Khelani's son's father, and Kemp would see to that.

"Any other kids? Ever been married before?"

"No, sir. For many years, my focus was my label. Not many can do what I did, and I knew that if I wanted to succeed that I would need to be one hundred percent focused. I dedicated all of my time to it, so that didn't leave much time for anything else."

That was another plus for Kyrie. Kemp was glad to see that he wasn't the type to spread his seed all over town. That showed that he was responsible. He had also heard from Kasim that Kyrie assisted him in killing the man who shot Khelani. Kemp was finally comfortable with the idea of Khelani being with a man and having his child. Kyrie seemed deserving of his daughter, but only time would tell. He could not only provide, but he could protect her as well.

Kemp had a few more questions for Kyrie, but dinner was pulled off without a hitch. Khelani was exhausted and full, so she showered and got into bed. Kyrie was in the study with Kemp, drinking and smoking cigars. He finally came in the room with red eyes. "I think he likes me."

"Yayyy." Khelani smiled but turned her head when he tried to kiss her. "I love your kisses, but that cigar stinks. I need you to shower and brush your teeth."

"Yes, ma'am." Despite what she said and that he seemed to agree, he still placed a quick peck on her lips and stole a kiss, which made her giggle.

Kyrie had to be something special if he wore her down and got Kemp's approval. Only time would tell where they would end up, but for the moment, Khelani was happy. The day she landed in Atlanta, she had no clue that it would be the best thing that ever happened to her.

"I'm having a birthday party in Vegas next month on the rooftop of a hotel. It's gon' be lit, and I'd love to fly you out as my date," Swag said to Anya.

He had been with damn near every thick industry chick there was, and he had his sights set on Anya. He met her one day when Khelani was styling him, and now here she was at Kyrie's Memorial Day weekend party for his label. Kyrie wasn't even at his own party because he was in Hawaii with Khelani, but the show still went on. Anya had met Kim on a few occasions, and she was cool, so Anya had no issue going to the party without her sister.

Swag was cute enough, and he was a rich rapper. Even though her bank account was a million dollars heavier, Anya still couldn't fuck with any broke niggas. She still didn't know what she wanted to do with her life, but she knew she could make a million dollars last while she figured it out. She didn't really want a lot of kids, but she wouldn't mind being a housewife. Who wouldn't want to be a kept bitch to a rich nigga? That way, she could spend his money and keep her own. And if the nigga started tripping, she could leave him and still be able to maintain whatever lifestyle she had with him. She doubted Swag would be that guy, but she could date until she found him.

Anya was just about to accept his invite when Tae walked over and gave Swag dap. He spoke to Swag, but his eyes were on Anya and the skimpy white dress she wore, which her areolas were damn near jumping out of.

"What up, homie?" Swag greeted Tae. "I was just inviting Anya to my party in Vegas as my date. You coming, right?"

Tae eyed Anya with a gleam in his eye. He came just in time because he wanted to hear what she was going to say. Anya had been all set to accept, but she couldn't for the life of her understand why she was hesitant to do so in front of Tae. "Ummm, I will definitely let you know," she said, and Tae smirked.

"She'll be there, but she'll be there with me. Anya didn't tell you she was my best friend?" He turned to Swag, and Swag groaned.

"Ahhh, shit. That must be code for y'all fucking." He held up his hands in surrender. "I'm out."

He walked off, and Anya laughed. "Don't be coming over here cock blocking. When you were on the phone with that chick last night, I was quiet as hell while she begged you to come through."

Tae stepped into her personal space. "But did I go?"

"That was your choice."

Since they got back from L.A., Tae and Anya were together every day. He spent a grip on her in L.A., buying her Chanel bags, shoes, and all kinds of good stuff. She was really starting to like him, and she kept her promise to him. Anya wasn't going to switch up and start tripping, so she didn't trip no matter how many females called him or texted him. No matter how much time they spent together, he wasn't her man.

"Fuck all that. We together all the time. We have sex damn near every day. We might as well do this shit."

"What shit?" Anya teased him. His words were unexpected, but she wasn't opposed to what he was saying.

"Stop fucking playing with me."

Anya giggled. "Okay, you know I'm cool and shit, but I can't deal with the cheating. I'm not the chick who will cry and leave though. I'm just gon' match your energy and go cheat too. We can go body for body 'til one of us gets tired."

Tae kissed his teeth. "Get the fuck outta here. You got me fucked up." Something told him she was serious though, so he knew what he had to do. He just wouldn't be cheating if he didn't want her to cheat. Tae felt like she was for sure worth it.

Anya smiled at him. "You wanna be my boyyyyfriend. I feel special. You have a lot of hoes to disappoint. You gonna break them up into days, do a group text, or what?"

He placed one hand on her waist. "You got all the jokes tonight. What you been sipping on?"

"Azul, and I had three edibles. I'm freakin' lit, bro."

Tae laughed. He had no second thoughts about his decision to settle down with Anya. She was like his spirit animal. They were both chill, laid-back, about their money, and they liked to have sex. He couldn't have found a better match.

Chapter 33

Anya was in the mall looking for something to wear to a classy event when she felt someone standing a little too close to her. When she looked up and saw who it was, her eyes narrowed. She didn't want to get kicked out of the mall for fighting, but she owed this bitch an ass whooping. Camila's dead ass couldn't get hers, but this bitch could. The look on Anya's face was so menacing that Caresha took a step back.

"I didn't come over here for all that. Look, you don't have to forgive me. It's cool if you don't, but I wanted to fight you that day over Snow. The shit was wrong on my behalf, but I never planned to jump you. I had no clue that Camila would jump in, and once the fight was over, I thought she was just being a good friend. A few weeks after Snow died, the police brought me his belongings. I tried to get in his phone for a minute, but I couldn't. Finally, I got in there, and I saw messages between him and Camila. I thought she was my friend, but she was having sex with my kids' father. I found out the day before she died, and I couldn't even go to her funeral. I'm sorry that she's dead, but Camila was a fucked-up person. She's gone and so is Snow, and I had some heavy thinking to do. I just didn't want unnecessary beef, but it's whatever. I'm sorry. Even if she hadn't jumped in, I should have never fought you because Snow was a dog."

Caresha said her piece and walked off. They would never be friends, and Anya didn't need her apology to be okay. She did decide, however, to just let the shit go. She had promised herself that the next time she saw Caresha it was on, but it was whatever. She could let the past go. She wasn't the same Anya she was when she came to Atlanta.

Anya found the perfect outfit and went to pay for it. Tonight would be epic.

Kyrie extended his arm toward Khelani, and she looped her arms through his. She almost had a meltdown at home because the dress she bought three days before was damn near too tight, and she thought she would never get it zipped. It was crazy that her belly had grown that much in three days. Khelani ate like a pig in Hawaii, and when she got home, the scale told her that she'd gained seven pounds in two weeks. Khelani knew she needed to slow down, but food was her best friend.

It was a special night for Kyrie. He was getting some kind of award, so she got her makeup professionally done and had her hair straightened. She wore a red gown that hung off her shoulders and hugged her body. On her feet were silver heels that she couldn't wait to take off. Even though her round belly was still small, she felt like her equilibrium was off and that she would fall. It was safe to say she wouldn't be one of those women who slayed heels her entire pregnancy.

He walked her into the banquet hall, and it took Khelani a moment to realize that they couldn't have been at an award ceremony for Kyrie because she spotted Kasim, Delante, Anya, and Tae. There were only about twenty people there, and it was a small, intimate gathering. Khelani stopped walking when she spotted Kemp and Courtney. She turned to look at Kyrie with her heart beating in her throat.

"What is this?"

The room was filled with roses. There must have been more than 200 of them. Everyone was dressed in either red or white, matching the couple, because Kyrie wore a red tuxedo. He got down on one knee, and Khelani thought she would pass out.

"When I was in Trinidad, I asked your father for your hand in marriage, and he gave me his blessing. We've barely known each other for six months, but when you know, you know. I want to live in the same house with you and my son. I want both of you to have my last name, and I want to spend the rest of my life calling you by that last name."

Khelani choked back tears as Kyrie flipped open a ring box that showcased the biggest diamond she'd ever seen up close. Kyrie had dropped $18,500 on the pear-shaped canary diamond that was surrounded by smaller diamonds. Khlenai's hand was trembling.

"Will you marry me?"

Words became tangled in her throat, and all she could do was nod, but that was good enough for Kyrie. He slid the ring on her finger, and everyone cheered. The rest of the night was like one big fairy tale. There was an open bar for the guests and a spread of shrimp cocktail, grilled salmon, rice pilaf, filet mignon, fried chicken, hush puppies, pasta salad, potato salad, and an assortment of cakes and pies. Everything seemed surreal to Khelani. The most important part was that her parents were there supporting her. Kyrie's aunt and uncle showed up, too, and it was the first time he saw them smile since Camila's death.

At the end of the night, when they got back in the car to be driven home, Khelani's feet were hurting so bad that she took her shoes off, and Kyrie began rubbing her feet. "When do you want to get married?"

She didn't even have to give it a lot of thought. "What are you doing tomorrow?"

Kyrie chuckled. "What?"

"What are you doing tomorrow? I can pay for a private jet to take us to Vegas, and we can get married over there at one of those little cheesy chapels. My parents can come, your aunt and uncle, Anya and Tae, and Kasim and Delante."

"You're serious?" Kyrie asked, confused, and she nodded.

"I don't need a big wedding or a long engagement, and you don't always have to take care of everything. I might not be as rich as you, but I'm something like a boss too." She grinned. "By the time my baby is born, I want us to be married."

All Kyrie could do was lean over and kiss her. Khelani never ceased to amaze him. She had given him a run for his money, but in the end, it had been more than worth it, and he was ready to spend forever with her stubborn ass.

Epilogue

Khelani stood in the doorway of Kevon's nursery, smiling at Kyrie's back. "Babe," she finally whispered, "let that baby sleep."

Kyrie turned around and saw Khelani standing there with a baby monitor in her hand. Their son had fallen asleep twenty minutes ago, and despite her having the monitor, he still left their guests in the backyard and came to check on the 5-month-old. Kyrie was in love with being a father. He smiled at Khelani and went over to her.

"And why are you here?"

"Because I had to pee, and I knew you were here."

It was his birthday, and they were leaving the next day for Santorini, Greece. He wanted to take the baby, but Khelani reminded him that they hadn't been anywhere since he'd been born. They both traded in industry parties, selling weed, and nights out to sit at home with their son, but Khelani wanted to have just a small break. She loved her son with everything in her, but a few days away wouldn't hurt.

"You've been peeing a lot, and I haven't even seen you drinking."

Khelani peered up at him. "That's because your pullout game is weak as fuck. My period is three days late, and I've been peeing like crazy. I already know what it is." She shook her head at the thought of having her body taken hostage again so soon after giving birth.

He clearly didn't feel the way she did, because he picked her up and spun her around. "I'm going to get you a test right now."

"There is no need for that. Please go back and enjoy your party," she laughed. "I have a test. I'll take it tonight, and after this one, there will be no more babies for at least three years. I am not playing," she warned in a stern voice.

"I love you so much." He looked at her with eyes full of admiration. Since Khelani had their son, his love for her had grown immensely. Seeing how protective she was with him and how she made her entire life about them made him realize that it was in her all along. He just had to bring it out of her.

She read to their son every day. She also went through great lengths to make Kyrie feel appreciated, wanted, and loved. Like putting together this birthday celebration for him with all of their friends and family. The trip to Greece was also planned and paid for by her.

"I love you too, but we're going to have to research birth control. I've been killing myself in the gym, and now I'm about to be fat again."

"And you're still the most beautiful woman in the world."

The pair walked down the stairs and out into their huge backyard, where their guests were eating, drinking, talking, dancing, and smoking. "'Bout time. I thought y'all were in there doing it," Anya stated.

"We aren't you and Tae," Khelani replied, referring to the time they were hosting a fight party at Anya's house and they dipped off to have sex.

Anya had taken $300,000 of the money her father gave her and had a house built from the ground up. She invested the rest of her money in an online boutique that sold clothes, swimsuits, shoes, and accessories. She was also about to start selling hair, lashes, and makeup. Tae had given her $10,000 for inventory. They didn't live together, but he stayed with her a few nights out of the week, and she did the same with him. Tae was still selling weed, and he also got legal money with Kyrie. He had used that to open a barbershop, and he was looking into purchasing some 18-wheelers. Tae was ready to flip his weed money into legal businesses so he could give the game all the way up.

Life was lit for all of them, and Khelani and Anya agreed that Atlanta would be home for good. Kasim and Delante had moved on to Dallas, and Kasim even had a girlfriend. Who said hustlers can't have a happily ever after?

The End

BOOK SERIES
AVAILABLE ON AMAZON KINDLE

TRAP WIVES OF CHARLOTTE 1-2
CAUGHT UP WITH A MAFIA BOSS 1-2
THE PLUGS GIRL 1-2
A BISSET CARTEL LOVE STORY 1-2
HER MAN HAS MY HEART
A BISSET CARTEL CHRISTMAS
FOREVER YOURS : A SAVAGE KIND OF LOVE 1-2
TAMMI, CAM, AND MEEK: A SCANDALOUS LOVE AFFAIR 1-2
THE HOTTEST SUMMER IN BROOKLYN 1-2
FALLIN FOR A HUSTLER LIKE ME 1-2

NATISHA RAYNOR   GIFTED_HUSTLER